The War Of Women
Vol. II

by

Alexandre Dumas

The War Of Women
Vol. II
by Alexandre Dumas

Copyright © 2024

All Rights reserved.

ISBN: 978-93-62205-22-3

Published by

DOUBLE 9 BOOKS
2/13-B, Ansari Road
Daryaganj, New Delhi – 110002
info@double9books.com
www.double9books.com
Tel. 011-40042856

This book is under public domain

ABOUT THE AUTHOR

French author and playwright Alexandre Dumas fils is best known for his romantic novel La Dame aux Camélias (The Lady of the Camellias), published in 1848. Giuseppe Verdi adapted it into his opera La traviata (The Fallen Woman), which debuted in 1853. Other notable works by Dumas fils include a number of stage and film adaptations, which are usually titled Camille in English-language adaptations. The playwright Alexandre Dumas père ("father"), the author of classic works including The Three Musketeers and The Count of Monte Cristo, was the father of Dumas fils (French for "son"). Dumas fils received the Légion d'honneur (Legion of Honour) in 1894 after being accepted into the Académie française (French Academy) in 1874. The illegitimate child of tailor Marie-Laure-Catherine Labay (1794–1868) and novelist Alexandre Dumas, Dumas was born in Paris, France. His father gave him official recognition in 1831 and made sure the young Dumas attended the Collège Bourbon and the Institution Goubaux for the greatest education available. The elder Dumas was then permitted by law to remove the child from his mother. The younger Dumas was driven to write about sad female characters by her anguish.

CONTENTS

THE ABBEY OF PEYSSAC

EPILOGUE

THE VICOMTESSE DE CAMBES

I

Two days later they came in sight of Bordeaux, and it became necessary to decide at once how they should enter the city. The dukes, with their army, were no more than ten leagues away, so that they were at liberty to choose between a peaceable and a forcible entry. The important question to be decided was whether it was better to have immediate possession of Bordeaux at all hazards, or to comply with the wishes of the Parliament. Madame la Princesse summoned her council of war, which consisted of Madame de Tourville, Claire, Lenet, and her maids of honor. Madame de Tourville knew her arch antagonist so well that she had persistently opposed his admission to the council, upon the ground that the war was a war of women, in which men were to be used only to do the fighting. But Madame la Princesse declared that as Lenet was saddled upon her by her husband, she could not exclude him from the deliberative chamber, where, after all, his presence would amount to nothing, as it was agreed beforehand that he might talk all he chose, but that they would not listen to him.

Madame de Tourville's precautions were by no means uncalled-for; she had employed the two days that had just passed in bringing Madame la Princesse around to the bellicose ideas which she was only too anxious to adopt, and she feared that Lenet would destroy the whole structure that she had erected with such infinite pains.

When the council was assembled, Madame de Tourville set forth her plan. She proposed that the dukes should come up secretly with their army, that they should procure, by force or by persuasion, a goodly number of boats, and go down the river into Bordeaux, shouting: "Vive Condé! Down with Mazarin!"

In this way Madame la Princesse's entry would assume the proportions of a veritable triumph, and Madame de Tourville, by a détour, would accomplish her famous project of taking forcible possession of Bordeaux, and thus inspiring the queen with a wholesome terror of an army whose opening move resulted so brilliantly.

Lenet nodded approval of everything, interrupting Madame de Tourville with admiring exclamations. When she had completed the exposition of her plan, he said:—

"Magnificent, madame! be good enough now to sum up your conclusions."

"That I can do very easily, in two words," said the good woman, triumphantly, warming up at the sound of her own voice. "Amid the hailstorm of bullets, the clanging of bells, and the cries, whether of rage or affection, of the people, a handful of weak women will be seen, intrepidly fulfilling their noble mission; a child in its mother's arms will appeal to the Parliament for protection. This touching spectacle cannot fail to move the most savage hearts. Thus we shall conquer, partly by force, partly by the justice of our cause; and that, I think, is Madame la Princesse's object."

The summing up aroused even more enthusiasm than the original speech. Madame la Princesse applauded; Claire, whose desire to be sent with a flag of truce to Île Saint-Georges became more and more earnest, applauded; the captain of the guards, whose business it was to thirst for battle, applauded; and Lenet did more than applaud; he took Madame de Tourville's hand, and pressed it with no less respect than emotion.

"Madame," he cried, "even if I had not known how great is your prudence, and how thoroughly you are acquainted, both by intuition and study, with the great civil and military question which engages our attention, I should assuredly be convinced of it now, and should prostrate myself before the most useful adviser that her Highness could hope to find."

"Is she not?" said the princess; "isn't it a fine scheme, Lenet? I agree with her entirely. Come, Vialas, give Monsieur le Duc d'Enghien the little sword I had made for him, and his helmet and coat of mail."

"Yes! do so, Vialas. But a single word first, by your leave, madame," said Lenet; while Madame de Tourville, who was all swollen up with pride, began to lose confidence, in view of her vivid remembrance of the subtle arguments with which Lenet was accustomed to combat her plans.

"Well," said the princess, "what is it now?"

"Nothing, madame, nothing at all; for no plan could be proposed more in harmony with the character of an august princess like yourself, and it could only emanate from your household."

These words caused Madame de Tourville to puff out anew, and brought back the smile to the lips of Madame la Princesse, who was beginning to frown.

"But, madame," pursued Lenet, watching the effect of this terrible *but* upon the face of his sworn foe, "while I adopt, I will not say simply without repugnance, but with enthusiasm, this plan, which seems to me the only available one, I will venture to propose a slight modification."

Madame de Tourville stiffened up, and prepared for defence. Madame la Princesse's smile disappeared.

Lenet bowed and made a motion with his hand as if asking permission to continue.

"My heart is filled with a joy I cannot express," he said, "in anticipation of the clanging of the bells, and the joyous acclamations of the people. But I haven't the confidence I would like to have in the hail-storm of bullets to which Madame has referred."

Madame de Tourville assumed a martial air. Lenet bowed even lower than before, and continued, lowering his voice a half-tone:—

"Assuredly it would be a grand spectacle to see a woman and her child walking calmly along in the midst of a tempest which would terrify most men. But I should fear that one of those same bullets, following a blind impulse, as brutal, unintelligent things are wont to do, might give Monsieur de Mazarin the advantage over us, and spoil our plan, which is so magnificent in other respects. I am of the opinion, expressed so eloquently by Madame de Tourville, that the young prince and his august mother should open up the way to the Parliament-house for us,—but by petition, not by arms. I think, in short, that it will be much better to move in that way the most savage hearts, than to conquer by other means the most valiant. I think that the former of these methods presents infinitely more chances of success, and that the object of Madame la Princesse is, before all else, to gain admission to Bordeaux. Now, I say that nothing is less sure than our success in gaining admission to Bordeaux, if we take the chances of a battle."

"You see," said Madame de Tourville, sourly, "that monsieur proposes, as usual, to demolish my plan, bit by bit, and quietly substitute a plan of his own therefor."

"I!" cried Lenet, while the princess reassured Madame de Tourville with a smile and a glance,—"I, the most enthusiastic of your admirers! no, a thousand times no! But I say that an officer in his Majesty's service named Dalvimar has arrived in the city from Blaye, whose mission is to arouse the officials and the people against her Highness. And I say that if Monsieur de Mazarin can put an end to the war at a single blow he will do it; that is why I fear Madame de Tourville's hail-storm of bullets, the more intelligent ones even more perhaps than the brutal, unreasoning ones."

This last argument seemed to make Madame la Princesse reflect.

"You always know everything, Monsieur Lenet," retorted Madame de Tourville, in a voice trembling with wrath.

"A good hot action would be a fine thing, however," said the captain of the guards, drawing himself up and marking time with his foot as if he were on the parade ground; he was an old soldier, whose sole reliance was upon force, and who would have shone in action.

Lenet trod upon his foot, looking at him the while with a most amiable smile.

"Yes, captain," said he; "but do you not think also that Monsieur le Duc d'Enghien is necessary to our cause, and that with him dead or a prisoner we are deprived of the real generalissimo of our armies?"

The captain of the guards, who knew that to bestow this pompous title of generalissimo upon a prince of seven years made himself, in reality, the commander-in-chief of the army, realized what a fool he had made of himself, and warmly supported Lenet's opinion.

Meanwhile Madame de Tourville had gone to the princess's side and was talking with her in an undertone. Lenet saw that the battle was not yet won; indeed, the next moment her Highness turned to him and said, testily:—

"It is very strange that you should be so bent upon demolishing what was so well constructed."

"Your Highness is in error," said Lenet. "I have never been persistent in offering such advice as I have had the honor to give you, and, if I demolish, it is with the intention of rebuilding. If, notwithstanding the arguments I have had the honor to submit to you, your Highness still desires to seek death with your son, you are at liberty to do so, and we will face death at your side; that is a very simple thing to do, and the first footman in your retinue, or the meanest scoundrel in the city will do as much. But if we wish to succeed, despite Mazarin, despite the queen, despite the Parliament, despite Mademoiselle Nanon de Lartigues, despite all the disadvantages inseparable from the feeble state to which we are reduced, this, in my opinion, is what we must do."

"Monsieur," cried Madame de Tourville, impetuously, catching Lenet's last sentence on the rebound, "there is no such thing as weakness, where we have on the one hand the name of Condé, and on the other two thousand of the men of Rocroy, Nordlingen, and Lens; and if we are weak under such circumstances, why, we are lost in any event, and no plan of yours, however magnificent it may be, will save us."

"I have read, madame," rejoined Lenet, calmly, enjoying in anticipation the effect of what he was about to say upon the princess, who was listening attentively in spite of herself, — "I have read that, in the reign of Tiberius, the widow of one of the most illustrious Romans, the noble-hearted Agrippina, who had been bereft of her husband Germanicus by persecution, a princess who could at will arouse to frenzy a whole army devoted to the memory of their dead general, preferred to enter Brundisium alone, to traverse Puglia and Campania clad in mourning, holding a child by each hand, pale-cheeked, eyes red with tears and bent upon the ground, while the children sobbed and gazed imploringly around; whereat all who saw — and from Brundisium to Rome there were above two million people — burst into tears, broke forth in threats and imprecations, and her cause was won, not at Rome alone, but before all Italy; not only in the judgment of her contemporaries, but in that of posterity; for she met with no shadow of resistance to her tears and lamentations, while lances would have been met with pikes, and swords with swords. To my mind there is a very strong resemblance between her Highness and Agrippina, between Monsieur le Prince and Germanicus, between Piso, the persecuting minister and poisoner, and Monsieur de Mazarin. With this strong resemblance between the personages concerned, the situation being almost identical, I ask that the same line of conduct be adopted; for, in my opinion, it is impossible that what succeeded so perfectly at one time could fail at another."

An approving smile played about Madame la Princesse's lips, and assured Lenet that his discourse had turned the tide of battle in his favor. Madame de Tourville took refuge in a corner of the room, veiling herself like an antique statue. Madame de Cambes, who had found a friend in Lenet, repaid him for his support in another matter, by nodding her head approvingly; the captain of the guards wept like a military tribune, and the little Duc d'Enghien cried: —

"Mamma, will you hold my hand, and dress me in mourning?"

"Yes, my son," the princess replied. "You know, Lenet, that it has always been my intention to present myself to the people of Bordeaux dressed in black."

"Especially," said Madame de Cambes, "as black is so wondrously becoming to your Highness,"

"Hush! little one," said the princess; "Madame de Tourville will cry it loud enough, without your saying it, even in a whisper."

The programme for the entry into Bordeaux was arranged according to Lenet's suggestions. The ladies of the escort were ordered to make their preparations. The young prince was dressed in a suit of white, trimmed with black and silver lace, and wore a hat with black and white plumes.

The princess herself was arrayed with an affectation of the greatest simplicity. In order to resemble Agrippina, by whom she was determined to take pattern in every respect, she wore plain black with no jewels of any sort.

Lenet, as the architect of the fête, exerted himself to the utmost to make it magnificent. The house in which he lived, in a small town some two leagues from Bordeaux, was constantly filled with partisans of Madame la Princesse, who were anxious to know, before she entered the city, what sort of entry would be most agreeable to her. Lenet, like a modern theatrical manager, suggested flowers, acclamations, and the ringing of bells; and, wishing to afford some satisfaction to the bellicose Madame de Tourville, he proposed that the princess should receive an artillery salute.

On the following day, May 31st, at the invitation of the Parliament, the princess set out for the city. One Lavie, *avocat-général* of Parliament, and a zealous partisan of Monsieur de Mazarin, had ordered the gates closed the night before, to prevent the entrance of the princess if she should present herself. But, on the other hand, the partisans of the Condés were not idle, and early in the morning the people, at their instigation, assembled in crowds amid shouts of, "Vive Madame la Princesse! Vive Monsieur le Duc d'Enghien!" and cut down the gates with axes; so that there was, finally, no opposition to this famous entry, which assumed the character of a triumph. Interested observers could estimate from these two occurrences the relative power of the leaders of the two factions which divided the city, for Lavie was acting directly under the advice of the Duc d'Épernon, while the leaders of the people were advised by Lenet.

The princess had no sooner passed through the gate than the scene which had been long in preparation was enacted upon a gigantic scale. A salute was fired by the vessels in the harbor, and the guns of the city replied. Plowers fell in showers from the windows, and were stretched in festoons across the street, so that the pavements were strewn with them and the air laden with their perfume. Loud acclamations arose from the lips of thirty thousand zealots of all ages and both sexes, whose enthusiasm increased with the interest inspired by Madame la Princesse and her son, and with their hatred for Mazarin.

However, the Duc d'Enghien was the cleverest actor in all the cast. Madame la Princesse gave up leading him by the hand, either because she feared to weary him, or so that he might not be buried under the roses; he was carried by his gentleman-in-waiting, so that his hands were free, and he sent kisses to right and left, and waved his plumed hat gracefully to the spectators.

The good people of Bordeaux are easily excited; the women soon reached a condition of frenzied adoration for the lovely child who wept so charmingly, and the old magistrates were moved to tears by the words of the little orator, who said: "Messieurs, take my father's place, for Monsieur le Cardinal has taken him away from me."

In vain did the partisans of the minister attempt to make some opposition; fists, stones, and even halberds enjoined discretion upon them, and they had no choice but to leave the triumphant rebels a clear field.

Meanwhile Madame de Cambes, with pale and serious face, drew the attention of many in the crowd as she walked along behind Madame la Princesse. As she reflected upon the glorious success of the day, she could not avoid the fear that it might bring forgetfulness of the resolution of the preceding day. She was walking along, as we have said, hustled and crowded by the adoring people, inundated with flowers and respectful caresses, shuddering with the fear of being taken up and carried in triumph, a fate with which some voices began to threaten Madame la Princesse, the Duc d'Enghien, and their suite, when Lenet noticed her embarrassment, and gave her his hand to assist her in reaching a carriage.

"Ah! Monsieur Lenet, you are very fortunate," she said to him, replying to her own thought. "You succeed always in enforcing your opinion, and your advice is always followed. To be sure," she added, "it is always good, and the best results—"

"It seems to me, madame," rejoined Lenet, "that you have no reason to complain, as the only suggestion you have made has been adopted."

"How so?"

"Wasn't it agreed that you should try to take Île Saint-Georges?"

"Yes, but when shall I be allowed to open my campaign?"

"To-morrow, if you promise to fail."

"Never fear; I am only too likely to fulfil your wishes in that regard."

"So much the better."

"I do not fully understand you."

"We need to have Île Saint-Georges make a stubborn resistance, in order to induce the Bordelais to call for our two dukes and their army, who,

I am free to say, although my opinion on that point comes dangerously near coinciding with Madame de Tourville's, seem to me eminently necessary under present circumstances."

"Unquestionably," said Claire; "but although I am not as learned in the art of war as Madame de Tourville, I had the impression that a place is not usually attacked until it has been summoned to surrender."

"What you say is perfectly true."

"Then you will send a flag of truce to Île Saint-Georges?"

"Most certainly!"

"Very well! I ask leave to carry the flag of truce."

Lenet's eyes dilated in surprise.

"You!" he said; "you! Why, have all our ladies become Amazons?"

"Gratify my whim, dear Monsieur Lenet."

"To be sure. The worst that can happen to us would be your taking Saint-Georges."

"It's agreed, then?"

"Yes."

"But promise me one thing."

"What is that?"

"That no one shall know the name or sex or rank of the flag of truce, unless her mission is successful."

"Agreed," said Lenet, giving Madame de Cambes his hand.

"When shall I start?"

"When you choose."

"To-morrow."

"To-morrow let it be."

"Good. See, Madame la Princesse and her son are just about going up on Monsieur le Président Lalasne's terrace. I leave my part in the triumph to Madame de Tourville. Pray excuse my absence to her Highness on the ground of indisposition. Bid the coachman drive me to the apartments assigned me. I will make my preparations, and reflect upon how I can best accomplish my mission, which naturally causes me some uneasiness, as it is the first of the kind I have ever undertaken, and everything in this world, they say, depends on one's beginning."

"Peste!" said Lenet. "I no longer wonder that Monsieur de La Rochefoucauld was upon the point of deserting Madame de Longueville for you; you are certainly her equal in many respects, and her superior in others."

"Possibly," said Claire. "I do not put the compliment aside altogether; but if you have any influence over Monsieur de La Rochefoucauld, dear Monsieur Lenet, I beg you to exert it to strengthen his devotion to his first flame, for his love terrifies me."

"We will do our best," said Lenet, with a smile. "This evening I will give you your instructions."

"You consent, then, to let me take Saint-Georges for you?"

"I must, since you wish it."

"And what about the dukes and the army?"

"I have in my pocket another means of bringing them hither."

Having given the address of Madame de Cambes to the coachman, Lenet smilingly took leave of her and returned to the princess.

II

On the day following Madame la Princesse's entry into Bordeaux, there was a grand dinner-party at Île Saint-Georges, Canolles having invited the principal officers of the garrison and the other governors of fortresses throughout the province.

At two o'clock in the afternoon, the hour appointed for the beginning of the repast, Canolles found himself surrounded by a dozen or more gentlemen, the majority of whom he then saw for the first time. As they described the great event of the preceding day, making sport of the ladies in Madame la Princesse's retinue, they bore but little resemblance to men about to enter upon what might be an obstinate conflict, and to whom the most momentous interests of the kingdom were intrusted.

Canolles, magnificent in his gold-laced coat, and with radiant face, set the example of gayety and animation. As dinner was about to be served, he said:—

"Messieurs, I beg your pardon, but there is still one guest missing."

"Who is it?" the young men asked, exchanging glances.

"The governor of Vayres, to whom I sent an invitation, although I do not know him, and who, just because I do not know him, is entitled to some indulgence. I beg, therefore, that you will pardon a delay of half an hour."

"The governor of Vayres!" exclaimed an old officer, accustomed to military regularity, and from whom the suggestion of delay brought forth a sigh,—"the governor of Vayres, if I mistake not, is the Marquis de Bernay; but he doesn't administer the government in person; he has a lieutenant."

"In that case," said Canolles, "if he doesn't come, his lieutenant will come in his place. He is himself undoubtedly at court, the fountain-head of favors."

"But, baron," said one of the guests, "it doesn't seem to me that he need be at court to secure promotion, for I know a certain commandant who has no reason to complain. *Dame!* captain, lieutenant-colonel, and governor, all within three months! That's a very pretty little road to travel, you must confess."

"And I do confess it," said Canolles, blushing, "and as I know not to whom to attribute such a succession of favors, I must, in good sooth, agree that there is some good genius in my household to bring me such prosperity."

"We have no question as to Monsieur le Gouverneur's good genius," said the lieutenant who received Canolles upon his arrival; "it is his merit."

"I do not deny the merit, far from it," said another officer; "I am the first to bear witness to it. But I will take the liberty of adding to it the patronage of a certain lady, the cleverest, most generous, most lovable of her sex,— after the queen, of course."

"No insinuations, count," rejoined Canolles, smiling at the last speaker; "if you have any secrets of your own, keep them for your own sake; if they concern your friends, keep them for your friends' sake."

"I confess," said an officer, "that when I heard a suggestion of delay, I supposed that our forgiveness was to be sought in favor of some gorgeous toilet. But I see that I was mistaken."

"Pray, do we dine without ladies?" asked another.

"*Dame!* unless I invite Madame la Princesse and her suite," said Canolles, "I hardly see whom we could have; besides, we must not forget, messieurs, that our dinner-party is a serious function; if we choose to talk business we shall bore nobody but ourselves."

"Well said, commandant, although the women do seem to be engaged in a veritable crusade against our authority at this moment; witness what Monsieur le Cardinal said in my presence to Don Luis de Haro."

"What did he say?" Canolles asked.

"'You are very fortunate! Spanish women think of nothing but money, flirting, and lovers, while the women of France refuse to take a lover now until they have sounded him on political questions; so that,' he added, despairingly, 'lovers pass their time discussing affairs of State.'"

"For that reason," said Canolles, "the present war is called the 'war of women;' a very flattering title for us."

At that moment, just as the half-hour's reprieve expired, the door opened, and a servant announced that Monsieur le Gouverneur was served.

Canolles requested his guests to follow him; but as the procession was about to start, another announcement was heard in the reception-room.

"Monsieur le Gouverneur de Vayres!"

"Ah!" said Canolles; "it's very kind of him."

He stepped forward to meet the colleague in whom he expected to find a stranger, but started back in amazement.

"Richon!" he cried; "Richon, governor of Vayres!"

"Myself, my dear baron," returned Richon, affably, but with his customary serious expression.

"Ah! so much the better! so much the better!" said Canolles, cordially pressing his hand. "Messieurs," he added, "you do not know him, but I do; and I say, emphatically, that it would be impossible to intrust an important appointment to a more honorable man."

Richon looked proudly about upon the guests, and as he detected no other expression in the looks which were bent upon him than polite surprise tempered with much good-will, he said:—

"My dear baron, now that you have answered for me so handsomely, present me, I beg you, to those of your guests whom I haven't the honor of knowing."

As he spoke he glanced significantly at three or four gentlemen to whom he was an entire stranger.

Thereupon ensued an interchange of civilities in the courtly manner characteristic of the time. Before half an hour had passed Richon was on the friendliest terms with all the young officers, and might have asked any one of them for his sword or his purse. His sponsors were his well-known gallantry, his spotless reputation, and the noble spirit written in his eyes.

"*Pardieu!* messieurs;" said the governor of Braunes, "there's no denying that, although he's a churchman, Monsieur de Mazarin has a keen eye for fighting-men, and has been managing matters well in that direction for some time. He scents war, and selects for governors, Canolles here, and Richon at Vayres."

"Is there to be fighting?" inquired Richon, carelessly.

"Is there to be fighting!" rejoined a young man fresh from the court. "You ask if there is to be fighting, Monsieur Richon?"

"Yes."

"Well! I ask you what condition your bastions are in?"

"They are almost new, monsieur; for in the three days I have been at the fort I have done more repairing and renovating than had been done in three years."

"Good! it won't be long before they will be tested," rejoined the young man.

"So much the better," said Richon. "What do fighting-men long for? War."

"The king can sleep soundly now," said Canolles, "for he holds the Bordelais in check by means of the two rivers."

"The person who put me where I am can count upon my devotion," said Richon.

"How long do you say you have been at Vayres, monsieur?"

"Three days. How long have you been at Saint-Georges, Canolles?"

"A week. Did you have a reception like mine, Richon? Mine was magnificent, and even yet I haven't thanked these gentlemen sufficiently. There were bells ringing and drums beating, and acclamations. Cannon were the only thing missing, but I have been promised some within a few days, and that consoles me."

"My reception, my dear Canolles, was as modest as yours was splendid. I was ordered to introduce a hundred men into the place, a hundred men of the Turenne regiment, and I was in a quandary how I was to do it, when my commission, signed by Monsieur d'Épernon, arrived at Saint-Pierre, where I then was. I set out at once, handed my commission to the lieutenant, and took possession of the place without drum or trumpet. At present I am there."

Canolles, who smiled at the beginning, was conscious of an indefinable presentiment of evil from the tone in which these last words were uttered.

"And you are settled there?" he asked Richon.

"I am putting things in order," Richon replied tranquilly.

"How many men have you?"

"In the first place, the hundred men of the Turenne regiment, old soldiers of Rocroy, who can be depended upon; also a company I am forming in the town; as fast as recruits come in, I take them in hand, tradesmen, workingmen, youths, about two hundred in all; lastly, I am expecting a re-enforcement of a hundred or a hundred and fifty men, levied by an officer of the province."

"Captain Ramblay?" inquired one of the guests.

"No, Captain Cauvignac."

"I don't know him," said several voices.

"I do," said Canolles.

"Is he a stanch royalist?"

"I should not dare to say. I have every reason to think, however, that Captain Cauvignac is a creature of Monsieur le Duc d'Épernon and very devoted to him."

"That answers the question; any man who is devoted to the duke is devoted to his Majesty."

"He's a sort of scout sent on ahead to beat up the country for the king," said the old officer, who was making up for the time lost in waiting. "I have heard of him in that connection."

"Is his Majesty on his way hither?" asked Richon, with his customary tranquil manner.

"He should be at least as far as Blois," replied the young man just from the court.

"Are you sure of it?"

"Quite sure. His army will be commanded by Maréchal de la Meilleraie, who is to effect a junction in this neighborhood with Monsieur le Duc d'Épernon."

"At Saint-Georges, perhaps?"

"Rather at Vayres," said Richon. "Monsieur de la Meilleraie comes from Bretagne, and Vayres is on his road."

"The man who happens to be where the two armies come together will have to look well to his bastions," said the governor of Braunes. "Monsieur de la Meilleraie has thirty guns, and Monsieur d'Épernon twenty-five."

"They will make a fine show," said Canolles; "unfortunately, we shall not see it."

"True," said Richon, "unless some one of us declares for the princes."

"But Canolles is sure to come in for a volley from somebody. If he declares for the princes he'll have Monsieur de la Meilleraie and Monsieur d'Épernon about his ears; if he remains true to his Majesty he'll taste the fire of the Bordelais."

"Oh! as to the latter," said Canolles, "I don't consider them very terrible, and I confess that I am a little ashamed to have no worthier antagonist. Unfortunately, I am for his Majesty body and soul, and I must be content with a tradesmen's war."

"They'll give you that, never fear," said Richon.

"Have you any basis for conjecture on that subject?" queried Canolles.

"I have something better than that," said Richon. "I have certain knowledge. The council of citizens has decided to take Île Saint-Georges first of all."

"Good," said Canolles, "let them come; I am ready for them."

The conversation had reached this stage and the dessert had just been served, when they heard drums beating at the entrance of the fortress.

"What does that mean?" said Canolles.

"*Pardieu!*" exclaimed the young officer who had brought the news from court, "it would be curious if they should attack you at this moment; an assault and escalade would be a delightful after-dinner diversion!"

"Deuce take me! it looks very much like it," said the old officer; "these wretched cads never fail to disturb you at your meals. I was at the outposts at Charenton at the time of the war in Paris, and we could never breakfast or dine in peace."

Canolles rang; the orderly on duty in the antechamber entered.

"What is going on?" Canolles asked.

"I don't know yet, Monsieur le Gouverneur; some messenger from the king or from the city, no doubt."

"Inquire, and let me know."

The soldier hastened from the room.

"Let us return to the table, messieurs," said Canolles to his guests, most of whom had left their seats. "It will be time enough to leave the table when we hear the cannon."

All the guests resumed their seats with smiling faces. Richon alone, over whose features a cloud had passed, still seemed restless, and kept his eyes fixed upon the door, awaiting the soldier's return. But an officer with drawn sword appeared in his stead.

"Monsieur le Gouverneur," said he, "a flag of truce."

"A flag of truce from whom?"

"From the princes."

"Coming from where?"

"From Bordeaux."

"From Bordeaux!" all the guests save Richon repeated in chorus.

"Oho! so war is really declared, is it," said the old officer, "that they send flags of truce?"

Canolles reflected a moment, and during that moment his features assumed as grave an expression as the circumstances demanded.

"Messieurs," said he, "duty before everything. I shall probably find myself confronted with a question not easy to solve in connection with this message from my Bordeaux friends, and I cannot say when I shall be able to join you again—"

"No! no!" cried the guests as one man. "Allow us to take our leave, commandant; this incident is notice to us to return to our respective posts, and we must separate at once."

"It was not for me to suggest it, messieurs," said Canolles, "but as the suggestion comes from you I am bound to say that it would be the more prudent course. Bring out the horses or carriages of these gentlemen."

As hurried in their movements as if they were already on the battlefield, the guests having been ferried ashore, vaulted into the saddle, or entered their carriages and rode rapidly away, followed by their escorts, in the direction of their respective residences.

Richon was the last to take his leave.

"Baron," said he, "I did not want to leave you as the others did, as we have known each other longer than you have known any of them. Adieu; give me your hand, and good luck to you!"

Canolles gave him his hand.

"Richon," said he, looking earnestly into his face, "I know you; you have something on your mind; you do not tell it to me, for it probably is not your secret. However, you are moved,—and when a man of your temperament is moved, it's for no small matter."

"Are we not about to part?" said Richon.

"Yes, and so were we about to part when we took leave of each other at Biscarros's inn, but you were calm then."

Richon smiled sadly.

"Baron," said he, "I have a presentiment that we shall never meet again!"

Canolles shuddered at the profoundly melancholy inflection in the partisan's ordinarily firm voice.

"Ah, well!" said he, "if we do not meet again, Richon, it will be because one of us has died the death of a brave man; and in that case the one who dies will be sure, at all events, of surviving in the heart of a friend! Embrace me, Richon; you wished me good luck; I wish you good courage!"

The two men embraced warmly, and for some seconds their noble hearts beat against each other.

When they parted, Richon wiped away a tear, the first, perhaps, that ever dimmed his proud glance; then, as if he feared that Canolles might see the tear, he hurried from the room, ashamed, no doubt, to have exhibited such a sign of weakness to a man whose courage was so well known to him.

III

The dining-hall was left untenanted, save by Canolles and the officer who announced the flag of truce, and who was still standing beside the door.

"What are Monsieur le Gouverneur's orders?" he said, after a brief pause.

Canolles, who was deep in thought, started at the voice, raised his head, and shook off his preoccupation.

"Where is the flag of truce?" he asked.

"In the armory, monsieur."

"By whom is he accompanied?"

"By two of the Bordeaux militia."

"What is he?"

"A young man, so far as I can judge; he wears a broad-brimmed hat, and is wrapped in a great cloak."

"In what terms did he announce himself?"

"As the bearer of letters from Madame la Princesse and the Parliament of Bordeaux."

"Request him to wait a moment," said Canolles, "and I will be at his service."

The officer left the room to perform his errand, and Canolles was preparing to follow him, when a door opened, and Nanon, pale and trembling, but with an affectionate smile upon her lips, made her appearance.

"A flag of truce, my dear," she said, grasping the young man's hand. "What does it mean?"

"It means, dear Nanon, that the good people of Bordeaux propose either to frighten me or seduce me."

"What have you decided?"

"To receive him."

"Is there no way to avoid it?"

"Impossible. It is one of the customs which must be followed."

"Oh! *mon Dieu!*"

"What's the matter, Nanon?"

"I'm afraid—"

"Of what?"

"Didn't you say that the mission of this flag of truce was to frighten you or seduce you?"

"Of course; a flag of truce is good for nothing else. Are you afraid he'll frighten me?"

"Oh, no! but he may perhaps seduce you—"

"You insult me, Nanon."

"Alas! my dear, I only say what I am afraid of—"

"You distrust me to that extent? For what do you take me, pray?"

"For what you are, Canolles; a noble heart, but easily moved."

"Well, well!" laughed Canolles; "in God's name, who is this flag of truce? Can it be Dan Cupid in person?"

"Perhaps."

"Why, have you seen him?"

"I haven't seen him, but I heard his voice. It's a very soft voice for a flag of truce."

"You are mad, Nanon! let me do my duty. It was you who made me governor."

"To defend me, my dear."

"Well, do you think me dastard enough to betray you? Really, Nanon, you insult me by placing so little confidence in me!"

"You are determined, then, to see this young man?"

"I must, and I shall take it very ill of you if you make any further objection to my fulfilling my duty in that respect."

"You are free to do as you please, my dear," said Nanon, sadly. "One other word—"

"Say it."

"Where shall you receive him?"

"In my cabinet."

"Canolles, one favor—"

"What is it?"

"Receive him in your bedroom instead of your cabinet."

"What have you in your head?"

"Don't you understand?"

"No."

"My room opens into yours."

"And you will listen?"

"Behind your bed-curtains, if you will allow me." "Nanon!"

"Let me be near you, dear. I have faith in my star; I shall bring you luck."

"But, Nanon, suppose this flag of truce—"

"Well?"

"Should have some State secret to tell me?"

"Can you not intrust a State secret to her who has intrusted her life and her fortune to you?"

"Very well! listen to us, Nanon, if you insist upon it; but don't detain me any longer; the messenger is waiting for me."

"Go, Canolles, go; but, first, accept my loving thanks for your kindness to me!"

And the young woman would have kissed her lover's hand.

"Foolish girl!" said Canolles, pressing her to his heart and kissing her on the forehead; "so you will be—"

"Behind the curtains of your bed. There I can see and hear."

"Whatever else you do, don't laugh, Nanon, for these are serious matters."

"Have no fear," said Nanon. "I won't laugh."

Canolles ordered the messenger to be introduced, and passed into his own apartment, a room of great size, furnished under Charles IX. in a style of severe simplicity. Two candelabra were burning upon the chimney-piece, but their feeble glimmer was quite inadequate to light the immense apartment; the alcove at the farther end was entirely in shadow.

"Are you there, Nanon?" Canolles asked.

A stifled "Yes" reached his ears.

At that moment he heard steps in the corridor. The sentinel presented arms; the messenger entered and followed his introducer with his eyes, until he was, or thought he was, alone with Canolles. Then he removed his hat and threw back his cloak; immediately a mass of blond locks fell down over a pair of shapely shoulders, the graceful, willowy form of a woman appeared under the gold baldric, and Canolles, by the sad, sweet expression of her face, recognized the Vicomtesse de Cambes.

"I told you that I would seek you," she said, "and I keep my word; here I am."

Canolles clasped his hands and fell upon a chair in speechless amazement, and an agony of fear.

"You! you!" he muttered. "*Mon Dieu!* why are you here; what seek you here?"

"I have come to ask you, monsieur, if you still remember me."

Canolles heaved a heart-breaking sigh, and put his hands before his eyes, seeking to banish the ravishing but fatal apparition.

Everything was made clear to him in an instant; Nanon's alarm, her pallor, her trembling, and, above all, her desire to be present at the interview. Nanon, with the keen eyes of jealousy, had detected a woman in the flag of truce.

"I have come to ask you," continued Claire, "if you are ready to carry out the engagement you entered into with me in the little room at Jaulnay, — to send your resignation to the queen, and enter the service of the princes."

"Oh! silence! silence!" cried Canolles.

Claire shuddered at the accent of utter dismay in the commandant's voice, and glanced uneasily about the room.

"Are we not alone here?" she asked.

"We are, madame; but may not some one hear us through the walls?"

"I thought that the walls of Fort Saint-Georges were more solid than that," said Claire with a smile.

Canolles made no reply.

"I have come to ask you," Claire resumed, "how it happens that I have heard nothing of you during the eight or ten days you have been here, — so that I should still know nothing as to who is governor of Île Saint-Georges, had not chance, or public rumor, informed me that it is the man who swore to me, barely twelve days since, that his disgrace was the best of good fortune, since it enabled him to devote his arm, his courage, his life, to the party to which I belong."

Nanon could not repress a movement, which made Canolles jump and Madame de Cambes turn her head.

"Pray, what was that?" she demanded.

"Nothing," Canolles replied; "one of the regular noises of this old room. There is no end to the dismal creaking and groaning here."

"If it is anything else," said Claire, laying her hand upon Canolles' arm, "be frank with me, baron, for you must realize the importance of this interview between us, when I decided to come myself to seek you."

Canolles wiped the perspiration from his brow, and tried to smile.

"Say on," said he.

"I reminded you a moment since of your promise, and asked you if you were ready to keep it."

"Alas, madame," said Canolles, "it has become impossible."

"Why so?"

"Because since that time many unforeseen events have happened, many ties which I thought broken forever have been formed anew; for the punishment which I knew I had merited, the queen has substituted a recompense of which I am unworthy; to-day I am united to her Majesty's party by—gratitude."

A sigh floated out upon the air. Poor Nanon doubtless was expecting a different word from the one that ended the sentence.

"Say by ambition, Monsieur de Canolles, and I can understand it. You are nobly born; at twenty-eight you are made lieutenant-colonel, and governor of a fortress; it's all very fine, I know; but it is no more than the fitting reward of your merit, and Monsieur de Mazarin is not the only one who appreciates it."

"Madame," said Canolles, "not another word, I beg."

"Pardon, monsieur," returned Claire, "but on this occasion it is not the Vicomtesse de Cambes who speaks to you, but the envoy of Madame la Princesse, who is intrusted with a mission to you,—a mission which she must now fulfil."

"Speak, madame," said Canolles, with a sigh which was much like a groan.

"Very well! Madame la Princesse, being aware of the sentiments which you expressed, in the first place at Chantilly, and afterwards at Jaulnay, and being anxious to know to what party you really belong, determined to send you a flag of truce to make an attempt to secure the fortress; this attempt, which another messenger might have made with much less ceremony, perhaps, I undertook to make, thinking that I should have more chance of success, knowing, as I do, your secret thoughts on the subject."

"Thanks, madame," said Canolles, tearing his hair; for, during the short pauses in the dialogue, he could hear Nanon's heavy breathing.

"This is what I have to propose to you, monsieur, in the name of Madame la Princesse, let me add; for if it had been in my own name," continued Claire, with her charming smile, "I should have reversed the order of the propositions."

"I am listening," said Canolles, in a dull voice.

"I propose that you surrender Île Saint-Georges on one of the three conditions which I submit to your choice. The first is this,—and pray remember that it does not come from me: the sum of two hundred thousand livres—"

"Oh, madame, go no further," said Canolles, trying to break off the interview at that point. "I have been intrusted by the queen with the post of commandant at Île Saint-Georges, and I will defend it to the death."

"Remember the past, monsieur," said Claire, sadly; "that is not what you said to me at our last interview, when you proposed to abandon everything to follow me, when you had the pen already in your hand to offer your resignation to the persons for whom you propose to sacrifice your life to-day."

"I might have had that purpose, madame, when I was free to choose my own road; but to-day I am no longer free—"

"You are no longer free!" cried Claire, turning pale as death; "how am I to understand that? What do you mean?"

"I mean that I am in honor bound."

"Very well! then listen to my second proposition."

"To what end?" said Canolles; "have I not told you often enough, madame, that my resolution is immovable? So do not tempt me; you would do so to no purpose."

"Forgive me, monsieur," said Claire, "but I, too, am intrusted with a mission, and I must go through with it to the end."

"Go on," murmured Canolles; "but you are very cruel."

"Resign your command, and we will work upon your successor more effectively than upon you. In a year, in two years, you can take service under Monsieur le Prince with the rank of brigadier."

Canolles sadly shook his head.

"Alas! madame," said he, "why do you ask nothing of me but impossibilities?"

"Do you make that answer to me?" said Claire. "Upon my soul, monsieur, I do not understand you. Weren't you on the point of signing your resignation once? Did you not say to her who was beside you at that time, listening to you with such delight, that you did it freely and from the bottom of your heart? Why, I pray to know, will you not do here, when I ask you, when I beg you to do it, the very thing that you proposed to do at Jaulnay?"

Every word entered poor Nanon's heart like a dagger-thrust, and Canolles seemed to share her agony.

"That which at that time was an act of trifling importance would to-day be treachery, infamous treachery!" said Canolles, gloomily. "I will never surrender Île Saint-Georges, I will never resign my post!"

"Stay, stay," said Claire in her sweetest voice, but looking about uneasily all the while; for Canolles' resistance, and, above all, the constraint under which he was evidently laboring seemed very strange to her. "Listen now to my last proposition, with which I would have liked to begin, for I knew, and I said beforehand, that you would refuse the first two. Material advantages, and I am very happy to have divined it, are not the things which tempt a heart like yours. You must needs have other hopes than those of ambition and of fortune; noble instincts require noble rewards. Listen—"

"In Heaven's name, madame," Canolles broke in, "have pity on me!"

And he made as if he would withdraw.

Claire thought that his resolution was shaken, and, confident that what she was about to say would complete her victory, she detained him, and continued:—

"If, instead of a mere mercenary recompense, you were offered a pure and honorable recompense; if your resignation were to be purchased,—and you can resign without blame, for, as hostilities have not begun, it would be neither defection nor treachery, but a matter of choice, pure and simple, — if, I say, your resignation were to be purchased by an alliance; if a woman, to whom you have said that you loved her, whom you have sworn always to love, and who, notwithstanding your oaths, has never responded directly to your passion, if that woman should come to you and say: 'Monsieur de Canolles, I am free, I am wealthy, I love you; be my husband, let us go hence together, — go wherever you choose, away from all these civil commotions, away from France,' — tell me, monsieur, would you not then accept?"

Canolles, despite Claire's blushes, despite her fascinating hesitation, despite the memory of the lovely little château de Cambes, which he could have seen from his window, had not the darkness come down from heaven during the scene we have been describing, — Canolles remained firm and immovable in his determination; for he could see in the distance, a white spot in the deep shadow, the pale, tear-stained face of Nanon, trembling with agony, peering out from behind the Gothic curtains.

"Answer me, in Heaven's name!" exclaimed the viscountess, "for I am at a loss to understand your silence. Am I mistaken? Are you not Monsieur le Baron de Canolles? Are you not the same man who told me at Chantilly that you loved me, and who repeated it at Jaulnay, — who swore that you loved me alone in all the world, and that you were ready to sacrifice every other love to me? Answer! answer! in Heaven's name, answer!"

A moan came from behind the curtains, this time so distinct and unmistakable that Madame de Cambes could no longer doubt that a third person was present at the interview; her frightened eyes followed the direction taken by Canolles' eyes, and he could not look away so quickly that the viscountess did not catch a glimpse of that pale, immovable face, that form like the form of a ghost, which followed, with breathless interest, every word that was uttered.

The two women exchanged a glance of flame through the darkness, and each of them uttered a shriek.

Nanon disappeared.

Madame de Cambes hastily seized her hat and cloak, and said, turning to Canolles: —

"Monsieur, I understand now what you mean by duty and gratitude. I understand what duty it is that you refuse to abandon or betray; I understand, in short, that there are affections utterly impervious to all seduction, and I leave you to those affections and to that duty and gratitude. Adieu, monsieur, adieu!"

She started toward the door, nor did Canolles, attempt to detain her; but a painful memory stopped her. "Once more, monsieur," said she, "in the name of the friendship that I owe you for the service you were pleased to render me, in the name of the friendship that you owe me for the service I rendered you, in the name of all those who love you and whom you love — and I except not one — do not engage in this struggle; to-morrow, day after to-morrow, perhaps, you will be attacked at Saint-Georges; do not cause me the bitter pain of knowing that you are either conquered or dead."

At the words the young man started and came to himself.

"Madame," said he, "I thank you on my knees for the assurance you give me of your friendship, which is more precious to me than I can tell you. Oh! let them come and attack me! *Mon Dieu!* let them come on! I look for the enemy with more ardor than will ever impel him to come to me. I feel the need of fighting, I feel the need of danger to raise me in my own esteem; let the struggle come, and the danger that attends it, aye, death itself! death will be welcome since I know that I shall die rich in your friendship, strong in your compassion, and honored by your esteem."

"Adieu, monsieur," said Claire, walking toward the door.

Canolles followed her. In the middle of the dark corridor he seized her hand, and said, in so low a tone that he himself could hardly hear the words he uttered: —

"Claire, I love you more than I have ever loved you; but it is my misfortune that I can prove my love only by dying far away from you."

A little ironical laugh was Claire's only reply; but no sooner was she out of the château than a pitiful sob burst from her throat, and she wrung her hands, crying: —

"Ah! my God, he doesn't love me! he doesn't love me! And I, poor miserable wretch that I am, do love him!"

IV

Upon leaving Madame de Cambes, Canolles returned to his apartment. Nanon was standing like a statue in the centre of the room. Canolles walked toward her with a sad smile; as he drew nearer she bent her knee; he held out his hand, and she fell at his feet.

"Forgive me," said she; "forgive me, Canolles! It was I who brought you here, I who procured this difficult and dangerous post to be given you; if you are killed I shall be the cause of your death. I am a selfish creature, and I thought of naught but my own happiness. Leave me now; go!"

Canolles gently raised her.

"Leave you!" said he; "never, Nanon, never; you are sacred in my sight; I have sworn to protect you, defend you, save you, and I will save you, or may I die!"

"Do you say that from the bottom of your heart, Canolles, without hesitation or regret?"

"Yes," said Canolles, with a smile.

"Thanks, my noble, honorable friend, thanks. This life of mine, to which I used to attach so much value, I would sacrifice for you to-day without a murmur, for not until to-day did I know what you have done for me. They offered you money,—are not my treasures yours? They offered you love,— was there ever in the world a woman who would love you as I love you? They offered you promotion? Look you, you are to be attacked; very good! let us buy soldiers, let us heap up arms and ammunition; let us double our forces and defend ourselves; I will fight for my love, you for your honor. You will whip them, my gallant Canolles; you will force the queen to say that she has no more gallant officer than you; and then I will look to your promotion; and when you are rich, laden with glory and honor, you can desert me, if you choose; I shall have my memories to console me."

As she spoke Nanon gazed at Canolles, and she awaited such a response as women always expect to their exaggerated words,—a response, that is to say, as absurd and hyperbolical as the words themselves. But Canolles sadly hung his head.

"Nanon," said he, "so long as I remain at Île Saint-Georges, you shall never suffer injury, never submit to insult. Set your mind at ease on that score, for you have nothing to fear."

"Thanks," said she, "although that is not all I ask. Alas! I am lost," she muttered inaudibly; "he loves me no longer."

Canolles detected the glance of flame which shone in her eyes like a lightning-flash, and the frightful momentary pallor which told of such bitter suffering.

"I must be generous to the end," he said to himself, "or be an infamous villain.—Come, Nanon, come, my dear, throw your cloak over your shoulders, take your man's hat, and let us take a breath of the night air; it will do you good. I may be attacked at any moment, and I must make my nightly round of inspection."

Nanon's heart leaped for joy; she arrayed herself as her lover bade her, and followed him.

Canolles was no make-believe officer. He entered the service when he was little more than a child, and had made a real study of his profession. So it was that he made his inspection not simply as commandant, but as engineer. The officers, when they saw that he came in the guise of a favorite, supposed that he was a mere ornamental governor. But when they were questioned by him, one after another, as to the provisions for attack and defence, they were compelled to recognize in this apparently frivolous young man an experienced captain, and even the oldest among them addressed him with respect. The only things with which they could find fault were the mildness of his voice when giving orders, and the extreme courtesy with which he questioned them; they feared that this last might be the mask of weakness. However, as every one realized the imminence of the danger, the governor's orders were executed with such celerity and accuracy that the chief conceived as favorable an opinion of his soldiers as they had formed of him. A company of pioneers had arrived during the day. Canolles ordered the construction of works, which were instantly begun. Vainly did Nanon try to take him back to the fort, in order to spare him the fatigue of a night passed in this way; Canolles continued his round, and gently dismissed her, insisting that she should return within the walls. Then, having sent out three or four scouts, whom the lieutenant recommended as the most intelligent of all those at his disposal, he stretched himself out upon a block of stone, whence he could watch the progress of the work.

But while his eyes mechanically followed the movement of mattocks and pickaxes, Canolles's mind wandered away from the material things which surrounded him, to pass in review, not only the events of the day, but all the extraordinary adventures of which he had been the hero since the day he first saw Madame de Cambes. But, strangely enough, his mind went back no farther than that day; it seemed to him as if his real life had begun at that time; that until then he had lived in another world,—a world of inferior instincts, of incomplete sensations. But from that hour there had been a light in his life which gave a different aspect to everything, and in the brightness of that new light, Nanon, poor Nanon, was pitilessly sacrificed to another passion, violent from its very birth, like every passion which takes possession of the whole life into which it enters.

After much painful meditation, mingled with thrills of heavenly rapture at the thought that he was beloved by Madame de Cambes, Canolles confessed to himself that it was duty alone which impelled him to act the part of a man of honor, and that his friendship for Nanon counted for nothing in his determination.

Poor Nanon! Canolles called his feeling for her friendship, and in love friendship is very near indifference.

Nanon also was keeping vigil, for she could not make up her mind to retire. Standing at a window, wrapped in a black cloak to avoid being seen, she followed, not the sad, veiled moon peering out through the clouds, not the tall poplars waving gracefully in the night wind, not the majestic Garonne, which seemed like a rebellious vassal gathering its strength to war against its master, rather than a faithful servant bearing its tribute to the ocean,—but the slow, painful struggle in her lover's mind; in that dark form outlined against the stone, in that motionless shadow lying beneath a lantern, she saw the living phantom of her past happiness. She, once so active and so proud and clever, had lost all her cleverness and pride and energy; it seemed as if her faculties, sharpened by her misery, became doubly acute and far-seeing; she felt another love springing into life in her lover's heart, as God, sitting aloft in the vast firmament, feels the blade of grass growing in the earth.

Not until dawn did Canolles return to his room. Nanon took her leave when she saw him coming, so that he had no idea that she had watched all night. He dressed himself with care, mustered the garrison anew, inspected by daylight the different batteries, especially those which commanded the left bank of the Garonne, ordered the little harbor to be closed by chains, stationed a number of boats provided with falconets and blunder-busses, reviewed his men, encouraged them with a few earnest, heartfelt words, and returned to his apartment once more, about ten o'clock.

Nanon was awaiting him with a smile upon her lips.

She was no longer the haughty, imperious Nanon, whose slightest caprice made Monsieur d'Épernon himself tremble; but a timid mistress, a shrinking slave, who had ceased to demand love for herself, but simply craved permission to love.

The day passed without other incident than the different developments of the drama which was being enacted in the hearts of the two young people. The scouts sent out by Canolles returned one after another. No one of them brought any definite news; but there was great excitement in Bordeaux, and it was evident that something was in preparation there.

Madame de Cambes, upon returning to the city, although she did not divulge the details of the interview, which lay hidden in the inmost recesses of her heart, made known its result to Lenet. The Bordelais loudly demanded that Île Saint-Georges should be taken. The people volunteered in crowds for the expedition.

The leaders could hold them hack only by alleging the absence of an experienced officer to take charge of the enterprise, and of regular troops to carry it through. Lenet seized the opportunity to whisper the names of the two dukes and offer the services of their army; the suggestion was received with enthusiasm, and the very men who had voted to close the gates a few days before, were loudest in demanding their presence.

Lenet hastened to make known the good news to the princess, who at once assembled her council.

Claire feigned fatigue in order to avoid taking part in any decision adverse to Canolles, and withdrew to her chamber to weep at her ease.

There she could hear the shouts and threats of the mob. Every shout, every threat was directed against Canolles.

Soon the drum began to beat, the companies assembled; the sheriffs distributed weapons to the people, who demanded pikes and arquebuses; the cannon were taken from the arsenal, powder was distributed, and two hundred boats were in readiness to ascend the Garonne with the evening tide, while three thousand men were to march up the left bank and attack by land.

The river army was to be commanded by Espagnet, councillor of Parliament, a brave and judicious man; and the land forces by Monsieur de La Rochefoucauld, who had entered the city with about two thousand gentlemen. Monsieur le Duc de Bouillon, with a thousand more, was to arrive two days later, and Monsieur de La Rochefoucauld hastened the attack as much as possible, so that his colleague should not be present.

V

On the second day following that on which Madame de Cambes presented herself in the guise of a flag of truce at Île Saint-Georges, as Canolles was making his round upon the ramparts about two in the afternoon, he was informed that a messenger with a letter for him desired to speak with him.

The messenger was at once introduced, and handed his missive to Canolles.

Evidently there was nothing official about the document; it was a small letter, longer than it was wide, written in a fine, slightly tremulous hand, upon perfumed bluish paper of fine quality.

Canolles felt his heart beat faster at the mere sight of the letter.

"Who gave it to you?" he asked.

"A man of fifty-five to sixty years of age."

"Grizzly moustache and royale?"

"Yes."

"Slightly bent?"

"Yes."

"Military bearing?"

"Yes."

"That's all."

Canolles gave the man a louis, and motioned to him to withdraw at once.

Then, with wildly beating heart, he concealed himself in the corner of a bastion, where he could read the letter at his ease.

It contained only these two lines:—

> "You are to be attacked. If you are no longer worthy of me,
> show yourself at least worthy of yourself."

The letter was not signed, but Canolles recognized Madame de Cambes as he had recognized Pompée; he looked to see if anybody was looking at him, and blushing like a child over his first love, he put the paper to his lips, kissed it ardently, and placed it upon his heart.

Then he mounted the crown of the bastion, whence he could follow the course of the Garonne well-nigh a league, and could see the whole extent of the surrounding plain.

Nothing was to be seen upon land or water.

"The day will pass like this," he muttered; "they won't come by daylight; they have probably halted to rest on the way, and will begin the attack this evening."

He heard a light step behind him, and turned. It was his lieutenant.

"Well, Monsieur de Vibrac, what news?" said Canolles.

"They say, commandant, that the princes' flag will float over Île Saint-Georges to-morrow."

"Who says that?"

"Two of our scouts who have just come in, and have seen the preparations the citizens are making."

"What answer did you make when they said that?"

"I answered, commandant, that it was all the same to me so long as I wasn't alive to see it."

"Ah! you stole my answer, monsieur."

"Bravo, commandant! we asked nothing better; and the men will fight like lions when they know that that is your answer."

"Let them fight like men, that's all I ask. What do they say as to the manner of the attack?"

"General, they are preparing a surprise for us," said De Vibrac, with a laugh.

"*Peste!* what sort of a surprise? this is the second warning I have received. Who leads the assailants?"

"Monsieur de La Rochefoucauld the land forces, Espagnet, councillor of Parliament, the naval forces."

"Very good!" said Canolles; "I have a little advice to give him."

"Whom?"

"The councillor."

"What is it?"

"To re-enforce the urban militia with some good, well-disciplined regiment, who can show the tradesmen how to receive a well-sustained fire."

"He hasn't waited for your advice, commandant; I think he must have been more or less of a soldier before he became a man of the law, for he has enlisted the services of the Navailles regiment for this expedition."

"The Navailles regiment?"

"Yes."

"My old regiment?"

"The same. It has gone over, it seems, bag and baggage, to the princes."

"Who is in command?"

"Baron de Ravailly."

"Indeed?"

"Do you know him?"

"Yes—a fine fellow, and brave as his sword. In that case it will be warmer than I supposed, and we shall have some fun."

"What are your orders, commandant?"

"That the posts be doubled to-night; that the troops retire fully dressed, with loaded muskets within reach. One half will stand guard, while the other half sleeps. Those who are on guard will keep out of sight behind the embankment. One moment—Have you informed anybody of the news brought by the scouts?"

"Nobody."

"Good; keep it secret for some little time yet. Select ten or twelve of your worst soldiers; you should have some fishermen, or poachers?"

"We have only too many of them, commandant."

"Well, as I was saying, select ten of them, and give them leave of absence till to-morrow morning. Let them go and throw their lines in the Garonne, and set their snares in the fields. To-night Espagnet and Monsieur de La Rochefoucauld will take them and question them."

"I don't understand—"

"Don't you understand that it is most essential that the assailants should believe that we are entirely unprepared for them? These men, who know nothing, will take their oaths with an air of sincerity, which will carry conviction because it will not be assumed, that we are sound asleep in our beds."

"Ah! excellent!"

"Let the enemy approach, let him disembark, let him plant his ladders."

"But when shall we fire on him?"

"When I give the word. If a single shot is fired from our ranks before I order it, the man who fires it shall die, my word for it!"

"The deuce!"

"Civil war is war twice over. It is important, therefore, that it be not carried on like a hunting party. Let Messieurs les Bordelais laugh, and laugh yourselves if it amuses you; but don't laugh until I give the word."

The lieutenant retired to transmit Canolles' commands to the other officers, who looked at one another in amazement. There were two men in the governor, — the courteous gentleman, and the implacable soldier.

Canolles returned to take supper with Nanon; but the supper was put ahead two hours, as he had determined not to leave the ramparts from dusk till dawn. He found Nanon running through a pile of letters.

"You can defend the place with confidence, dear Canolles," said she, "for it won't be long before you are re-enforced. The king is coming, Monsieur de La Meilleraie is coming with his army, and Monsieur d'Épernon is coming with fifteen thousand men."

"But, meanwhile, they have a week or ten days before them. Nanon," added Canolles, with a smile, "Île Saint-Georges is not impregnable."

"Oh! while you are in command I have no fear."

"Yes; but just because I am in command I may be killed. Nanon, what would you do in that case? Have you thought about it?"

"Yes," replied Nanon, smiling back at him.

"Very good! have your boxes ready. A boatman will be waiting at a certain spot; if you have to take to the water, four of my people who are good swimmers will be at hand, with orders not to leave you, and they will take you ashore."

"All precautions are useless, Canolles; if you are killed I shall need nothing."

Supper was announced. Ten times, while they sat at table, Canolles rose and went to the window, which looked upon the river, and before the end of the repast he left the table altogether; night was beginning to fall.

Nanon would have followed him.

"Nanon," said he, "go to your room, and give me your word that you will not leave it. If I knew that you were outside, exposed to the slightest danger, I would not answer for myself. Nanon, my honor is at stake; do not trifle with my honor."

Nanon offered Canolles her carmine lips, more brilliant in hue from the pallor of her cheeks, and went to her room, saying:—

"I obey you, Canolles; I choose that enemies and friends alike should know the man I love; go!"

Canolles left the room. He could not withhold his admiration from this strong nature, so quick to comply with his wishes, so responsive to his will. He had hardly reached his post ere the night came down, threatening and awe-inspiring, as it always is when it conceals in its dark depths a bloody secret.

Canolles took up his position at the end of the esplanade, which overlooked the course of the stream and both its banks. There was no moon; a veil of dark clouds overhung the earth. There was no danger of being seen, but it was almost impossible to see.

About midnight, however, it seemed to him that he could distinguish dark masses moving upon the left bank, and gigantic shapes gliding along the surface of the stream. But there was no other noise than the moaning of the night wind among the branches.

The masses ceased to move, the shapes became stationary at some distance. Canolles thought that he must have been mistaken, but he redoubled his watchfulness; his eager eyes pierced the darkness, his ear was awake to the slightest sound.

The clock on the fortress struck three, and the slow, mournful reverberation died away in the darkness.

Canolles was beginning to think that the warning he had received was a hoax, and he was on the point of retiring, when Lieutenant de Vibrac, who stood beside him, suddenly placed one hand upon his shoulder and pointed with the other toward the river.

"Yes, yes," said Canolles, "there they are; we have no time to lose. Go and wake the men who are off duty, and station them behind the wall. You told them, didn't you, that I would kill the first man who fired?"

"Yes."

"Well, tell them again."

By the first streaks of dawn long boats laden with men, who were laughing and talking in low tones, could be seen approaching the island, and there was a very pronounced eminence on the bank, which did not exist the night before. It was a battery of six guns which Monsieur de La Rochefoucauld had set up during the night, and the men in the boats had delayed their arrival because the battery was not ready to begin operations.

Canolles asked if the weapons were loaded, and upon being answered in the affirmative, bade the troops reserve their fire.

The boats came nearer and nearer, and there was soon light enough for Canolles to distinguish the cross-belts and peculiar hats worn by the Navailles regiment, to which, as we know, he formerly belonged. In the prow of one of the foremost boats was Baron de Ravailly, who had succeeded him in command of his company, and at the stern the lieutenant, who was his foster brother, a great favorite among his comrades because of his joyous nature, and his inexhaustible store of jokes.

"You will see," said he, "that they won't stir, and Monsieur de La Rochefoucauld will have to wake them up with his cannon. *Peste!* how they sleep at Saint-Georges; I'll surely come here when I'm ill."

"Dear old Canolles plays his rôle of governor like a paterfamilias," said Ravailly; "he's afraid his men will take cold if he makes them mount guard at night."

"Upon my soul," said another, "there's not a sentinel to be seen!"

"*Holà!*" cried the lieutenant, stepping ashore, "wake up, up there, and lend us a hand to come up."

Shouts of laughter arose along the whole line at this last pleasantry, and while three or four boats pulled toward the harbor, the rest of the force disembarked.

"I see how it is," said Ravailly; "Canolles prefers to have it appear that he was taken by surprise in order not to get into trouble at court. Let us return him courtesy for courtesy, messieurs, and kill no one. Once in the fort, mercy for all, except for the women, who may not ask it, *sarpejeu!* Don't forget that this is a war between friends, boys; I '11 run through the first man who unsheathes his sword."

The merriment broke out afresh at this command, which was given with true French gayety, and the soldiers joined in with the officers.

"Ah! my friends," said the lieutenant, "it does one good to laugh, but we mustn't let it interfere with what we have to do. Ladders and grappling-hooks!"

The soldiers thereupon drew forth long ladders from the boats, and advanced toward the wall.

At that, Canolles rose with his cane in his hand, and his hat on his head, like a man who was taking the fresh morning air for pleasure, and approached the parapet, which reached only to his waist.

It was light enough for him to be recognized.

"Ah! good-morning, Navailles," he said to the regiment; "good-morning, Ravailly; good-morning, Remonenq."

"Look, it's Canolles!" exclaimed the young officers; "are you awake at last, baron?"

"Why, yes! what would you have? we live like the King of Yvetot here,—early to bed, and late to rise; but what the devil are you doing at this time of night?"

"*Pardieu!*" said Ravailly, "I should think that you might see. We are here to besiege you, that's all."

"Well, why are you here to besiege me?"

"To take your old fort."

Canolles began to laugh.

"Come," said Ravailly, "you surrender, don't you?"

"But I must know first to whom I am surrendering. How happens it that Navailles is serving against the king?"

"Faith, my dear fellow, because we have turned rebels. On thinking it over we concluded that Mazarin was a downright rascal, unworthy to be served by gallant gentlemen; so we went over to the princes. And you?"

"My dear fellow, I am an enthusiastic Épernonist."

"Pshaw! leave your people there and come with us."

"Impossible—Ho! hands off the drawbridge chains down there! You know that those things are to be looked at from a distance, and it brings bad luck to touch them. Ravailly, bid them not touch the chains, or I'll fire on them," continued Canolles, frowning; "and I warn you, Ravailly, that I have some excellent marksmen."

"Bah! you are joking!" rejoined the captain. "Let yourself be taken; you are not in force."

"I am not joking. Down with the ladders! Ravailly, beware, I beg you, for it's the king's house you are besieging!"

"Saint-Georges the king's house!"

"*Pardieu!* look up and you will see the flag on the crown of the embankment. Come, push your boats off into the water, and put the ladders aboard, or I fire. If you want to talk, come alone or with Remonenq, and we will breakfast together, and talk as we eat. I have an excellent cook at Île Saint-Georges."

Ravailly began to laugh, and encouraged his men with a glance. Meanwhile another company was preparing to land.

Canolles saw that the decisive moment had arrived; and, assuming the firm attitude and serious demeanor befitting a man burdened with so heavy a responsibility as his, he cried:—

"Halt there, Ravailly! A truce to jesting, Remonenq! not another word or step, or I fire, as truly as the king's flag is above, and as your arms are raised against the lilies of France."

Suiting the action to the threat, he overturned with his strong arm the first ladder that showed its head over the stones of the rampart.

Five or six men, more eager than their fellows, were already on the ladder, and were overturned with it. They fell, and a great shout of laughter arose from besiegers and besieged alike; one would have said they were schoolboys at play.

At that moment a signal was given to indicate that the besiegers had passed the chains drawn across the mouth of the harbor.

Ravailly and Remonenq at once seized a ladder and prepared to go down into the moat, shouting:—

"This way, Navailles! Escalade! escalade! up! up!"

"My poor Ravailly," cried Canolles, "I beseech you to stop where you are."

But at the same instant the shore battery, which had kept silent hitherto, flashed and roared, and a cannon-ball ploughed up the dirt all around Canolles.

"Go to!" said Canolles, extending his cane, "if you will have it so! Fire, my lads, fire all along the line!"

Thereupon, although not a man could be seen, a row of muskets appeared, pointing down at the parapet, a girdle of flame enveloped the crown of the wall, while the detonation of two huge pieces of artillery answered Monsieur de La Rochefoucauld's battery.

Half a score of men fell; but their fall, instead of discouraging their comrades, inspired them with fresh ardor. The shore battery replied to the battery on the rampart; a cannon-ball struck down the royal standard, and another killed one of Canolles' lieutenants, named D'Elboin.

Canolles looked around and saw that his men had reloaded their weapons.

"Fire!" he cried, and the order was executed as promptly as before.

Ten minutes later not a single pane of glass was left on the island. The stones trembled and burst in pieces; the cannon-balls knocked holes in the walls, and were flattened on the great flags; a dense smoke overhung the fort, and the air was filled with shrieks and threats and groans.

Canolles saw that Monsieur de La Rochefoucauld's artillery was doing the greatest amount of damage. "Vibrac," said he, "do you look out for Ravailly, and see that he doesn't gain an inch of ground in my absence. I am going to our battery."

He ran to the two pieces which were returning Monsieur de La Rochefoucauld's fire, and himself attended to loading and sighting them; in an instant three of the six guns on shore were dismounted, and fifty men were stretched on the ground. The others, who were not anticipating such a resistance, began to scatter and fly.

Monsieur de La Rochefoucauld, trying to rally them, was struck by a fragment of stone, which knocked his sword out of his hands.

Canolles, content with this result, left the captain of the battery to do the rest, and ran back to repel the assault, which was continued by the Navailles regiment, supported by Espagnet's men.

Vibrac had maintained his ground, but had received a bullet in his shoulder.

Canolles, by his mere presence, redoubled the courage of his troops, who welcomed him with joyful shouts.

"Pray pardon me," he cried to Ravailly, "for leaving you for a moment, my dear friend; I did it, as you may see, to dismount Monsieur de La Rochefoucauld's guns; but be of good cheer, here I am again."

As the captain, who was too excited to reply to the jest,—indeed, it may be that he failed to hear it amid the terrific uproar of artillery and musketry,—led his men to the assault for the third time, Canolles drew a pistol from his belt, and taking aim at his former comrade, now his enemy, fired.

The ball was guided by a firm hand and sure eye; it broke Ravailly's arm.

"Thanks, Canolles!" he cried, for he saw who fired the shot. "Thanks, I will pay you for that."

Notwithstanding his force of will, the young captain was forced to halt, and his sword fell from his hands. Remonenq ran to him and caught him in his arms.

"Will you come into the fort and have your wound dressed, Ravailly?" cried Canolles. "I have a surgeon who's as skilful in his line as my cook in his."

"No; I return to Bordeaux. But expect me again at any moment, for I will come, I promise you. The next time, however, I will select my own hour."

"Retreat! retreat!" cried Remonenq. "They are running over yonder. Au revoir, Canolles; you have the first game."

Remonenq spoke the truth; the artillery had done tremendous execution among the forces on shore, which had lost a hundred men or more. The naval contingent had fared little better. The greatest loss was sustained by the Navailles regiment, which, in order to uphold the honor of the uniform, had insisted upon marching ahead of D'Espagnet's citizen soldiers.

Canolles raised his pistol.

"Cease firing!" said he; "we will let them retreat unmolested; we have no ammunition to waste."

Indeed, it would have been a waste of powder to continue the fire. The assailants retired in hot haste, taking their wounded with them, but leaving the dead behind.

Canolles mustered his men and found that he had four killed and sixteen wounded. Personally he had not received a scratch.

"*Dame!*" he exclaimed, as he was receiving Nanon's joyful caresses ten minutes later, "they were not slow, my dear, to make me earn my governor's commission. What absurd butchery! I have killed a hundred and fifty men at least, and broken the arm of one of my best friends, to prevent his being killed outright."

"Yes," said Nanon, "but you are safe and sound, aren't you?"

"Thank God! surely you brought me luck, Nanon. But look out for the second bout! The Bordelais are obstinate; and, more than that, Ravailly and Remonenq promised to come again."

"Oh, well," said Nanon, "the same man will be in command at Saint-Georges, with the same troops to sustain him. Let them come, and the second time they will have a warmer reception than before, for between now and then you will have time to strengthen your defences, won't you?"

"My dear," said Canolles, confidentially, "one doesn't get to know a place all at once. Mine is not impregnable, I have discovered that already; and if my name were La Rochefoucauld, I would have Île Saint-Georges to-morrow morning. By the way, D'Elboin will not breakfast with us."

"Why not?"

"Because he was cut in two by a cannon-ball."

VI

The return of the attacking party to Bordeaux presented a doleful spectacle. The worthy tradesmen had left home triumphantly on the previous day, relying upon their numbers and upon the ability of their leaders; in fact, their minds were entirely at ease as to the result of the expedition, from sheer force of habit, which sometimes answers all the purposes of confidence to men who are in danger. For who was there among them who had not in his young days haunted the woods and fields of Île Saint-Georges? Where could you find a Bordelais who had not handled the oar, the fowling-piece, or the fisherman's net in the neighborhood which they were about to revisit as soldiers.

Thus the defeat was doubly depressing to the honest fellows; the locality shamed them no less than the enemy. So it was that they returned with hanging heads, and listened resignedly to the lamentation and wailing of the women, who ascertained the losses sustained by the vanquished forces, by counting them after the manner of the savages of America.

The great city was filled with mourning and consternation. The soldiers returned to their homes to describe the disaster, each in his own way. The chiefs betook themselves to the apartments occupied by the princess at the house of the president.

Madame de Condé was at her window awaiting the return of the volunteers. Sprung as she was from a family of warriors, wife of one of the greatest conquerors in the world, and brought up to look with scorn upon the rusty armor and absurd headgear of the militia, she could not restrain a feeling of uneasiness as she thought that those same citizens, her partisans, had gone out to contend against a force of old, well-disciplined soldiers. But there were three considerations from which she derived some comfort: in the first place, Monsieur de La Rochefoucauld was in command; in the second place the Navailles regiment had the right of the line; in the third place, the name of Condé was inscribed upon the banners.

But every one of these considerations, which gave the princess ground for hope, was the source of bitter grief to Madame de Cambes; even so did everything that grieved the illustrious dame become a source of triumph to the viscountess.

The Duc de La Rochefoucauld was the first to make his appearance, covered with dust and blood; the sleeve of his black doublet was torn open, and there were spots of blood upon his shirt.

"Is this true that I hear?" cried the princess, darting to meet him.

"What do you hear, madame?" he asked, coolly.

"That you were repulsed."

"You have not heard the whole, madame; to put it frankly, we have been beaten."

"Beaten!" cried the princess, turning pale; "beaten! it isn't possible!"

"Beaten!" murmured the viscountess; "beaten by Monsieur de Canolles!"

"How did it happen, I pray to know?" demanded Madame de Condé, in a freezing tone eloquent of her bitter indignation.

"It happened, madame, as all miscalculations happen, in play, in love, in war; we attacked those who were more clever or stronger than ourselves."

"Pray is this Monsieur de Canolles such a gallant fellow?" queried the princess.

Madame de Cambes' heart throbbed with delight.

"Oh! *mon Dieu!*" replied La Rochefoucauld with a shrug, "not more so than another! But as he had fresh soldiers, stout walls, and was on the lookout for us, having probably received warning of our attack, he had the advantage of our good Bordelais. Ah! madame, let me remark parenthetically that they are sorry soldiers! They ran away at the second volley."

"And Navailles?" cried Claire, heedless of the imprudence of such a demonstration.

"Madame," replied La Rochefoucauld, "the only difference between Navailles and the militia is that the militia ran away, and Navailles fell back."

"The only thing we lack now is to lose Vayres!"

"I don't say that we shall not," retorted La Rochefoucauld, coolly.

"Beaten!" exclaimed the princess, tapping the floor with her foot; "beaten by upstarts, commanded by a Monsieur de Canolles! the very name is absurd."

Claire blushed to the whites of her eyes.

"You think the name absurd, madame," rejoined the duke, "but Monsieur de Mazarin thinks it sublime. And I should almost venture to say," he added with a swift, keen glance at Claire, "that he's not alone in his opinion. Names are like colors, madame," he continued with his bilious smile; "there's no accounting for tastes concerning them."

"Do you think Richon is the man to allow himself to be whipped?"

"Why not? I have allowed myself to be whipped! We must wait until the vein of bad luck is exhausted; war is a game; one day or another we shall have our revenge."

"This wouldn't have happened," said Madame de Tourville, "if my plan had been adopted."

"That's very true," said the princess; "they are never willing to do what we suggest, on the ground that we are women and know nothing about war. The men have their own way and get beaten."

"*Mon Dieu*, yes, madame; but that happens to the greatest generals. Paulus Æmilius was beaten at Cannae, Pompey at Pharsalia, and Attila at Chalons. There are none but Alexander and yourself, Madame de Tourville, who have never been beaten. Let us hear your plan."

"My plan, Monsieur le Duc," said Madame de Tourville in her primmest manner, "was to lay siege to the fortress in regular form. They wouldn't listen to me, but preferred a *coup de main*. You see the result."

"Answer madame, Monsieur Lenet," said the duke; "for my own part I do not feel sufficiently strong in strategy to maintain the conflict."

"Madame," said Lenet, whose lips thus far had opened only to smile, "there was this to be said against your idea of a regular siege, that the Bordelais are not soldiers but citizens; they must have supper under their own roof and sleep in their own bed. Now, a regular siege requires those concerned in it to dispense with a multitude of conveniences to which our worthy burghers are accustomed. So they went out to besiege Île Saint-Georges as amateurs; do not blame them for having failed to-day; they will travel the four leagues and recommence the struggle as often as need be."

"You think that they will begin again?" the princess inquired.

"Oh! as to that, madame," said Lenet, "I am quite sure of it; they are too fond of their island to leave it in the king's hands."

"And they will take it?"

"Most assuredly, some day or other."

"Very good! on the day that they take it," cried Madame la Princesse, "I propose that this insolent Monsieur de Canolles shall be shot unless he surrenders at discretion."

Claire felt a deathly shudder run through her veins.

"Shot!" echoed the duke; "*peste!* if that's according to your Highness's ideas of war, I congratulate myself most sincerely that I am numbered among your friends."

"Let him surrender, then."

"I would like to know what your Highness would say if Richon were to surrender."

"We're not talking of Richon, Monsieur le Duc; Richon is not in question now. Bring me a citizen, a sheriff, a councillor,—somebody to whom I can talk and assure myself that this cup is not without bitterness to those who have put it to my lips."

"Luckily enough," said Lenet, "Monsieur d'Espagnet is even now at the door, soliciting the honor of an audience of your Highness."

"Admit him," said the princess.

Throughout this scene Claire's heart had beaten at times as if it would burst, and again had felt as if it would never beat again. She said to herself that the Bordelais would make Canolles pay dear for his triumph.

But it was much worse when Espagnet, by his protestations surpassed Lenet's confident anticipations.

"Madame," said he to the princess, "I beg that your Highness will have no fear; instead of four thousand men we will send eight thousand; instead of six pieces of cannon, we will take along twelve; instead of one hundred men, we will lose two, three, four hundred, if need be, but we will take Saint-Georges!"

"Bravo! monsieur," cried the duke; "spoken like a man! You know that I am with you, whether as your leader or as a volunteer, as often as you undertake this task. But bear in mind, I beg, that at the rate of five hundred men lost for each of four expeditions like this one, our army will be reduced one-fifth."

"Monsieur le Duc," rejoined Espagnet, "we have thirty thousand men in condition to bear arms at Bordeaux; we will drag all the cannon from the arsenal to the fortress, if necessary; we will discharge enough ammunition to reduce a mountain of granite to powder; I will myself cross the river at the head of the sappers, and we will take Saint-Georges; we have just sworn a solemn oath to do it."

"I doubt whether you will take Saint-Georges so long as Monsieur de Canolles is alive," said Claire in an almost inaudible voice.

"Then we will kill him, or have him killed, and take Saint-Georges afterward," rejoined Espagnet.

Madame de Cambes stifled the cry of dismay that came to her lips.

"Do you desire to take Saint-Georges?"

"Do we desire it!" cried the princess; "I should say as much; we desire little else."

"Very well!" said Madame de Cambes, "let me have my way, and I will put the place in your hands."

"Bah!" exclaimed the princess; "you promised much the same thing once before and failed."

"I promised your Highness to make an attempt to win over Monsieur de Canolles. That attempt failed because I found Monsieur de Canolles inflexible."

"Do you expect to find him more easy to approach after his triumph?"

"No; for that reason I did not say this time that I would turn over the governor to you, but the place itself."

"How so?"

"By admitting your soldiers into the very heart of the fortress."

"Are you a fairy, madame, that you undertake such a task?" La Rochefoucauld asked her.

"No, monsieur, I am a landowner," said the viscountess.

"Madame is pleased to jest," retorted the duke.

"Not at all, not at all," said Lenet. "I can imagine a world of meaning in the three words just uttered by Madame de Cambes."

"Then that is all I require," said the viscountess; "Monsieur Lenet's approval means everything to me. I say again that Saint-Georges is as good as taken, if I may be allowed to say four words in private to Monsieur Lenet."

"Madame," chimed in Madame de Tourville, "I too can take Saint-Georges, if I can have my way."

"Let Madame de Tourville first set forth her plan so that we can all hear," said Lenet, checking the effort Madame de Cambes was making to lead him into a corner; "then you shall whisper yours to me."

"Say on, madame," said the princess.

"I would start at night with twenty boats carrying two hundred musketeers; another party, equal in number, would creep along the right bank; four or five hundred more would ascend the left bank; meanwhile ten or twelve hundred Bordelais—"

"Bear in mind, madame," interposed La Rochefoucauld, "that you already have ten or twelve hundred men engaged."

"I will take Saint-Georges with a single company," said Claire; "give me Navailles, and I will answer for the result."

"'Tis worth considering," said the princess, while Monsieur de La Rochefoucauld, with his most contemptuous smile, gazed pityingly at these women who presumed to discuss military questions which embarrassed the boldest and most enterprising men.

"I will listen to you now, madame," said Lenet. "Come this way."

He led Claire to a window recess, where she whispered her secret in his ear.

Lenet emitted a joyful exclamation.

"Indeed, madame," said he, turning to the princess, "if you will give Madame de Cambes *carte blanche*, Saint-Georges is ours."

"When?" the princess demanded.

"When you please."

"Madame is a great captain!" sneered La Rochefoucauld.

"You may judge for yourself, Monsieur le Duc," said Lenet, "when you enter Saint-Georges in triumph, without firing a single shot."

"When that time comes I will approve."

"If it's as certain as you say," said the princess, "let everything be prepared for to-morrow."

"On such day and at such hour as your Highness pleases," said Claire. "I will await your commands in my apartment."

With that she bowed and withdrew; the princess, who had passed in an instant from wrath to hope, did the same, followed by Madame de Tourville. Espagnet, having renewed his protestations, took his departure, and the duke was left alone with Lenet.

VII

"My dear Monsieur Lenet," said the duke, "as the women seem to have taken charge of the war, I think it would be a good plan for the men to do a little intriguing. I have heard of a certain Captain Cauvignac, whom you commissioned to raise a company, and who is represented to me as an exceedingly clever sort of fellow. I sent for him; is there any way for me to see him?"

"He is waiting, monseigneur," said Lenet.

"Let him come in, then."

Lenet pulled a bell-cord, and a servant appeared.

"Send Captain Cauvignac hither," said Lenet.

An instant after, our old acquaintance appeared in the doorway; but, prudent as always, there he halted.

"Come hither, captain," said the duke; "I am Monsieur le Duc de La Rochefoucauld."

"I know you perfectly well, monseigneur," said Cauvignac.

"Ah! so much the better, then. You received a commission to raise a company?"

"It is raised."

"How many men have you at your disposal?"

"A hundred and fifty."

"Well armed and equipped?"

"Well armed, poorly equipped. I looked out for the weapons first of all, as the most essential thing. As to their equipment, as I am a very disinterested youth, and as I am moved principally by my affection for Messieurs les Princes, I came rather short of money, Monsieur Lenet having given me but ten thousand livres."

"You have enrolled a hundred and fifty men with ten thousand livres?"

"Yes, monseigneur."

"That's a marvellous achievement."

"I have methods known to myself alone, monseigneur, to which I have resorted."

"Where are your men?"

"They are here; you will see a fine company, monseigneur, especially in respect to their morals, — all men of rank; not a single nobody among them."

Monsieur de La Rochefoucauld walked to the window, and saw in the street a hundred and fifty individuals of all ages, sizes, and conditions, drawn up in two lines, and kept in place by Ferguzon, Barrabas, Carrotel, and their two colleagues, arrayed in their most magnificent attire. The rank and file resembled a party of bandits much more nearly than a company of soldiers.

As Cauvignac had said, they were very much out at elbows, but remarkably well armed.

"Have you received any orders concerning the place where your men are to be stationed?" the duke inquired.

"I have been ordered to lead them to Vayres, and I am simply awaiting the ratification of that order by Monsieur le Duc to turn over my company to Monsieur Richon, who is expecting its arrival."

"But do not you remain at Vayres with them?"

"My principles, monseigneur, forbid my ever doing such a foolish thing as to shut myself up within four walls, when I am at liberty to go where I please. I was born to lead the life of the patriarchs."

"Very good; go where you choose; but despatch your men to Vayres as soon as possible."

"Then they are really to form part of the garrison of that place?"

"Yes."

"Under Monsieur Richon's orders?"

"Yes."

"But, monseigneur, what are my men to do in the fort, where there are already about three hundred men?"

"You are very inquisitive."

"Oh! it's not mere curiosity that makes me ask, monseigneur; it is fear."

"What are you afraid of?"

"That they will be condemned to inaction, which would be a great pity; any man makes a mistake who allows a good weapon to rust."

"Don't be alarmed, captain, they won't rust; in a week they will have a chance to fight."

"In that case they may be killed!"

"It's very likely,—unless, in addition to your secret method of recruiting soldiers, you have a secret method of making them invulnerable."

"Oh! it's not that; but before they are killed I would like to have them paid for."

"Didn't you tell me that you had received ten thousand livres?"

"Yes, on account. Ask Monsieur Lenet; he is a man of method, and I am sure he will remember our agreement."

The duke turned to Lenet.

"It is true, Monsieur le Duc," said the straightforward counsellor; "we gave Monsieur Cauvignac ten thousand livres by way of advance for the first outlay; but we promised him a hundred crowns per man."

"In that case," said the duke, "we owe the captain thirty-five thousand francs?"

"Just so, monseigneur."

"They will be given you."

"Might it not be done now, Monsieur le Duc?"

"No, impossible."

"Why so?"

"Because you are one of us, and strangers must be settled with first of all. You understand that only those people we fear have to be coaxed."

"An excellent maxim!" said Cauvignac; "in all bargains, however, it is customary to fix a time for payment."

"Very well, let us say a week," said the duke.

"A week it is," said Cauvignac.

"But suppose that when the week has elapsed we have not paid?" suggested Lenet.

"In that case I resume control of my men."

"That is no more than fair," the duke agreed.

"And I can do what I choose with them?"

"Of course, as they belong to you."

"But—" Lenet began.

"Nonsense!" said the duke in a low tone,—"when we have them safely shut up in Vayres!"

"I don't like this sort of bargain," said Lenet, shaking his head.

"They are very common in Normandy," said Cauvignac; "they are called conditional sales."

"Is it agreed?" asked the duke.

"It is," Cauvignac replied.

"When will your men start?"

"At once, if you so order."

"I do so order."

"Then they are off, monseigneur."

The captain went down into the street and said two words in Ferguzon's ear, and the Cauvignac company, followed by all the idlers whom its strange appearance had attracted, marched away toward the harbor, where the three boats were waiting which were to transport it up the Dordogne to Vayres, while its commander, faithful to the principle of freedom of action just enunciated by him to Monsieur de La Rochefoucauld, stood watching his men affectionately as they moved away.

Meanwhile the viscountess in her own apartments was sobbing and praying.

"Alas!" she moaned, "I could not save his honor unimpaired, but I will at least save the appearance of honor. He must not be conquered by force; for I know him so well that I know that he would die in defence of the place; it must be made to seem to him that he is overcome by treason. Then, when he knows what I have done for him, and, above all, my object in doing it, beaten as he is, he will bless me still."

Consoled by this hope, she rose, wrote a few words which she hid in her breast, and returned to Madame la Princesse, who had sent to ask her to go with her to look to the needs of the wounded and carry consolation and material assistance to the widows and orphans.

Madame la Princesse called together all who had taken part in the expedition. In her own name and that of the Dc d'Enghien, she praised the exploits of those who had distinguished themselves; talked a long time with Ravailly, who, although he carried his arm in a sling, declared his readiness to begin again the next morning; laid her hand upon Espagnet's shoulder, and told him that she looked upon him and his gallant Bordelais as the firmest supporters of her party; in fine, she succeeded so well in inflaming their minds that the most disheartened swore that they would have their revenge, and would have started for Île Saint-Georges on the instant.

"No, not at this moment," said the princess; "take to-day and to-night for rest, and day after to-morrow you shall be in possession there forever."

This assurance was welcomed by noisy demonstrations of warlike ardor. Every shout sank deep into the heart of the viscountess, for they were like so many daggers threatening her lover's existence.

"You hear what I have agreed, Claire," said the princess; "it is for you to see that I do not break my word to these good people."

"Never fear, madame," was the reply. "I will perform what I have promised."

That same evening a messenger set out in hot haste for Saint-Georges.

VIII

The next day, while Canolles was making his morning round, Vibrac approached him and handed him a note and a key which had been brought to the fortress during the night by a strange man, who left them with the lieutenant of the guard, saying that there was no reply.

Canolles started as he recognized the handwriting of Madame de Cambes, and his hand trembled as he broke the seal.

This is what the letter contained:—

> "In my last note I gave you warning that Saint-Georges would be attacked during the night; in this, I warn you that Saint-Georges will be taken to-morrow; as a man, as an officer of the king, you run no other risk than that of being made prisoner; but Mademoiselle de Lartigues is in a very different situation, and the hatred which is entertained for her is so great that I would not answer for her life if she should fall into the hands of the Bordelais. Therefore persuade her to fly; I will furnish you with the means of flight.

> "At the head of your bed, behind a curtain upon which are embroidered the arms of the lords of Cambes, to whom Île Saint-Georges formerly belonged,—Monsieur le Vicomte de Cambes, my late husband, presented it to the king,—you will find a door to which this is the key. It is one of the entrances to an extensive underground passage which passes beneath the bed of the river, and comes out at the manor of Cambes. Persuade Mademoiselle Nanon de Lartigues to fly through that passage—and, if you love her, fly with her.

> "I answer for her safety upon my honor.

> "Adieu. We are quits.

> "VICOMTESSE DE CAMBES."

Canolles read and re-read the letter, shivering with fear at every word, growing paler with every reading; he felt that a mysterious power, which he could not fathom, enveloped him, and directed his actions. Might not this same underground passage, from his bedroom to the Château de Cambes, which was to serve to assure Nanon's safety, serve equally well, if the secret were generally known, to deliver Saint-Georges to the enemy?

Vibrac followed, upon the governor's expressive features, the emotions which were reflected there.

"Bad news, commandant?" he asked.

"Yes, it seems that we are to be attacked again to-night."

"The fanatics!" said Vibrac. "I should have supposed we had given them a sufficient dressing-down, and were not likely to hear of them again for a week at least."

"I have no need to enjoin the strictest watchfulness upon you," said Canolles.

"Have no fear, commandant. Probably they will try to surprise us, as they did before?"

"I have no idea; but let us be ready for anything, and take the same precautions that we took before. Finish my round of inspection for me; I must go to my room; I have some orders to give."

Vibrac touched his hat and strode away with the soldierly indifference to danger often exhibited by those whose profession brings them face to face with it at every step.

Canolles went to his room, taking every possible precaution not to be seen by Nanon; and having made sure that he was alone, locked himself in.

At the head of his bed were the arms of the lords of Cambes, upon a tapestry hanging surrounded by a band of gold.

Canolles raised the band, which was not attached to the tapestry, and disclosed the crack of a door. With the aid of the key which accompanied the viscountess's letter, he opened the door, and found himself confronted by the gaping orifice of a subterranean passage.

For a moment Canolles was struck dumb, and stood motionless, with the sweat pouring from his brow. This mysterious opening into the bowels of the earth terrified him in spite of himself.

He lighted a candle and prepared to inspect it.

First, he descended twenty steep stairs, then kept on down a gentler slope farther and farther into the depths.

Soon he heard a dull, rumbling noise, which alarmed him at first, because he could not think to what cause to attribute it; but as he went forward he recognized it as the roar of the river flowing above his head.

The water had forced its way through the arch in divers places at one time or another, but the crevices had evidently been detected in time and filled with a sort of cement, which became harder in course of time than the stones it bound together.

For about ten minutes Canolles heard the water rolling over his head; then the noise gradually died away until it was hardly more than a murmur. At last even the murmuring ceased, to be succeeded by perfect silence; and after walking a hundred feet or more in the silence, Canolles reached a staircase similar to the one by which he had descended, and closed at the top by a massive door which the united strength of ten men could not have moved, and which was rendered fire-proof by a thick iron plate.

"Now I understand," said Canolles; "she will await Nanon at this door and help her to escape."

He retraced his steps beneath the river-bed, ascended the staircase, re-entered his room, replaced the gold band, and betook himself deep in thought to Nanon's apartments.

IX

Nanon was, as usual, surrounded by maps, letters, and books. In her own way the poor woman was carrying on the war in the king's interest. As soon as she saw Canolles, she gave him her hand joyfully.

"The king is coming," said she, "and in a week we shall be out of danger."

"He is always coming," returned Canolles, with a sad smile; "unfortunately, he never arrives."

"Ah! but this time my information is reliable, my dear baron, and he will surely be here within the week."

"Let him make what haste he may, Nanon, he will arrive too late for us."

"What do you say?"

"I say that instead of wearing yourself out over these maps and papers, you would do better to be thinking of means of escape."

"Of escape? Why so?"

"Because I have bad news, Nanon. A new expedition is preparing, and this time I may be forced to yield."

"Very well, my dear; didn't we agree that I should share your fate and your fortune, whatever they may be?"

"No that cannot be; I shall be too weak, if I have to fear for you. Did they not propose at Agen to burn you at the stake? Did they not try to throw you into the river? Nanon, in pity for me, do not insist upon remaining, for your presence would surely make me do some cowardly thing."

"*Mon Dieu*, Canolles, you frighten me."

"Nanon, I implore you to give me your word that you will do what I bid you, if we are attacked."

"Why should I make such a promise?"

"To give me the strength to do my duty. Nanon, if you do not promise to obey me blindly, I swear that I will take the first opportunity to seek my own death."

"Whatever you wish, Canolles; I swear it by our love!"

"Thank God! Dear Nanon, my mind is much more at ease now. Get together your most valuable jewels. Where is your money?"

"In a small iron-bound chest."

"Have it all ready. You must take it with you."

"Oh! Canolles, you know that the real treasure of my heart is neither gold nor jewels. Canolles, is this all a mere pretext to send me away from you?"

"Nanon, you deem me a man of honor, do you not? Very good; upon my honor, what I now do is inspired solely by my dread of the danger that threatens you."

"You seriously believe that I am in danger?"

"I believe that Île Saint-Georges will be taken to-morrow."

"How, pray?"

"That I cannot say, but I believe it."

"And suppose I consent to fly?"

"I will do everything in my power to preserve my life, Nanon, I swear."

"Do you command, my dear, and I will obey," said Nanon, giving her hand to Canolles, regardless, in the intensity of her gaze, of two great tears which were rolling down her cheeks.

Canolles pressed her hand and left the room. Had he remained a moment longer, he would have wiped away those two pearls with his lips; but he placed his hand on the viscountess's letter, and that gave him strength to tear himself away.

It was a cruel day. The positive, definite threat, "To-morrow Île Saint-Georges will be taken," rang incessantly in Canolles' ears. How?—by what means? What ground had the viscountess for speaking with such conviction? Was he to be attacked by water or by land? From what quarter was this invisible yet indubitable disaster to burst upon him? He was well-nigh mad.

So long as the daylight lasted, Canolles burned his eyes out in the glaring sunshine, looking everywhere for the enemy. After dark he strained his eyes trying to peer into the depths of the forest, scanning the sky-line of the plain, and the windings of the river; all to no purpose, he could see nothing.

When night had fallen altogether, he spied a light in one wing of the Château de Cambes; it was the first time he had detected the slightest sign of life there while he had been at Île Saint-Georges.

"Ah!" said he, with a long-drawn sigh, "there are Nanon's saviors at their post."

What a strange, mysterious problem is that of the workings of the human heart! Canolles no longer loved Nanon, Canolles adored Madame de Cambes, and yet, at the moment of separation from her whom he no longer loved, he felt as if his heart would break; it was only when he was far away from her, or when he was about to leave her, that Canolles felt the full force of the singular sentiment with which he regarded that charming person.

Every man in the garrison was on duty upon the ramparts. Canolles grew weary of gazing, and questioning the silence of the night. Never was darkness more absolutely dumb, or apparently more solitary. Not the slightest sound disturbed the perfect calmness, which seemed like that of the desert.

Suddenly it occurred to Canolles that it might be that the enemy proposed to make their way into the fort by the underground passage he had explored. It seemed highly improbable, for in that case they would have been unlikely to give him warning; but he resolved none the less to guard the passage. He ordered a barrel of powder to be prepared with a slow-match, selected the bravest man among his sergeants, rolled the barrel down upon the last step of the subterranean staircase, lighted a torch, and placed it in the sergeant's hand. Two other men were stationed near him.

"If more than six men appear in this passage," he said to the sergeant, "call upon them to withdraw; if they refuse, set fire to the match and give the barrel a roll; as the passage slopes down, it will burst in the midst of them."

The sergeant took the torch; the two soldiers stood motionless behind him, in its reddish glare, with the barrel of powder at their feet.

Canolles ascended the stairs with his mind at rest, in that direction at least; but as he stepped into his room he saw Nanon, who had seen him come down from the ramparts and return indoors, and had followed him in quest of news. She stared in open-mouthed dismay, at this yawning orifice of which she had no knowledge.

"Oh! *mon Dieu!*" said she, "what is that door?"

"The door of the passage through which you are to fly, dear Nanon."

"You promised me that you wouldn't require me to leave you except in case you were attacked."

"And I renew my promise."

"Everything about the island seems to be quiet, my dear."

"Everything seems quiet within, too, does it not? And yet there are a barrel of powder, a man, and a torch within twenty feet of us. If the man should put the torch to the powder, in one second not one stone would be left upon another in the whole fort. That is how quiet everything is, Nanon."

The color fled from the young woman's cheeks.

"Oh! you make me shudder!" she cried.

"Nanon, call your women," said Canolles, "and bid them come hither with all your packages, and your footman with your money. Perhaps I am mistaken, perhaps nothing will happen to-night; but never mind, let us be ready."

"Qui vive?" cried the sergeant's voice in the underground passage.

Another voice replied, but in a friendly tone.

"Hark," said Canolles, "they have come for you."

"There is no attack as yet, dear heart; all is quiet. Let me stay with you; they will not come."

As Nanon ceased to speak, the cry of "Qui vive?" rang out thrice in the inner court-yard, and the third time it was followed by the report of a musket.

Canolles darted to the window, and threw it open.

"To arms!" cried the sentinel, "to arms!"

Canolles saw a black, moving mass in one corner; it was the enemy pouring forth in floods from a low, arched doorway opening into a cellar used as a wood-house, to which there was no doubt some secret issue.

"There they are!" cried Canolles; "hurry! there they are!"

As he spoke the sentinel's shot was answered by a score of muskets. Two or three bullets shattered the glass in the window, which Canolles hastily closed.

He turned back into the room and found Nanon on her knees. Her women and her man-servant came running in from her apartment.

"There's not an instant to lose, Nanon!" cried Canolles: "come! come!"

He took her in his arms as if she weighed no more than a feather, and plunged into the underground passage, calling to her people to follow him.

The sergeant was at his post, torch in hand; the two soldiers, with matches lighted, were ready to fire upon a group of men, among whom was our old acquaintance, Master Pompée, pale with fear, and uttering profuse protestations of friendliness.

"Ah! Monsieur de Canolles," he cried, "pray tell them that you were expecting us; what the devil! one doesn't indulge in pleasantry of this sort with one's friends."

"Pompée," said Canolles, "I place madame in your charge; one whom you know has agreed upon her honor to answer to me for her; you shall answer to me for her upon your head."

"Yes, I will answer for everything," said Pompée.

"Canolles! Canolles! I will not leave you!" cried Nanon, clinging to the young man's neck; "Canolles, you promised to go with me."

"I promised to defend Saint-Georges while one stone stands upon another, and I propose to keep my promise."

Despite Nanon's shrieks and tears and entreaties, Canolles gave her into Pompée's hands, and he, with the assistance of two or three servants of Madame de Cambes and the poor girl's own attendants, carried her off into the dark passage.

For an instant Canolles looked after the fair, white phantom, as it was borne away with arms outstretched toward him. But suddenly he remembered that he was expected elsewhere, and rushed back to the stairway, shouting to the sergeant and the two soldiers to follow him.

Vibrac was in the governor's room, pale and hatless, with his drawn sword in his hand.

"Commandant," he cried as soon as he caught sight of Canolles, "the enemy!—the enemy!"

"I know it."

"What must we do?"

"*Parbleu!* a pretty question!—sell our lives dearly, of course!" and Canolles darted down into the court-yard. On the way he spied a miner's axe, and took possession of it.

The court-yard was full of the invading force; sixty soldiers of the garrison stood in a group, trying to defend the door leading to the governor's apartments. In the direction of the ramparts, there was much shouting and firing, and it was evident that fighting was in progress everywhere.

"Commandant! Here's the commandant!" cried the soldiers, when they saw Canolles.

"Yes," he shouted back, "the commandant has come to die with you. Courage, my lads, courage! they have surprised us by treachery, because they couldn't whip us in a fair fight."

"All's fair in war," said the mocking voice of Ravailly, who, with his arm in a sling was urging his men on to take Canolles. "Surrender, Canolles, surrender, and you shall have good terms."

"Ah! is it you, Ravailly?" was the reply. "I thought I had paid you my debt of friendship; but you are not content. Wait a moment—"

As he spoke, Canolles darted forward five or six steps, and hurled the axe he held in his hand at Ravailly with such force that it cut through the helmet and gorget of a militia officer, who stood beside the captain of Navailles, and who fell dead.

"Damnation!" exclaimed Ravailly; "how courteously you reply to proffered courtesies! I ought, though, to be well-used to your ways. He's mad, boys! fire on him! fire!"

At the word a brisk volley came from the enemy's ranks, and five or six men about Canolles fell.

"Fire!" cried he; "fire!"

But only four or five muskets responded. Taken by surprise, just when they were least expecting it, and confused by the darkness, Canolles' troops had lost their courage.

He saw that there was no hope.

"Go in," he said to Vibrac, "go in and take your men with you; we will barricade ourselves, and we won't surrender at all events until they have carried the fort by assault."

"Fire!" shouted two new voices, those of Espagnet and La Rochefoucauld. "Remember your dead comrades, who are crying out for vengeance. Fire!"

The storm of lead came whistling again about Canolles without touching him, but decimating his little troop once more.

"Back!" cried Vibrac, "back!"

"At them! at them!" cried Ravailly; "forward, my lads, forward!"

His men obeyed and rushed forward; Canolles, with hardly more than a half a score of men, sustained the shock; he had picked up a dead soldier's gun, and used it as a club.

The soldiers entered the governor's house, Vibrac and he bringing up the rear. With their united efforts they succeeded in closing the door, despite the efforts of the assailants to prevent them, and secured it with an enormous bar of iron.

There were bars at the windows.

"Axes, crow-bars, cannon if necessary!" cried the voice of Duc de La Rochefoucauld; "we must take them all, dead or alive."

His words were followed by an appalling discharge; two or three bullets pierced the door, and one of them shattered Vibrac's thigh.

"'Faith, commandant," said he, "my account is settled; do you look now to settling yours; I am done with it all."

He lay down by the wall, unable to stand erect.

Canolles glanced about him; a dozen men were still in fighting trim, among them the sergeant he had stationed in the underground passage.

"The torch!" said Canolles; "what did you do with the torch?"

"I threw it down beside the barrel, commandant."

"Is it still burning?"

"Probably."

"Good. Send out all your men through the rear doors and windows. Obtain for them and for yourself the best terms you can; the rest is my affair."

"But, commandant—"

"Obey!"

The sergeant bent his head and bade his soldiers follow him. In a twinkling they all disappeared toward the rear of the house; they understood the purpose Canolles had in mind, and were not at all solicitous to be blown up with him.

Canolles listened for an instant. They were at work on the door with axes, but the fusillade did not abate; they were firing at random, mostly at the windows, where they thought that the besieged might be lying in ambush.

Suddenly a loud shout announced that the door had yielded, and Canolles heard the assailants rushing from room to room with cries of joy.

"Ah me!" he muttered, "five minutes hence these cries of joy will change to shrieks of despair."

He rushed into the underground passage, where he found a young man sitting on the barrel, with the torch at his feet, and his face buried in his hands.

He raised his head at the sound of footsteps and Canolles recognized Madame de Cambes.

"Ah! here you are at last!" she cried, as she rose.

"Claire!" murmured Canolles, "why have you come here?"

"To die with you, if you are determined to die."

"I am dishonored, ruined, and there is nothing for me But to die."

"You are saved and your honor is secure,—saved by me."

"Ruined by you! Do you hear them? they are coming; here they are! Claire, make your escape while you may; you have five minutes, it is more than enough."

"I will not fly, I will remain."

"But do you know why I came down here? Do you know what I propose to do?"

Madame de Cambes picked up the torch, and put it near the barrel of powder.

"I have a suspicion," said she.

"Claire!" cried Canolles in dismay. "Claire!"

"Say again that you propose to die, and we will die together."

The pale face of the viscountess indicated such resolution that Canolles realized that she was quite capable of doing what she said; and he stopped.

"Tell me what you wish," he said.

"I wish you to surrender."

"Never!"

"Time is precious," continued the viscountess; "surrender. I offer you life and honor, for I give you the excuse that you were surprised by treachery."

"Let me fly, then; I will lay my sword at the king's feet, and beseech him to give me an opportunity to have my revenge."

"You shall not fly."

"Why not?"

"Because I can live in this way no longer; because I cannot live apart from you; because I love you."

"I surrender! I surrender!" cried Canolles, throwing himself at Madame de Cambes' knees, and hurling away the torch she still held in her hand.

"Ah!" she murmured, "now I have him, and no one can take him away from me again."

There was one very peculiar thing, which is capable of explanation, however; namely, that love acted so differently upon these two women.

Madame de Cambes, shy, timid, and gentle by nature, had become resolute, bold, and strong.

Nanon, capricious and wilful, had become shy, timid, and gentle.

Herein lies the explanation of the phenomenon: Madame de Cambes felt more and more confident that she was beloved by Canolles; Nanon felt that Canolles' love for her was growing less day by day.

X

The second return of the army of the princes to Bordeaux was very different from the first. On this occasion there were laurels for everybody, even for the vanquished.

Madame de Cambes with consummate tact had assigned an honorable rôle to Canolles, who, as soon as he had entered the city, side by side with his friend Ravailly, whom he was so near killing on two occasions, was surrounded and congratulated as a great captain and a gallant soldier.

They who had been so soundly whipped but two days before, especially those of them who had suffered any damage at that time, retained some hard feeling against their conqueror. But Canolles was so handsome and sweet-tempered; his manners were so simple; he bore himself in his new position so good-humoredly and yet with such becoming dignity; the friends who surrounded him were so demonstrative in their evidences of affection for him; both officers and men of the Navailles regiment were so loud in their praise of him as their captain, and as governor of Île Saint-Georges,—that the Bordelais soon forgot their rancor. Moreover, they had other things to think of.

Monsieur de Bouillon arrived a day or two later, and they had most precise information that the king would be at Libourne in a week at the latest.

Madame de Condé was dying with curiosity to see Canolles; she stood behind the curtains at her window, and watched him pass, and was impressed with his distinguished bearing, which fully justified the reputation he had acquired among friends and foes alike.

Madame de Tourville's opinion did not coincide with that of Madame la Princesse; she claimed that he lacked distinction. Lenet declared that he considered him a gallant fellow, and Monsieur de La Rochefoucauld said simply:—

"Aha! so that's the hero, is it?"

Quarters were assigned Canolles in the principal fortress of the city, the Château Trompette. By day he was free to go where he pleased throughout the city, on business or pleasure as the case might be. At taps he returned to the fortress. His word was taken that he would not attempt to escape nor to correspond with any one outside the city.

Before accepting this last condition, he asked permission to write a few lines: and the permission being granted, he sent Nanon the following letter:—

> "A prisoner, but at liberty upon my word of honor to correspond with no one outside the walls of Bordeaux, I write you these few words, dear Nanon, to assure you of my affection, which my silence might cause you to doubt. I depend upon you to defend my honor in the sight of the king and queen.
>
> "Baron de Canolles."

In these very mild conditions the influence of Madame de Cambes was very perceptible.

It was four or five days before he came to the end of the banquets and festivities of all sorts, with which his friends entertained him; he was seen constantly with Ravailly, who walked about with his left arm in that of Canolles and his right in a sling. When the drums beat and the Bordelais set out upon some expedition or hurried to quell an uprising, they were sure to see Canolles somewhere on the way, either with Ravailly on his arm, or alone, with his hands behind his back, interested, smiling, and inoffensive.

Since his arrival he had seen Madame de Cambes very rarely, and had hardly spoken to her; the viscountess seemed to be content so long as he was not with Nanon, and she was happy to know that he was in her neighborhood.

Canolles wrote to her to complain, mildly, whereupon she procured for him invitations to one or two houses in the city.

More than that. Canolles, through Lenet's intercession, had obtained permission to pay his respects to Madame de Condé, and the comely prisoner appeared sometimes at her receptions, dancing attendance upon the ladies of her suite.

It would be impossible, however, to imagine a man less interested than Canolles in political matters. To see Madame de Cambes and exchange a few words with her; if he could not succeed in speaking to her, to receive an affectionate smile and nod from her, to press her hand when she entered her carriage, and, Huguenot though he was, to offer her holy water at church,— such were the main points of interest in the prisoner's day.

At night he thought over what had taken place during the day.

It was not long, however, before this mild distraction ceased to satisfy the prisoner. As he fully realized the exquisite delicacy of Madame de Cambes, who was even more solicitous for his honor than her own, he sought to enlarge the circle of his distractions. In the first place he fought with an officer of the garrison and with two bourgeois, which helped to while away a few hours. But as he disarmed one of his opponents and wounded the others, that form of amusement soon failed him for lack of persons disposed to amuse him.

Then he indulged in one or two little love-affairs. This was not to be wondered at, for not only was Canolles, as we have said, an extremely well-favored youth, but since he had been a prisoner he had become immeasurably more interesting. For three whole days and the morning of the fourth his captivity was the talk of the town; more could hardly be said of that of Monsieur le Prince.

One day when Canolles hoped to see Madame de Cambes at church, — and when Madame de Cambes, perhaps for fear of meeting him there, did not appear, — as he stood at his post by the pillar he offered the holy water to a charming creature whom he had not before seen. It was not the fault of Canolles, but of Madame de Cambes; for if she had come, he would have thought of none but her, would have seen none but her, and would have offered holy water to none but her.

That same day, as he was wondering in his own mind who the charming brunette could be, he received an invitation to pass the evening with Lavie, the *avocat-général*, the same man who had undertaken to interfere with the entry of Madame la Princesse, and who, in his capacity of upholder of the royal authority, was detested almost as cordially as Monsieur d'Épernon. Canolles, who felt more and more imperatively the need of being amused, accepted the invitation with thankfulness, and betook himself to the *avocat-général's* house at six o'clock.

The hour may seem strange to our modern entertainers; but there were two reasons why Canolles made his appearance so seasonably: in the first place, as people in those days dined at noon, evening parties began vastly earlier; in the second place, as Canolles invariably reported at Château Trompette as early as half-after nine, he must needs arrive among the first if he wished to do anything more than show himself for a moment.

As he entered the salon he uttered an exclamation of delight; Madame Lavie was no other than the bewitching brunette to whom he so gallantly presented the holy water that very morning.

Canolles was greeted in the *avocat-général's* salon as a royalist who had been tried and found not wanting. He had no sooner been presented than he was overwhelmed with compliments fit to turn the head of one of the seven wise men of Greece. His defence, at the time of the first attack, was compared with that of Horatius Codes, and his final defeat to the fall of Troy brought about by the artifices of Ulysses.

"My dear Monsieur de Canolles," said the *avocat-général*, "I know from the best authority that you have been much talked of at court, and that your gallant defence has covered you with glory; the queen has declared that she will exchange you as soon as possible, and that when you return to her service it shall be as colonel or brigadier; now, do you wish to be exchanged?"

"'Faith, monsieur," replied Canolles, with a killing glance at Madame Lavie, "I assure you that I desire nothing so much as that the queen will not hurry. She would have to exchange me for a sum of money, or for some good soldier; I am not worth the expense of the one, nor do I deserve the honor of the other. I will wait until her Majesty has taken Bordeaux, where I am extremely comfortable just at present; then she will have me for nothing."

Madame Lavie smiled affably.

"The devil!" said her husband, "you speak very lukewarmly of your freedom, baron."

"Well, why should I get excited over it? Do you imagine that it would be very agreeable for me to return to active service, where I am exposed day after day to the risk of killing some of my dearest friends?"

"But what sort of a life are you leading here?" rejoined the *avocat-général*, —"a life altogether unworthy of a man of your calibre, taking part in no council and in no enterprise for the good of the cause, forced to see others serving the cause in which they believe, while you sit with folded arms, useless to yourself and to everybody else; the situation ought to be burdensome to you."

Canolles looked at Madame Lavie, who happened to be looking at him.

"No," said he, "you are mistaken; I am not bored in the least. You busy yourself with politics, which is a very wearisome pursuit, while I make love, which is very amusing. You people in Bordeaux are on the one hand the servants of the queen, on the other hand the servants of the princess, while I attach myself to the fortunes of no one sovereign, but am the slave of all the ladies."

The retort was much enjoyed, and the mistress of the house expressed her opinion of it by a smile.

Soon they sat down at the card-tables, and Madame Lavie went shares with Canolles against her husband, who lost five hundred pistoles.

The next day the populace, for some unknown reason, thought best to organize an *émeute*. A partisan of the princes, somewhat more fanatical in his devotion than his fellows, proposed that they should go and throw stones at Monsieur Lavie's windows. When the glass was all broken, another proposed to set fire to his house. They were already running to fetch firebrands when Canolles arrived with a detachment of the Navailles regiment, escorted Madame Lavie to a place of safety, and rescued her husband from the clutches of half a score of maniacs, who, as they had failed to burn him, were determined to hang him.

"Well, my man of action," said Canolles to the *avocat-général*, who was positively blue with terror, "what do you think now of my idleness? Is it not better for me to do nothing?"

With that he returned to Château Trompette, as taps were just sounding. He found there upon his table a letter, the shape of which made his heart beat faster, and the writing made him jump.

It was written by Madame de Cambes.

Canolles hastily opened it and read:—

> "To-morrow, about six in the evening, be at the Carmelite Church, alone, and go to the first confessional on the left as you enter. You will find the door open."

"Well, that's an original idea," said Canolles.

There was a postscript.

> "Do not boast," it said, "of having been where you were yesterday and to-day. Bordeaux is not a royalist city, remember, and the fate Monsieur *l'Avocat-général* would have suffered but for you should make you reflect."

"Good!" said Canolles, "she is jealous. And so, whatever she may say, I did very well to go to Monsieur Lavie's yesterday and to-day."

XI

It must be said that since his arrival at Bordeaux, Canolles had undergone all the torture of unrequited love. He had seen the viscountess courted and caressed and flattered, while he himself was forbidden to devote himself to her, and had to take what comfort he could in an occasional glance bestowed upon him by Claire when the gossips were looking the other way. After the scene in the underground passage, after the passionate words they had exchanged at that critical moment, the existing state of things seemed to him to denote something worse than lukewarmness on her part. But, as he felt sure that beneath her cold exterior she concealed a real and deep affection for him, he looked upon himself as the most to be pitied of all happy lovers that ever lived. His frame of mind is easily understood. By virtue of the promise he had been made to give, that he would carry on no correspondence with the outside world, he had relegated Nanon to that little corner of the conscience which is set aside for the accommodation of that variety of remorse. As he heard nothing of her, and consequently was spared the ennui caused by tangible reminders of the woman to whom one is unfaithful, his remorse was not altogether unbearable.

And yet, sometimes, just when the most jovial of smiles overspread the young man's features, when his voice was heard giving utterance to some bright and witty remark, a cloud would suddenly pass across his brow, and a sigh would escape from his lips at least, if not from his heart. The sigh was for Nanon; the cloud was the memory of the past casting its shadow over the present.

Madame de Cambes had remarked these moments of melancholy; she had sounded the depths of Canolles' heart, and it seemed to her that she could not leave him thus abandoned to his own resources. Between an old love which was not altogether extinct, and a new passion which might spring up in his heart, it was possible that his surplus ardor, which was formerly expended upon the proper performance of his military duties and the functions of his responsible position, might tend to check the growth of the pure flame which she sought to inspire. Moreover she simply desired to gain time until the memory of so many romantic adventures should fade away, after keeping the curiosity of all the courtiers of the princess on the *qui vive.* Perhaps Madame de Cambes was injudicious; perhaps, if she had made no concealment of her love, it would have created less sensation, or the sensation would have been less long-lived.

But Lenet was the one who followed the progress of this mysterious passion with the most attention and success. For some time his observant eye had detected its existence without feeling sure of its object; nor had he been able to guess its precise situation, whether it was or was not reciprocated. But Madame de Cambes, sometimes tremulous and hesitating, sometimes firm and determined, and almost always indifferent to the pleasures which those about her enjoyed, seemed to him to be stricken to the heart in very truth. Her warlike ardor had suddenly died away; she was neither tremulous nor hesitating nor firm nor determined; she was pensive, smiled for no apparent motive, wept without cause, as if her lips and her eyes responded to the vagaries of her thought, the contrary impulses of her mind. This transformation had been noticeable for six or seven days only, and it was six or seven days since Canolles was taken prisoner. Therefore there was little doubt that Canolles was the object of her love.

Lenet, be it understood, was quite ready to further a passion which might some day result in enrolling so gallant a warrior among the partisans of Madame la Princesse.

Monsieur de La Rochefoucauld was perhaps farther advanced than Lenet in the exploration of Madame de Cambes' heart. But the language of his gestures and his eyes, as well as of his mouth, was so closely confined to what he chose to permit them to say, that no one could say whether he himself loved or hated Madame de Cambes. As to Canolles, he did not mention his name or look at him, or take any more notice of him than if he had not existed. For the rest, he assumed a more warlike attitude than ever, posing constantly as a hero,—a pretension in which he was justified to some extent by his undeniable courage, and his equally undeniable military skill; day by day he attributed increased importance to his position as lieutenant to the generalissimo. Monsieur de Bouillon, on the other hand, a cold, mysterious, calculating personage, whose political ends were admirably served by attacks of gout, which sometimes came so in the nick of time that people were tempted to question their reality, was forever negotiating, and concealed his real thoughts as much as possible, being unable to realize the tremendous distance that lay between Mazarin and Richelieu, and being always fearful for his head which he was very near losing upon the same scaffold with Cinq-Mars, and saved only by giving up Sedan, his own city, and renouncing in fact, if not in name, his rank as a sovereign prince.

The city itself was carried away by the flood of dissipation and profligacy which poured in upon it from all sides. Between two fires, with death and ruin of one sort or another staring them in the face, the Bordelais were never sure of the morrow, and they felt the need of doing what they could to sweeten their precarious existence, which could count the future only by seconds.

They remembered La Rochelle and its demolition by Louis XIII., and the profound admiration of Anne of Austria for that exploit. Why did not Bordeaux afford the hatred and ambition of that princess an opportunity to duplicate the fate of La Rochelle?

They constantly forgot that the man who imposed his levelling instrument upon all heads and walls that seemed to him too high was dead, and that Cardinal de Mazarin was hardly equal to the shadow of Cardinal de Richelieu.

So it was that every one let himself go with the tide, Canolles with the rest. It is no less true that there were times when he was inclined to doubt everything, and in his fits of scepticism he doubted the love of Madame de Cambes, as he doubted everything else. At such times Nanon's image would once more fill a large space in his heart, in absence more affectionate and devoted than ever. At such times, if Nanon had appeared before him in the flesh, the inconstant creature would have fallen at her feet.

While his thoughts and emotions were in this incoherent state, which only those hearts can understand that have at some time hesitated between two loves, Canolles received the viscountess's letter. We need not say that every other thought instantly disappeared. After reading the letter he could not understand how he could ever have dreamed of loving any other than Madame de Cambes, and after reading it a second time he was sure that he had never loved any other than her.

He passed one of those feverish, restless nights which do not bring exhaustion in their train, because happiness furnishes a counterpoise to insomnia. Although he had hardly closed his eyes during the night, he rose with the dawn.

Every one knows how a lover passes the hours preceding a meeting with his beloved,—in looking at his watch, running aimlessly hither and thither, and jostling his dearest friends without recognizing them. Canolles performed every mad feat that his state of mind demanded.

At the precise moment (it was the twentieth time he had entered the church) he went to the confessional, the door of which stood open. Through the small window filtered the last rays of the setting sun; the whole interior of the religious edifice was lighted up by that mysterious light, so sweet to those who pray, and those who love. Canolles would have given a year of his life rather than lose a single hope at that moment.

He looked around to make sure that the church was deserted, and when he was convinced that there was no one to see him, entered the confessional and closed the door behind him.

XII

An instant later Claire, enveloped in a thick cloak, herself appeared at the door, leaving Pompée outside as sentinel; then having satisfied herself that she was in no danger of being seen, she knelt at one of the prie-Dieus in the confessional.

"At last, madame," said Canolles, "at last you have taken pity upon me!"

"I could do no less, since you were ruining yourself," Claire replied; it disturbed her peace of mind to tell even so harmless a falsehood as that, at the tribunal of truth.

"I am to understand then, madame," said Canolles, "that I owe the favor of your presence here to no other sentiment than compassion. Surely you will agree that I was entitled to expect something more than that from you."

"Let us speak seriously," said Claire, trying in vain to steady her trembling voice, "and as we ought to speak in a holy place. You are ruining yourself, I say again, by frequenting Monsieur Lavie's house, who is the princess's sworn enemy. Yesterday Madame de Condé heard of it from Monsieur de La Rochefoucauld, who knows everything, and she said this, which alarmed me greatly:—

"'If we have to guard against plotting by our prisoners, we must be as severe as we have been indulgent. Precarious situations demand decisive measures; we are not only ready to take such measures, but resolved to carry them out.'"

The viscountess's voice was under better control as she said this; she had faith to believe that God would pardon the action in consideration of the excuse; it was a sort of sop thrown to her conscience.

"I am not her Highness's knight, madame, but yours," said Canolles. "I surrendered to you, to you alone; you know under what circumstances, and on what conditions."

"I did not think," said Claire, "that any conditions were agreed on."

"Not by word of mouth, perhaps, but in the heart. Ah! madame, after what you said to me, after the happiness you led me to anticipate, after the hope you authorized me to entertain!—ah! madame, confess that you have been very cruel."

"My friend," said Claire, "is it for you to reproach me because I cared as much for your honor as for my own? And do you not understand without forcing me to make the admission—surely you must divine that I have suffered as much as yourself, yes, more than you, for I had not the strength to bear my suffering. Listen to what I say, and may my words, which come from the bottom of my heart, sink as deep into yours. My friend, as I told you, I have suffered more keenly than you, because I am haunted by a fear which you cannot have, knowing as you do that I love you alone. In your enforced abode here, do you ever regret her who is not here? In your dreams of the future, have you any hope of which I am not a part?"

"Madame," said Canolles, "you appeal to my frankness, and I will speak frankly to you. Yes, when you leave me to my sorrowful reflections; when you leave me alone face to face with the past; when by your absence you condemn me to wander among gambling-hells and brothels with these beplumed idiots; when you turn your eyes away from me, or compel me to pay so dearly for a word, a gesture, a glance, of which I may be unworthy,—at such times I reproach myself bitterly because I did not die in harness; I blame myself for capitulating; I suffer from regret, and from remorse."

"Remorse?"

"Yes, madame, remorse; for as truly as God is upon that holy altar before which I tell you that I love you, there is at this hour a woman, a weeping, moaning woman, who would give her life for me, and yet she must say to herself that I am either a dastard or a traitor."

"Oh! monsieur!—"

"It is so, madame! Did she not make me all that I am? Had not she my oath to save her?"

"Well, but you did save her, or I am much mistaken."

"Yes, from the enemies who would have made her suffer physical torture, but not from the despair which rends her heart, if she knows that it was you to whom I surrendered."

Claire hung her head and sighed.

"Ah! you do not love me," said she.

Canolles answered her sigh with another.

"I have no wish to tempt you, monsieur," she continued; "I have no wish to deprive you of a friend, whom I cannot hope to rival; and yet, you know that I love you. I came here to ask you for your love, your devoted, single-hearted love. I came to say to you: 'I am free, here is my hand. I offer it to you because you have no rival in my heart,—because I know no one who is superior to you.'"

"Ah! madame," cried Canolles, "you make me the happiest of men!"

"Nay, nay, monsieur," she rejoined, sadly, "you do not love me."

"I love you, I adore you; but I cannot describe what I have suffered from your silence and your reserve."

"*Mon Dieu!*" exclaimed Claire, "is it impossible for you men to divine anything that you are not told in words? Did you not understand that I was unwilling to make you play a ridiculous rôle; that I would not give people a pretext for believing that the surrender of Saint-Georges was arranged between us beforehand? No, it was my intention that you should be exchanged by the queen, or ransomed by me, when you would belong to me without reserve. Alas! you could not wait."

"But now, madame, I will wait. One hour like this, one word from your sweet voice to tell me that you love me, and I will wait hours, days, years."

"You still love Mademoiselle de Lartigues!" said Madame de Cambes, shaking her head.

"Madame," rejoined Canolles, "were I to say to you that I had not a feeling of grateful friendship for her, I should lie to you; take me, I pray you, with that feeling. I give you all the love that I have to give, and that is much."

"Alas!" said Claire, "I know not if I ought to accept, for your words prove that you possess a very noble, but also a very loving heart."

"Hear me," said Canolles, "I would die to spare you one tear, but without a pang I cause her you name to weep incessantly. Poor woman! she has many enemies, and they who do not know her, curse her. You have only friends; they who know you not respect you, and they who know you love you; judge, then, of the difference between these two sentiments, one of which has its birth in my conscience, the other in my heart."

"Thanks, my friend. But perhaps your present impulse is due to my presence, and you may be sorry for it hereafter. I implore you, therefore, to consider my words carefully. I give you until to-morrow to reply. If you wish to send any message to Mademoiselle de Lartigues, if you wish to join her, you are free to do so, Canolles; I myself will take you by the hand and lead you outside the walls of Bordeaux."

"Madame," replied Canolles, "it is useless to wait until to-morrow; I say it with a burning heart, but a cool head. I love you, I love you alone, I shall never love any other than you!"

"Ah! thanks, thanks, my love," cried Claire, giving him her hand. "My hand and my heart alike are yours."

Canolles seized her hand and covered it with kisses.

"Pompée signals to me that it is time to go," said Claire. "Doubtless they are about to close the church. Adieu, my love, or rather, au revoir. To-morrow you shall know what I intend to do for you, that is to say, for us. To-morrow you will be happy, for I shall be happy."

Unable to control the impulse which drew her toward him, she put his hand to her lips, kissed the ends of his fingers, and glided away, leaving Canolles as happy as the angels, whose heavenly voices seemed to find an echo in his heart.

XIII

Meanwhile, as Nanon had said, the king, the queen, the cardinal, and Monsieur de La Meilleraie were on their way to chastise the rebellious city which had dared openly to espouse the cause of the princes; they were approaching slowly, but they were approaching.

On his arrival at Libourne the king received a deputation from the Bordelais, who came to assure him of their respect and devotion. Under the circumstances this assurance had a strange sound; and so the queen received the ambassadors from the topmost pinnacle of her Austrian high-mightiness.

"Messieurs," said she, "we propose to continue our march by way of Vayres, so that we shall soon be able to judge if your respect and devotion are as sincere as you pretend."

At the mention of Vayres, the members of the deputation, who were doubtless in possession of some fact unknown to the queen, looked at one another with some uneasiness. Anne of Austria, whom nothing escaped, did not fail to observe the exchange of glances.

"We shall go at once to Vayres," said she. "Monsieur le Duc d'Épernon assures us that it is a strong place, and we will establish the king's headquarters there."

She turned to the captain of her guards.

"Who commands at Vayres?" she asked.

"I am told, madame," Guitaut replied, "that it is a new governor."

"A trustworthy man, I hope?" said the queen, with a frown.

"An adherent of Monsieur le Duc d'Épernon."

The cloud vanished from the queen's brow.

"If that is so, let us go on at once," she said.

"Madame," said the Duc de La Meilleraie, "your Majesty will of course be guided by your own judgment, but I think that we ought not to go forward more rapidly than the army. A warlike entry at Vayres would work wonders; it is well that the king's subjects should realize the extent of the forces at his Majesty's command; that will encourage the faithful and discourage traitors."

"I think that Monsieur de La Meilleraie is right," said Cardinal de Mazarin.

"And I say that he is wrong," rejoined the queen. "We have nothing to fear between this and Bordeaux; the king is strong in himself, and not in his troops; his household will suffice."

Monsieur de La Meilleraie bowed his acquiescence.

"It is for your Majesty to command," said he; "your will is law."

The queen summoned Guitaut and bade him order the guards, the musketeers and the light-horse to fall in. The king mounted his horse and took his place at their head. Mazarin's niece and the maids of honor entered their carriage.

The line of march was at once taken up for Vayres. The army followed on, and as the distance was but ten leagues, was expected to arrive three or four hours after the king, and pitch its camp upon the right bank of the Dordogne.

The king was barely twelve years old, and yet he was already a finished horseman, managing his steed with ease and grace, and exhibiting in his every movement that pride of race which made him in the sequel the most punctilious of monarchs in matters of etiquette. Brought up under the queen's eye, but constantly harassed by the everlasting niggardliness of the cardinal, who forced him to go without the most necessary things, he was awaiting with furious impatience the hour when he would attain his majority,—which hour would strike on the fifth of September following; and sometimes, amid his childish caprices, he indulged by anticipation in true kingly explosions which indicated what he would be some day.

This campaign was to him a very agreeable episode; it was in some sort a farewell to his pagehood, an apprenticeship in the trade of war, an essay at kingship. He rode proudly along, sometimes at the carriage-door, saluting the queen and making eyes at Madame de Fronsac, with whom he was said to be in love, and again at the head of his household, talking with Monsieur de La Meilleraie and old Guitaut of the campaigns of Louis XIII. and of the mighty prowess of the late cardinal.

The miles flew by as they talked, and at last the towers and outer galleries of the fort of Vayres came in sight. The weather was magnificent, and the country picturesque in the extreme; the sun's rays fell obliquely upon the river; for aught there was in the surroundings to indicate the contrary, they might have been riding out for pleasure. The king rode between Monsieur de La Meilleraie and Guitaut, looking through his glass at the fort, where no sign of life could be discovered, although it was more than probable that the sentinels, who could be seen standing like statues on the walls, had discovered and reported the approach of this brilliant advance-guard of the king's army.

The queen's carriage was driven rapidly forward to the king's side.

"I am surprised at one thing, Monsieur le Maréchal," said Mazarin.

"What is that, monseigneur?"

"It is my impression that careful governors generally know what is going on in the neighborhood of their fortresses, and that when the king takes the trouble to come their way, they should at least send him an escort."

"Nonsense!" said the queen, with a harsh, forced laugh; "mere ceremony! it's of no consequence; I care more for fidelity."

Monsieur de La Meilleraie put his handkerchief to his face to hide a grin; or if not that, his longing to indulge in one.

"But it's true that no one stirs," said the young king, annoyed at such disregard of the rules of etiquette, upon which his future grandeur was to be founded.

"Sire," replied Anne of Austria, "Monsieur de La Meilleraie here, and Guitaut too, will tell you that the first duty of a governor, especially in an enemy's country, is to remain under cover behind his walls, for fear of surprise. Do you not see yon banner, the banner of Henri IV. and François I., floating over the citadel?"

And she pointed proudly to that significant emblem, which seemed to prove that her confidence was most abundantly justified.

The procession rode forward, and in a few moments came upon an outwork which had evidently been thrown up within a few days.

"Aha!" said the marshal, "the governor seems to be at home in the profession. The position of this outwork is well selected, and the work itself well designed."

The queen put her head out through the window, and the king stood up in his stirrups.

A single sentinel was pacing to and fro upon the half-moon; but except for him the outwork seemed as silent and deserted as the fort itself.

"Although I am no soldier," said Mazarin, "and although I do not understand the military duties of a governor, it seems to me that this is very extraordinary treatment of a royal personage."

"Let us go forward all the same," said the marshal; "we shall soon see."

When the little troop was within a hundred yards of the half-moon, the sentinel came to a halt. After scrutinizing them for a moment, he cried:—

"Qui vive?"

"The king!" Monsieur de La Meilleraie replied.

At that word Anne of Austria expected to see officers and soldiers come running forth, drawbridges lowered, gates thrown open, and swords waving in the air.

But she saw nothing of all this.

The sentinel brought his right leg up beside his left, drew a bead upon the new-comers, and said in a loud, firm voice, the one word:—

"Halt!"

The king turned pale with rage; Anne of Austria bit her lips until the blood came; Mazarin muttered an Italian oath which was little used in France, but of which he had never succeeded in breaking himself; Monsieur le Maréchal de La Meilleraie did no more than glance at their Majesties, but it was a most eloquent glance.

"I love to have all possible precautionary measures taken in my service," said the queen, striving to deceive herself; for despite the confident expression she forced herself to maintain, she began to be disturbed at the bottom of her heart.

"I love respect for my person," murmured the young king, gazing with sullen wrath at the impassive sentinel.

XIV

Meanwhile the words, "The king! the king!" repeated by the sentinel rather as a warning to his fellows than as a mark of respect, were taken up by several voices, and at last reached the fort. Thereupon a man appeared upon the crown of the ramparts, and the whole garrison gathered about him.

He raised his staff of office; immediately the drums beat the salute, the soldiers presented arms, and a heavy gun boomed solemnly.

"You see," said the queen, "they are coming to their senses at last,— better late than never. Let us go on."

"Pardon, madame," said Maréchal de La Meilleraie, "but I cannot see that they are making any movement to throw open the gates, and we cannot enter unless the gates are open."

"They have forgotten to do it in the surprise and excitement caused by this august and unexpected visit," a courtier ventured to suggest.

"Such things are not forgotten, monsieur," the marshal replied. "Will your Majesties deign to listen to a word of advice from me?" he added, turning to the king and queen.

"What is it, marshal?"

"Your Majesties should withdraw to the distance of five Hundred yards with Guitaut and the guards, while I ride forward with the musketeers and light-horse, and reconnoitre the place."

The queen replied with a single word.

"Forward!" said she. "We will see if they will dare refuse to let us pass."

The young king, in his delight, drove his spurs into his horse, and galloped ahead of the others.

The marshal and Guitaut darted forward and overtook him.

"You cannot pass!" said the sentinel, still maintaining his hostile attitude.

"It is the king!" cried the pages.

"Halt!" cried the sentinel, with a threatening gesture. At the same moment the hats and muskets of the soldiers assigned to the defence of the outermost intrenchment appeared above the parapet.

A prolonged murmur greeted the sentinel's words and hostile demonstrations. Monsieur de La Meilleraie seized the bit of the king's horse, and turned him around, at the same time bidding the queen's coachman to turn and drive back. The two insulted majesties withdrew some seven or eight hundred yards, while their attendants scattered like a flock of birds at the report of the hunter's rifle.

Maréchal de La Meilleraie, master of the situation, left some fifty men as escort for the king and queen, and with the rest of his force rode back toward the fortifications.

When he was within a hundred yards of the moat, the sentinel, who had resumed his calm and measured tread, halted once more.

"Take a trumpet, put a handkerchief on the end of your sword, Guitaut," said the marshal, "and summon this insolent governor to open his gates."

Guitaut obeyed; he hoisted the emblem of peace, which affords protection to heralds in all civilized countries, and went forward toward the intrenchment.

"Qui vive?" cried the sentry.

"Flag of truce," Guitaut replied, waving his sword, with the bit of cloth at the end.

"Let him approach," said the same man who had previously appeared upon the rampart of the main fort, and who had doubtless reached the outwork by an underground passage.

The gate opened, and a drawbridge was lowered.

"What is your errand?" demanded an officer who was awaiting Guitaut at the gate.

"To speak to the governor," he replied.

"I am he," said the man, who had been seen twice already.

Guitaut noticed that he was very pale, but tranquil and courteous.

"Are you the governor of Vayres?" Guitaut asked.

"Yes, monsieur."

"And you decline to open the doors of your fortress to his Majesty the king, and the queen regent?"

"I regret that I must so decline."

"What do you demand?"

"The liberty of Messieurs les Princes, whose captivity is bringing ruin and desolation upon the kingdom."

"His Majesty does not chaffer with his subjects."

"Alas! monsieur, we know it; and for that reason we are prepared to die, knowing that we shall die in his Majesty's service, although we seem to be making war upon him."

"'Tis well," said Guitaut; "that is all we wished to know."

With a brusque nod to the governor, who replied with a most courteous salute, he withdrew.

There was no movement discernible upon the bastion.

Guitaut rejoined the marshal, and reported the result of his mission.

"Let fifty men ride at full speed to yonder village," said the marshal, pointing toward the hamlet of Isson, "and bring hither instantly all the ladders they can find."

Fifty men rode off at a gallop, and very soon reached the village, which was only a short distance away.

"Now, messieurs," said the marshal, "dismount. Half of you, armed with muskets, will cover the other half, as they scale the ramparts."

The command was greeted with joyful shouts. Guards, musketeers, and light-horse were on the ground in an instant, loading their weapons.

Meanwhile the fifty foragers returned with some twenty ladders.

Everything was quiet within the fortification; the sentinel paced up and down, and the ends of the musket-barrels and the peaked hats could still be seen over the parapet.

The king's household marched forward, led by the marshal in person. It was composed of about four hundred men in all, half of whom made ready to carry the outwork by assault, and the other half to cover the operation.

The king, the queen, and their suite followed the movements of the little troop from afar, with keen anxiety.

The queen seemed to have lost all her assurance. In order to have a better view of what was taking place, she caused her carriage to be partly turned, so that it stood side wise to the fortification.

The assailants had taken but a few steps when the sentinel came to the outer edge of the rampart.

"Qui vive?" he cried in a stentorian voice.

"Make no reply," said Monsieur de La Meilleraie, "but march on."

"Qui vive?" cried the sentinel a second time, putting his musket to his shoulder.

"Qui vive?" the challenge rang out a third time, and the sentinel levelled his weapon.

"Fire on the villain!" said Monsieur de La Meilleraie.

Instantly the royalist ranks poured forth a volley; the sentinel staggered, dropped his musket, which rolled down into the moat, and fell, crying:—

"To arms!"

This beginning of hostilities was answered by a single cannon-shot. The ball whistled over the heads of the first rank, ploughed through the second and third, killed four men, and eventually disembowelled one of the horses attached to the queen's carriage.

A cry of alarm went up from the party in attendance upon their Majesties; the king was forced to fall back still farther; Anne of Austria was near fainting with rage, and Mazarin with fear. The traces of the dead horse were cut, and those of the living horses as well, for they threatened to wreck the carriage with their terrified plunging and rearing. Eight or ten of the guards took their places, and drew the queen out of range.

Meanwhile the governor unmasked a battery of six pieces.

When Monsieur de La Meilleraie saw that battery, which would be likely to make short work of his three companies, he thought that it would be injudicious to proceed further with the attack, and ordered a retreat.

The moment that the king's household took its first backward step, the hostile preparations exhibited in the fortress disappeared.

The marshal returned to the queen, and requested her to select some spot in the neighborhood for her headquarters. Thereupon the queen, looking about, espied the small house on the other side of the Dordogne, standing by itself among the trees.

"Ascertain to whom yonder house belongs," she said to Guitaut, "and request accommodations for me therein."

Guitaut crossed the river in the Isson ferry-boat, and soon returned, to say that the house was unoccupied save by a sort of intendant, who said that it belonged to Monsieur le Duc d'Épernon, and was altogether at her Majesty's service.

"Let us go thither, in that case," said the queen; "but where is the king?"

The little fellow was found to have ridden apart a short distance; he returned when he heard them calling him, and although he tried to hide his tears, it was very evident that he had been weeping.

"What's the matter, sire?" the queen asked him.

"Oh! nothing, madame," the child replied, "except that some day I shall be king, and then—woe to them who have injured me!"

"What is the governor's name?" the queen inquired.

No one was able to tell her, until they asked the question of the ferryman, who replied that his name was Richon.

"'Tis well," said the queen. "I will remember that name."

"And so will I," said the young king.

XV

About a hundred men of the king's household crossed the Dordogne with their Majesties; the others remained with Monsieur de La Meilleraie, who, having decided to besiege Vayres, was awaiting the arrival of the army.

The queen was no sooner installed in the little house—which, thanks to Nanon's luxurious tastes, she found infinitely more habitable than she anticipated—than Guitaut waited upon her to say that an officer, who claimed to have important matters to discuss with her, requested the honor of an audience.

"Who is the man?" demanded the queen.

"Captain Cauvignac, madame."

"Is he of my army?"

"I do not think it."

"Ascertain that fact, and if he is not of my army, say that I cannot receive him."

"I crave your Majesty's pardon for venturing to differ with you on that point," said Mazarin, "but it seems to me that if he is not of your army, that is the very best of reasons for receiving him."

"Why so?"

"Because, if he is of your Majesty's army, and seeks an audience, he cannot be other than a faithful subject; whereas, if he belongs to the enemy's army, he may be a traitor. At this moment, madame, traitors are not to be despised, for they may be extremely useful."

"Admit him," said the queen, "since Monsieur le Cardinal so advises."

The captain was at once introduced, and presented himself with an easy and assured demeanor which amazed the queen, accustomed as she was to produce a far different effect upon all who approached her.

She eyed Cauvignac from head to foot, but he sustained the royal scrutiny with marvellous self-possession.

"Who are you, monsieur?" said she.

"Captain Cauvignac," was the reply.

"In whose service are you?"

"I am in your Majesty's service, if such be your pleasure."

"If such be my pleasure? Surely! Indeed, is there any other service in the kingdom? Are there two queens in France?"

"Assuredly not, madame; there is but one queen in France, and she it is at whose feet I have the honor to lay my most humble respect; but there are two contrary opinions in France,—at least, I thought as much just now."

"What mean you, sirrah?" demanded the queen, with a frown.

"I mean, madame, that I was riding about in this vicinity, and as I happened to be upon the summit of a slight eminence which overlooks the whole country-side, admiring the landscape, which, as your Majesty must have noticed, is surpassingly beautiful, I thought I saw that Monsieur Richon did not receive your Majesty with all the respect to which you are entitled; that fact confirmed a suspicion I had previously entertained, namely, that there are two ways of thinking in France, the royalist way and another, and that Monsieur Richon is of that other way of thinking."

Anne of Austria's brow grew darker and darker.

"Ah! you thought you saw that?" said she.

"Yes, madame," Cauvignac replied with the most innocent candor. "I even thought that I saw that a cannon was fired from the fort, and that the ball with which it was loaded had something to say to your Majesty's carriage."

"Enough. Did you seek audience of me, monsieur, only to indulge in such absurd remarks as these?"

"Ah! you are discourteous," was Cauvignac's mental reflection; "you shall pay the dearer for that."

"No, madame, I sought an audience to say to you that you are a very great queen, and that my admiration for you knows no bounds."

"Indeed!" said the queen, dryly.

"Because of your grandeur, and my admiration, which is its natural consequence, I resolved to devote myself heart and soul to your Majesty's cause."

"Thanks," said the queen, ironically. "Guitaut," she added, turning to the captain of the guards, "show this prating fool the door."

"Pardon, madame," said Cauvignac, "I will go without being driven out; but if I go you will not have Vayres."

Whereupon he saluted her Majesty with perfect grace, and turned upon his heel.

"Madame," said Mazarin, in an undertone, "I think that you are ill-advised to send this man away."

"Stay a moment," said the queen, "and say what you have to say; after all, you are a strange fellow, and most amusing."

"Your Majesty is very kind," said Cauvignac, bowing low.

"What were you saying about obtaining possession of Vayres?"

"I was saying that if your Majesty still entertains the purpose, which I fancied I detected this morning, of gaining admission to Vayres, I will make it my duty to show you the way in."

"How so?"

"I have a hundred and fifty men of my own at Vayres."

"Of your own?"

"Yes, of my own."

"Even so?"

"I turn over those one hundred and fifty men to your Majesty."

"What then?"

"What then?"

"Yes."

"Why, then, it seems to me that the devil's in it if with a hundred and fifty doorkeepers your Majesty cannot cause a door to be opened."

"'T is a witty knave," said the queen, with a smile.

Cauvignac evidently guessed that a compliment was intended, for he bowed a second time.

"What is your price, monsieur?" she asked.

"Oh! *mon Dieu*, madame!—five hundred livres for each doorkeeper; those are the wages I pay my men."

"You shall have them."

"And for myself?"

"Ah! you must have something for yourself also?"

"I should be proud to hold a commission by virtue of your Majesty's munificence."

"What rank do you demand?"

"I should love to be governor of Braune. I have always longed to be a governor."

"Granted."

"In that case, save for a trifling formality, the bargain is concluded."

"What is that formality?"

"Will your Majesty deign to sign this bit of paper, which I prepared in advance, hoping that my services would be acceptable to my magnanimous sovereign?"

"What is the paper?"

"Read it, madame."

With a graceful movement of his arm, and bending his knee with the utmost deference, Cauvignac presented a paper to the queen, who read as follows:—

"'On the day that I enter Vayres, without striking a blow, I will pay to Captain Cauvignac the sum of seventy-five thousand livres, and will make him governor of Braune.'

"And so," the queen continued, restraining her indignation, "Captain Cauvignac has not sufficient confidence in our royal word, but demands a written promise!"

"In matters of importance, madame, a written promise seems to me most desirable," rejoined Cauvignac, with a bow. '*Verba volant,*' says an old proverb; 'words fly away,' and, saving your Majesty's presence, I have been robbed."[1]

"Insolent knave!" exclaimed the queen, "begone!"

"I go," said Cauvignac, "but you will not have Vayres."

Again the captain turned upon his heel and walked toward the door; and Anne of Austria, whose irritation was far deeper than before, did not recall him.

Cauvignac left the room.

"See to it that that man is secured," said the queen.

Guitaut started to execute the order.

[1] There is a play upon words here which cannot be reproduced in a translation,—the same French word, *voler*, meaning to fly, and to steal or rob.

"Pardon, madame," said Mazarin, "but I think that your Majesty is wrong to yield to an angry impulse."

"Why so?"

"But I fear that we may need this man later, and that, if your Majesty molests him in any way, you will then have to pay double for his services."

"Very well," said the queen, "we will pay him what we must; but meanwhile let him be kept in sight."

"Oh! that's another matter, and I am the first to approve that precaution."

"Guitaut, see what becomes of him," said the queen.

Guitaut went out, and returned half an hour later.

"Well! what has become of him?" the queen demanded.

"Your Majesty may be perfectly easy in your mind, for your man shows not the least inclination to leave the neighborhood. I made inquiries, and found that he is domiciled at the inn of one Biscarros, within three hundred yards of this house."

"And has he gone thither?"

"No, madame; he had gone to the top of a hill near by, and is watching Monsieur de La Meilleraie's preparations for forcing the intrenchments. That spectacle seems to possess great interest for him."

"What of the rest of the army?"

"It is coming up, madame, and drawing up in line of battle as fast as it arrives."

"In that case the marshal proposes to attack at once?"

"In my opinion, madame, it would be much better to give the troops a night's rest before risking an attack."

"A night's rest!" cried the queen; "the royal army to be delayed a night and day by such a paltry affair as this! Impossible! Guitaut, go and order the marshal to attack the fort at once. The king proposes to lie tonight at Vayres."

"But, madame," murmured Mazarin, "it seems to me that the marshal's precaution—"

"And it seems to me," retorted Anne of Austria, "that when the royal authority has been outraged, it cannot be avenged too swiftly. Go, Guitaut, and say to Monsieur de La Meilleraie that the queen's eye is upon him."

Dismissing Guitaut with a majestic gesture, the queen took her son by the hand and left the room; and, without looking to see if she was followed, ascended a staircase leading to a terrace. This terrace commanded a view of the surrounding country by means of vistas most artfully designed.

The queen cast a rapid glance in every direction. Two hundred yards behind her was the Libourne road, with the hostelry of our friend Biscarros gleaming white in the sunlight. At her feet flowed the Dordogne, calm, swift, and majestic. At her right arose the fort of Vayres, silent as a ruin; the redoubts newly thrown up formed a circle around it. A few sentinels were pacing back and forth upon the gallery; five pieces of cannon showed their bronze necks and yawning mouths through the embrasures. At her left Monsieur de La Meilleraie was making his dispositions to camp for the night. The main body of the army had arrived and was drawn up in close order around the marshal's position.

Upon a hillock stood a man following attentively with his eyes every movement of besiegers and besieged; it was Cauvignac.

Guitaut crossed the river on the ferry-boat.

The queen stood like a statue upon the terrace, with contracted brow, holding the hand of little Louis XIV., who gazed on the scene before him with an interest beyond his years, and from time to time said to his mother:

"Madame, please let me mount my battle-horse, and go with Monsieur de La Meilleraie to punish these insolent fellows."

At the queen's side was Mazarin, whose crafty, mocking features had assumed for the moment that cast of serious thought which they wore on great occasions only; and behind the queen and the minister were the maids of honor, who took pattern by their mistress's silence, and hardly dared exchange a few hurried words in undertones.

In all this there was an appearance of peace and tranquillity; but it was the tranquillity of the mine, which a spark is soon to change into a destructive tempest.

The eyes of all were fixed with special intentness upon Guitaut, for from him was to come the explosion which was awaited with such diverse emotions.

The army likewise was in a state of painful suspense; and the messenger had no sooner stepped ashore upon the left bank of the Dordogne and been recognized than every eye was turned upon him. Monsieur de La Meilleraie, as soon as he caught sight of him, left the group of officers in the centre of which he was standing, and went to meet him.

Guitaut and the marshal talked together for a few seconds. Although the river was quite wide at that point, and although the distance was considerable between the royal party and the two officers, it was not so great that the surprised expression upon the marshal's face could not be detected. It was evident that the order conveyed to him seemed ill-advised and unseasonable, and he looked doubtfully toward the group in which the queen could be distinguished. But Anne of Austria, who understood his thought, made so imperative a gesture with both head and hand that the marshal, who knew his imperious sovereign of old, bent his head in token of acquiescence, if not of approbation.

Instantly, at a word from him, three or four captains, who exercised the functions of *aides-de-camp* of the present day, leaped into the saddle and galloped away in three or four different directions. Wherever they went the work of pitching the camp, which had just been begun, was at once broken off, and at the beat of the drums and the shrill call of the bugles, the soldiers let fall the armfuls of straw they were carrying, and the hammers with which they were driving in the tent-stakes. All ran to their weapons, which were stacked in due order; the grenadiers seized their muskets, the common soldiers their pikes, the artillerymen their various instruments; for a moment there was incredible confusion, caused by all these men running in all directions; but gradually order succeeded chaos, and every man was in his proper place,—the grenadiers in the centre, the king's household on the right, the artillery on the left; the drums and trumpets were silent.

A single drum was heard behind the intrenchments; then it too ceased and deathlike silence prevailed.

Suddenly an order was given in a clear, sharp tone. The queen was too far away to hear the words, but she saw the troops form instantly in columns; she drew her handkerchief and waved it, while the young king cried excitedly, stamping upon the ground: "Forward! forward!"

The army replied with a shout of "Vive le roi!" The artillery set off at a gallop, and took up its position upon a slight elevation, and the columns moved forward as the drums beat the charge.

It was not a siege in regular form, but a simple escalade. The intrenchments thrown up in haste by Richon were earthworks; there were no trenches to be opened therefore,—it was a matter of carrying them by assault. Every precaution had been taken by the energetic commandant of Vayres, and he had availed himself of every possible advantage in the lay of the land, with unusual science.

It was clear that Richon had determined not to fire first under any circumstances, for again he waited for the provocation to come from the king's troops; but again, as on the former occasion, that terrible row of muskets, which had done such execution upon the king's household, was seen to be pointing down at them.

As the forward movement began, the six guns drawn up on the little hill were discharged, and the cannon-balls threw up showers of dirt on the crown of the ramparts.

The response was not long delayed; the artillery within the intrenchments roared forth in its turn, ploughing broad furrows in the ranks of the royal army; but at the voice of the officers, these bleeding gaps disappeared; the lips of the wound opened for an instant, then closed again; the main column, which was momentarily shaken, moved forward once more.

While the cannon were being reloaded it was the turn of the musketry.

Five minutes later, the great guns on both sides discharged their volleys again, with but a single report, like two tempests in fierce combat with each other, like two peals of thunder coming at the same instant.

As it was perfectly calm, and a dense smoke hung over the battle-field, besiegers and besieged soon disappeared in a cloud, which was rent from time to time by the vivid flash of the artillery.

From time to time men could be seen coming out from the cloud in the rear of the royal army, dragging themselves along with difficulty, and leaving a bloody track behind them, until they fell exhausted.

The number of wounded rapidly increased, and the roar of the musketry and artillery continued. The royal artillery, however, were firing irregularly and at random; for amid the dense smoke the gunners could not distinguish friends from foes. The gunners in the fort on the other hand had none but foes in front of them, and their fire was more constant and more deadly than ever.

At last the royal artillery ceased firing altogether; it was evident that the assault had begun in good earnest, and that a hand-to-hand combat was in progress.

There was a moment of keenest anxiety on the part of the spectators, during which the smoke, the firing having greatly slackened, rose slowly into the air. The royal army was then seen to be falling back in disorder, leaving heaps of dead at the foot of the ramparts. A sort of breach had been made; a few palisades were torn away, leaving an opening; but that opening bristled with men and pikes and muskets, and amid those men, covered with blood, and yet as calm and cool as if he were a disinterested spectator of the tragedy in which he was playing so terrible a part, stood Richon, holding in his hand an axe all notched by the blows he had struck with it.

Some invisible power seemed to protect him, for he was constantly in the thickest of the firing, always in the front rank, always standing erect and with uncovered head, and yet no bullet had struck him, no pike had touched him; he was as invulnerable as he was impassive.

Thrice Maréchal de La Meilleraie in person led the royal troops to the assault; thrice the royal troops were beaten back before the eyes of the king and queen.

Great tears rolled silently down the pale cheeks of the boy king; Anne of Austria wrung her hands and muttered:—

"Oh! that man! that man! If he ever falls into my hands I will make a terrible example of him!"

Luckily flight was close at hand, and spread a veil, so to speak, over the royal blushes. Maréchal de La Meilleraie ordered the bugles to blow the recall.

Cauvignac left his post, descended the hill, and sauntered across the field toward the hostelry of Master Biscarros, with his hands in his pockets.

"Madame," said Mazarin, waving his hand in Cauvignac's direction, "there's a man who for a little gold would have spared you all this bloodshed."

"Nonsense!" said the queen. "Monsieur le Cardinal, that is strange language for economical man like yourself."

"True, madame," rejoined the cardinal: "I know the value of gold, but I know the value of blood also; and at this moment blood is more valuable to us than gold."

"Be assured," said the queen, "that the blood that has been shed shall be avenged. Comminges," she added, addressing the lieutenant of her guards, "seek out Monsieur de La Meilleraie and bring him to me."

"Bernouin," said the Cardinal to his valet, pointing to Cauvignac, who was within a few steps of the Golden Calf, "do you see that man?"

"Yes, monseigneur."

"Very good! go to him from me, and bring him secretly to my room to-night."

XVI

On the day following the interview with her lover in the Carmelite church, Madame de Cambes waited upon the princess with the intention of performing the promise she had given Canolles.

The whole city was in commotion; news had just come to hand of the king's arrival before Vayres, and of the admirable defence of Richon, who, with five hundred men, had twice repulsed the royal army of twelve thousand. Madame la Princesse was among the first to learn the news, and, in her transports of joy she cried, clapping her hands:—

"Oh! had I a hundred captains like my gallant Richon!"

Madame de Cambes swelled the chorus of admiration, doubly happy to be able to applaud openly the glorious conduct of a man she esteemed, and to find an opportunity ready made to put forward a request, of which the news of a defeat might have rendered doubtful the success, while on the other hand its success was well-nigh made certain by the news of a victory.

But even in her joy the princess had so much upon her mind that Claire dared not risk her request. The question under consideration was the sending Richon a reinforcement of men, of which it was not hard to realize his pressing need, in view of the approaching junction of Monsieur d'Épernon's army with the king's. The method of despatching this reinforcement was being discussed in council. Claire, seeing that politics had precedence for the moment over affairs of the heart, assumed the dignified demeanor of a councillor of State, and for that day the name of Canolles was not mentioned.

A very brief but very loving note advised the prisoner of this delay. It was less cruel to him than one might suppose, for the anticipation of that which we ardently desire is almost as pleasant as the reality. Canolles had too much of the true lover's delicacy in his heart not to take pleasure in what he called the antechamber of happiness. Claire asked him to wait patiently; he waited almost joyfully.

The next day the reinforcement was organized, and at eleven in the morning it started up the river; but, as mud and current were both adverse, they did not expect to arrive until the day following, being obliged to rely entirely upon their oars. Captain Ravailly, who was in command of the expedition was instructed to reconnoitre at the same time the fort of Braune, which belonged to the queen, and was known to be without a governor.

Madame la Princesse passed the morning superintending the preliminaries and the details of the embarkation. The afternoon was to be devoted to holding a grand council of war, the purpose being to devise means, if possible, to prevent the junction between Monsieur d'Épernon and the Maréchal de La Meilleraie, or at least to delay it until the reinforcement sent to Richon should have made its way into the fort.

Claire had no choice then but to wait another twenty-four hours; about four o'clock, however, she had an opportunity to wave her hand and nod to Canolles as he passed under her window, and those gestures were so eloquent of regret and affection that Canolles was almost happy that he was compelled to wait.

During the evening, in order to make sure that the delay would be prolonged no farther, and to leave herself no other alternative than to confide to the princess a secret as to which she felt some embarrassment, Claire requested a private audience for the next day,—a request which was, of course, granted without demur.

At the hour named, Claire waited upon the princess, who received her with her most charming smile. She was alone, as Claire had requested.

"Well, little one," she said, "what is the grave matter that leads you to ask me specially for a private audience, when you know that I am at my friends' service at all hours of the day?"

"Madame," the viscountess replied, "amid the felicity which is your Highness's due, I beg you to cast your eyes upon your faithful servant, who also feels the need of a little happiness."

"With great pleasure, my dear Claire, and all the happiness God could send you would not equal that which I desire for you. Say on, pray; what favor do you desire? If it is in my power to grant, look upon it as granted before it is asked."

"Widow as I am, and free,—too free, indeed, for my liberty is more burdensome to me than slavery would be,—I desire to exchange my loneliness for a happier lot."

"That is to say that you wish to marry, eh, little one?" queried Madame de Condé, with a smile.

"I think so," replied Claire, blushing.

"Very well! That is our affair."

Claire made a deprecatory gesture.

"Have no fear; we will be tender of your pride; you must have a duke and peer, viscountess. I will look up one for you among our faithful adherents."

"Your Highness is too kind; I did not propose to give you that trouble."

"That may be, but I propose to take it, for I am bound to repay in happiness what you have given me in devotion; you will wait till the end of the war, won't you?"

"I will wait the shortest possible time, madame," replied the viscountess, with a smile.

"You speak as if your choice were already made, as if you had in hand the husband you ask me to give you."

"Indeed, the fact is as your Highness suggests."

"Upon my word! Who is the lucky mortal, pray? Speak, have no fear."

"Oh, madame," said Claire; "I know not why, but I am trembling all over."

The princess smiled, took Claire's hand, and drew her to her side.

"Child!" said she, and added, with a look which redoubled Claire's embarrassment, "Do I know him?"

"I think that your Highness has seen him several times."

"I need not ask if he is young?"

"Twenty-eight."

"And nobly born?"

"He is of good family."

"And brave?"

"His reputation is established."

"And rich?"

"I am."

"Yes, little one, yes, and we have not forgotten it. You are one of the wealthiest nobles in our dominion, and we are happy to remember, that in the present war, the louis d'or of Monsieur de Cambes, and the crowns of your peasants have relieved our embarrassment more than once."

"Your Highness honors me by recalling my devotion."

"Very good. We will make him a colonel in our army if he is only a captain, and a brigadier-general if he is only a colonel; for he is faithful to us, I presume?"

"He was at Lens, madame," Claire replied with a craft in which she had lately become proficient by virtue of her diplomatic experiences.

"Excellent! Now there is but one thing left for me to learn," said the princess.

"What is that, madame?"

"The name of the very fortunate gentleman who already possesses the heart, and will soon possess the hand, of the loveliest warrior in my whole army."

Claire, driven into her last intrenchments, was summoning all her courage to pronounce the name of Canolles, when suddenly they heard a horse gallop into the court-yard, and in another moment the confused murmur of many voices, indicating the arrival of important news.

The princess ran to the window. A courier, begrimed with dust and reeking with perspiration, had just leaped from his horse, and was surrounded by a number of persons, to whom he seemed to be giving the details of some occurrence; and as the words fell from his lips, his listeners were overwhelmed with grief and consternation. The princess could not contain her curiosity, but opened the window and called: "Let him come up!"

The messenger looked up, recognized the princess, and darted to the stairway. In a few moments he was ushered into her apartment, covered with mud as he was, with disordered hair, and a hoarse, parched voice.

"Pray pardon me, your Highness," said he, "for appearing before you in my present condition! But I am the bearer of news at the mere utterance of which doors give way; Vayres has capitulated!"

The princess started back; Claire let her arms fall despairingly; Lenet, who entered behind the messenger, turned pale.

Five or six other persons, who had so far forgotten the respect due the princess as to invade her chamber, were stricken dumb with dismay.

"Monsieur Ravailly," said Lenet,—for the messenger was no other than our captain of Navailles,—"repeat what you said, for I find it hard to credit."

"I say again, monsieur: Vayres has capitulated!"

"Capitulated!" echoed the princess; "what of the reinforcements you led thither?"

"We arrived too late, madame! Richon was in the act of surrendering at the very moment of our arrival."

"Richon surrendered!" cried Madame la Princesse; "the coward!"

This exclamation sent a shiver down the back of everybody who heard it; but all remained mute, save Lenet.

"Madame," said he, sternly, heedless of wounding Madame de Condé's pride, "do not forget that the honor of men is at the mercy of princes, as their lives are in the hands of God. Do not brand with the name of coward the bravest of your servants, unless you would see all the most faithful abandon you to-morrow, when they see how you treat their fellows, leaving you alone, accursed and lost."

"Monsieur!" exclaimed the princess.

"Madame," rejoined Lenet, "I say again to your Highness that Richon is not a coward,—that I will answer for him with my head; and if he capitulated, it was certainly because he could not do otherwise."

The princess, pale with rage, was about to hurl at Lenet one of the aristocratic invectives which she deemed a sufficient substitute for good sense; but when she saw the averted faces, and eyes that avoided her own, Lenet with head erect, and Ravailly looking down at the floor, she realized that her cause would indeed be lost if she persevered in that fatal system; so she resorted to her usual argument.

"Unfortunate princess that I am," said she; "every one abandons me, fortune as well as men! Ah! my child, my poor child, you will undergo the same fate as your father!"

This wail of womanly weakness, this burst of maternal grief, found, as always, an echo in the hearts of those who stood by. The comedy, which the princess had so often enacted with success, once more accomplished its purpose.

Meanwhile Lenet made Ravailly repeat all that he could tell him concerning the capitulation of Vayres.

"Ah! I knew it must be so!" he suddenly ejaculated.

"What did you know?" the princess asked him.

"That Richon was no coward, madame."

"What has confirmed you in that opinion?"

"The fact that he held out two days and two nights; that he would have been buried beneath the ruins of his fort had not a company of recruits rebelled and forced him to capitulate."

"He should have died, monsieur, rather than surrender," said the princess.

"Ah! madame, can one die when one chooses?" said Lenet. "I trust," he added, turning to Ravailly, "that he obtained honorable terms."

"No terms at all, I fear," Ravailly replied. "I was told that the negotiations were conducted by a lieutenant, so that there may have been some treachery, and instead of having an opportunity to make terms Richon was betrayed."

"Yes, yes," cried Lenet, "he must have been betrayed! I know Richon, and I know that he is incapable, I will not insult him by saying of a cowardly act, but of an act of weakness. Oh, madame!" continued Lenet, "betrayed, do you understand? Let us look to his safety at once. Surrender negotiated by a lieutenant, Monsieur Ravailly? There is some great misfortune hovering over poor Richon's head. Write quickly, madame; write, I entreat you!"

"Write?" said the princess, sourly; "why should I write, pray?"

"Why, to save him, madame."

"Nonsense! when a man surrenders a fortress, he takes measures to ensure his own safety."

"But do you not understand that he didn't surrender it, madame? Do you not hear what the captain says, that he was betrayed, sold perhaps, — that it was a lieutenant who signed the capitulation, and not he?"

"What would you have me do for your Richon?"

"What would I have you do for him? Do you forget, madame, the subterfuge to which we resorted to put him in command at Vayres?—that we made use of a paper, signed in blank by Monsieur d'Épernon, and that he has resisted a royal army commanded by the queen and king in person?— that Richon is the first man to raise the standard of rebellion, and that they will surely make an example of him? Ah! madame, in Heaven's name, write to Monsieur de La Meilleraie; send a messenger, a flag of truce."

"Upon what errand should the messenger, or flag of truce, be sent?"

"To prevent at all hazards the death of a gallant officer; for if you do not make haste—Oh! I know the queen, madame, and perhaps the messenger will arrive too late as it is!"

"Too late?" said the princess; "pray, have we no hostages? Have we not some officers of the king as prisoners at Chantilly, at Montrond, and here?"

Claire rose from her chair in terror.

"Oh, madame! madame!" she cried, "do what Monsieur Lenet says: reprisals will not restore Monsieur Richon's liberty."

"It's not a question of his liberty, but of his life," said Lenet, with gloomy persistence.

"Very well," said the princess, "what they do, we will do; prison for prison, scaffold for scaffold."

Claire cried out and fell upon her knees.

"Ah! madame," said she, "Monsieur Richon is one of my friends. I have just asked you to grant me a favor, and you promised to do so. I ask you to put forth all your influence to save Monsieur Richon."

Claire was kneeling. The princess seized the opportunity to grant at her entreaty what she declined to grant in obedience to the somewhat harsh advice of Lenet. She walked to a table, seized a pen, and wrote to Monsieur de La Meilleraie a request for the exchange of Richon for such one of the officers whom she held as prisoners as the queen might select. Having written the letter she looked about for a messenger. Thereupon, suffering as he still was from his wound, and worn out by his recent expedition, Ravailly offered his services, on the single condition that he should have a fresh horse. The princess authorized him to take whatever horse he chose from her stables, and the captain left the room, animated by the cries of the crowd, the exhortations of Lenet, and the entreaties of Claire.

An instant after, they heard the murmuring of the people outside as Ravailly explained his errand to them; in their joy, they shouted at the top of their voices:—

"Madame la Princesse! Monsieur le Duc d'Enghien!"

Worn out by these daily exhibitions of herself, which she had been making in obedience to what resembled commands much more than invitations, the princess for an instant thought of refusing to comply with the popular desire; but, as commonly happens under such circumstances, the crowd was obstinate, and the shouts soon became roars.

"So be it," said Madame la Princesse, taking her son by the hand; "slaves that we are, let us obey!" and, affecting her most gracious smile, she appeared upon the balcony and saluted the people, whose slave she was and queen at the same time.

XVII

At the moment that the princess and her son showed themselves upon the balcony, amid the enthusiastic acclamations of the multitude, the sound of drums and fifes was heard in the distance, accompanied by loud cheering.

Instantly the noisy crowd which was besieging Président Lalasne's house to have a sight of Madame de Condé turned their heads in the direction from which the uproar seemed to proceed, and, with little heed to the laws of etiquette, began to melt away. The explanation of their action was not far to seek. They had already seen Madame la Princesse ten, twenty, perhaps a hundred times, while there was a promise of something new and unfamiliar in this noise which was coming constantly nearer.

"They are honest at least," murmured Lenet, with a smile, from behind the indignant princess. "But what is the meaning of all this music and shouting? I confess that I am almost as eager to know as yonder wretched courtiers."

"Very well," said the princess, "do you too, leave me, and go running about the streets with them."

"I would do it upon the instant, madame," said Lenet, "if I were sure of bringing you good news."

"Oh! as for good news," said the princess, with an ironical glance, apparently directed to the glorious blue sky over her head, "I hardly expect anything of the sort. We are not in a lucky vein."

"Madame," said Lenet, "you know that I am not easily deceived; I am very much mistaken, however, if all this noise does not mean that something favorable has happened."

Indeed the joyous character of the constantly increasing uproar, and the appearance of an excited multitude at the end of the street, with arms and handkerchiefs waving in the air, convinced the princess herself that what she was about to hear must be good news. She listened therefore with an eager attention which made her forget for a moment the desertion of her admirers, and distinguished these words:—

"Braune! the governor of Braune! the governor's a prisoner!"

"Aha!" said Lenet, "the governor of Braune a prisoner! That's not half bad. In him we have a hostage whom we can hold to answer for Richon."

"Have we not the governor of Île Saint-Georges?" said the princess.

"I am very happy," said Madame de Tourville, "that my plan for taking Braune has succeeded so well."

"Madame," said Lenet, "let us not flatter ourselves yet upon so complete a victory; chance mocks at the plans of man, sometimes even at the plans of woman."

"But; monsieur," retorted Madame de Tourville, bristling up as usual, "if the governor is taken, the place must be taken."

"Your logic is not absolutely unanswerable, madame; but have no fear that I shall not be the first to congratulate you, if to you we owe a twofold result of such importance."

"The most surprising thing to me in all this," said the princess, beginning to cast about already for something, in the anticipated good news, wounding to the aristocratic pride which was her most prominent characteristic, — "the most surprising thing to me is that I was not the first person to be informed of what had taken place; it is an unpardonable neglect of propriety, like everything that Monsieur le Duc de La Rochefoucauld does."

"Why, madame," said Lenet, "we haven't soldiers enough to do the fighting, and yet you would have us take some of them from their posts to make couriers of them! Alas! let us not be too exacting, and when good news arrives, let us take it as God sends it, and not ask how it came."

Meanwhile the crowd continued to increase in size, as all the detached groups joined the main body, even as the small streams flow into a great river. In the centre of this main body, composed of perhaps a thousand persons, was a little knot of soldiers, thirty men at most, and, surrounded by these thirty men, a prisoner whom they seemed to be protecting from the fury of the mob.

"Death! death!" cried the populace; "death to the governor of Braune!"

"Ah!" exclaimed the princess, with a triumphant smile, "it seems that they really have a prisoner, and that the prisoner is the governor of Braune!"

"Yes," said Lenet; "but look, madame; it seems also that the prisoner's life is in danger. Do you hear the threats? Do you see the fierce gestures? Why, madame, they are trying to force their way through the soldiers; they mean to tear him in pieces! Oh! the tigers, they smell the flesh, and thirst for blood!"

"Well, let them drink it!" said the princess, with the ferocity peculiar to women when their bad passions are aroused; "let them drink it! it's the blood of an enemy."

"Madame," said Lenet, "yonder prisoner is under safeguard of the honor of the Condés, remember that; and furthermore, who can say that at this moment Richon, our gallant Richon, is not exposed to the same danger as this poor wretch? Ah! they will force the soldiers back; if they reach him, he is lost! Twenty volunteers this way!" cried Lenet, turning about. "Twenty volunteers to help in driving back this canaille! If a hair on the prisoner's head is injured, your heads will answer for it; go!"

At the word, twenty musketeers of the civic guard, belonging to the best families of the city, rushed like a torrent down the stairs, forced the crowd aside by dint of dealing blows right and left with clubbed muskets, and reinforced the escort. It was high time, for a few claws, longer and sharper than the rest, had already torn some pieces from the prisoner's blue coat.

"I' faith, messieurs, I thank you," said the prisoner, "for you came just in time to prevent my being devoured by these cannibals; it was very well done of you. *Peste!* if they eat men up in this way, on the day that the royal army attempts an assault upon your city they will devour it raw."

With that he shrugged his shoulders carelessly and began to laugh.

"Ah! he's a brave man!" cried the crowd, observant of the somewhat artificial calmness of the prisoner; and they repeated the pleasantry, which flattered his self-esteem. "He's a true hero! he's not afraid. Long live the governor of Braune!"

"Gad, yes!" cried the prisoner, "long live the governor of Braune! That would suit me wonderfully well."

In a twinkling the popular rage changed to admiration, and this last sentiment was expressed in most emphatic terms. A veritable ovation took the place of the threatened martyrdom of the governor of Braune, in other words, of our old friend Cauvignac. For as our readers have undoubtedly guessed ere this, it was Cauvignac who was making this melancholy entry into the capital of Guyenne.

Meanwhile, protected by his guards, and by his presence of mind, the prisoner of war was taken to the house of Président Lalasne, and was haled before the princess by half of the escort, while the other half stood guard at the door.

Cauvignac entered Madame de Condé's apartment with proud and tranquil bearing; but truth compels us to state that his heart was beating wildly beneath this heroic exterior.

At the first glance he was recognized, despite the deplorable condition in which the mob had left his fine blue coat, his gold lace, and his feather.

"Monsieur Cauvignac!" cried Lenet.

"Monsieur Cauvignac, governor of Braune!" added the princess. "Ah! monsieur, this much resembles downright treason."

"What said your Highness?" queried Cauvignac, realizing that now, if ever, he must summon to his aid all his impudence, and all his wit. "I thought that I heard the word 'treason'!"

"Yes, monsieur, treason; for what is this title under which you appear before me?"

"The title of governor of Braune, madame."

"Treason, as you see. By whom is your commission signed?"

"By Monsieur de Mazarin."

"Treason! two-fold treason, as I said! You are governor of Braune, and it was your company that surrendered Vayres; the title was the fitting reward of the base deed."

At these words Cauvignac's face expressed the most unbounded amazement. He looked all about, as if seeking the person to whom this extraordinary language was addressed; and convinced at last that the princess's accusation was aimed at no other than himself, he let his hands fall by his sides with a despairing gesture.

"My company surrendered Vayres!" he exclaimed. "Does your Highness make such a charge against me?"

"Yes, monsieur, I do. Pretend to know nothing of it; affect amazement; you are evidently a clever comedian; but you will not make me the dupe of your grimaces or your words, although they harmonize so perfectly with one another."

"I pretend nothing, madame. How can your Highness say that I know what took place at Vayres, when I have never been there?"

"Subterfuge, monsieur, subterfuge!"

"I have nothing to say in reply to such words, madame, except that your Highness seems displeased with me. I pray your Highness to forgive the frankness of my character for the freedom with which I make bold to defend myself,—I was of the opinion that I had reason to complain of you."

"To complain of me, monsieur!" cried the princess, amazed at his audacity.

"Most assuredly, madame," rejoined Cauvignac, with undiminished self-possession; "relying upon your word and that of Monsieur Lenet here present, I levy a company of gallant fellows, and I enter into agreements with them, which are the more sacred in that they are in almost every instance merely verbal agreements. And lo! when I ask your Highness for the amount agreed upon,—a mere trifle, thirty or forty thousand livres,—to be used, not for myself, observe, but for the new defenders of the cause of Messieurs les Princes recruited by me, your Highness refuses to give them to me; yes, refuses me! I appeal to Monsieur Lenet."

"It is true," said Lenet; "when monsieur made his demand, we had no money."

"And could you not wait a few days, monsieur? Was your fidelity and that of your men a matter of a moment?"

"I waited the length of time that Monsieur de La Rochefoucauld himself asked me to wait, madame,—a week. At the end of the week I made my appearance again, and was then met with a formal refusal; once more I appeal to Monsieur Lenet."

The princess turned to her adviser with compressed lips, and eyes darting fire from beneath her frowning brow.

"Unfortunately," said Lenet, "I am forced to admit that what monsieur says is the exact truth."

Cauvignac drew himself up triumphantly.

"Tell me, madame," said he, "what would a schemer have done under such circumstances? He would have sold himself and his men to the queen. But I, who have a horror of intrigue, dismissed my company, and released every man from his agreement; and, being left entirely alone, I maintained absolute neutrality; I did what the sage advises the man who is in doubt to do,—I held aloof."

"But your soldiers, monsieur, your soldiers!" cried the princess, excitedly.

"Madame," Cauvignac retorted, "as I am neither king nor prince, but a simple captain; as I have neither subjects nor vassals, I call no soldiers mine, save those whom I pay; and as those whom you call mine were, as Monsieur Lenet affirms, not paid at all, they were free. Thereupon they turned against their new leader. What was I to do? I confess that I do not know."

"But what have you to say, monsieur, as to having taken the king's part yourself?—that your neutrality was a burden to you?"

"No, madame; but my neutrality, honest as it was, aroused the suspicion of his Majesty's partisans. One fine morning I was arrested at the Golden Calf inn on the Libourne road, and taken before the queen."

"And then you came to terms with her?"

"Madame," Cauvignac replied, "a man of heart has his sensitive spots, which a keen-sighted sovereign is sure to select for attack. My heart was embittered because I had been driven out of a party which I had rushed into blindly, with all the ardor and good faith of youth. I appeared before the queen between two soldiers who were ready to kill me; I expected reproaches, insults, death; for, after all, I had served the cause of the princes in intention. But, contrary to my expectations, instead of punishing me by depriving me of liberty, by consigning me to prison, or to the gallows, that great princess said to me:—

"'My gallant but deluded gentleman, I can with a word cause your head to fall; but you have met with ingratitude over yonder,—here you shall find us grateful. In the name of Saint-Anne, my patron saint, you shall be numbered henceforth among my retainers. Messieurs,' she continued, addressing my guards, 'treat this officer with respect, for I appreciate his meritorious qualities, and I make him your chief. And as for yourself,' she added, turning again to me, 'I make you governor of Braune; this is how a queen of France avenges herself.'

"What could I reply?" pursued Cauvignac, resuming his natural tone and attitude, after mimicking, in a half-comic, half-sentimental way, the voice and gestures of Anne of Austria. "Nothing. I was disappointed in my fondest hopes; I was disappointed in the result of my action in laying my devotion unrewarded at your Highness's feet, after I had had the good fortune, as it gives me great joy to remember, to render you a slight service at Chantilly. I followed the example of Coriolanus and sought the tents of the Volscii."

This discourse, delivered in a dramatic voice, and with majestic bearing, made a profound impression upon those who heard it. Cauvignac realized that he had triumphed when he saw the princess turn pale with rage.

"In Heaven's name, monsieur," said she, "to whom are you faithful?"

"To those who appreciate the delicacy of my conduct," was Cauvignac's retort.

"Be it so. You are my prisoner."

"I have that honor, madame; but I trust that you will treat me as a gentleman. I am your prisoner, it is true, but without having borne arms against your Highness. I was on my way to my post with my baggage, when I fell in with a party of your troops, who arrested me. I did not for an instant think of concealing my rank or my opinions. I say again, therefore, that I demand to be treated as a gentleman and as an officer of high rank."

"You will be so treated, monsieur," said the princess. "You will have the city for your prison; but you must swear to make no attempt to leave the city."

"I will swear whatever your Highness chooses to demand."

"'T is well. Lenet, repeat the formula to monsieur; we will receive his oath."

Lenet dictated the terms of the oath which Cauvignac was required to take.

Cauvignac raised his hand and solemnly swore that he would not leave the city until relieved from his oath.

"You may now withdraw," said the princess; "we rely upon your honor as a gentleman and a soldier."

Cauvignac did not wait to be told twice; but as he went out he detected a gesture of the councillor which signified:—

"He has put us in the wrong, madame; this is what comes of a niggardly policy."

The fact is that Lenet, who was quick to appreciate merit of every variety, recognized Cauvignac's exceeding shrewdness, and, for the very reason that he was in no wise deceived by any of his specious arguments, admired the skill with which the prisoner had extricated himself from one of the most difficult dilemmas in which a turn-coat could be involved.

Cauvignac meanwhile went slowly downstairs deep in thought, with his chin in his hand, saying to himself:

"Now the question is how I can sell them my hundred and fifty men again for a hundred thousand livres, which is quite possible, as the upright and intelligent Ferguzon has obtained full liberty for himself and his men. I shall find an opportunity one day or another. After all, I see that I did not make such a very great blunder in allowing myself to be taken as I at first thought."

XVIII

Let us now take a step backward, and direct the attention of our readers to the events that had taken place at Vayres, with which they are as yet only imperfectly acquainted.

After several assaults, which were the more terrible in that the royalist general sacrificed his men recklessly in order to save time, the outworks were carried; but their brave defenders, after contesting the ground foot by foot and heaping up the dead and wounded at the foot of the ramparts, retired by the underground passage, and intrenched themselves in the main fortification. Now Monsieur de La Meilleraie did not fail to realize that, if he had lost five or six hundred men in carrying a wretched earthwork surmounted by a palisade, he was practically certain to lose six times as many in carrying a fort surrounded by stout walls, and defended by a man whose strategic skill and soldierly gallantry he had discovered to his cost.

He had determined therefore to open trenches and lay siege to the place in due form, when he spied the advance guard of the Duc d'Épernon's army, which had effected its junction with his own, so that the royal forces were doubled. This put an entirely different face upon the affair. It was at once decided to undertake with twenty-four thousand men what they dared not undertake with twelve thousand, and to make an assault on the following day.

By the cessation of work upon the trenches, by the new dispositions which were seen to be in progress, and above all by the appearance of strong reinforcements, Richon understood that the besiegers proposed to give him no rest; and apprehending an assault upon the morrow, he called his men together, in order to make sure of the state of feeling among them, although he had no reason to doubt their zeal, in view of the manner in which they had supported him in the defence of the outworks.

His astonishment knew no bounds, therefore, when he discovered the change in the attitude of the garrison. His men gazed gloomily and uneasily at the royal army, and threatening murmurs arose in the ranks.

Richon had no patience with pleasantry in war-time, especially pleasantry of that sort.

"Who's muttering there?" he demanded, turning toward the spot where the sounds were most distinct.

"I!" replied one man, bolder than his fellows.

"You?"

"Yes, I."

"Come forward, and answer my questions."

The man left the ranks and approached his chief.

"What do you lack that you dare to complain?" said Richon, folding his arms and fixing his eyes sternly upon the malcontent.

"What do I lack?"

"Yes, what do you lack? Have you your ration of bread?"

"Yes, commandant."

"Your ration of wine?"

"Yes, commandant."

"Are your quarters unsatisfactory?"

"No."

"Are any arrears due you?"

"No."

"Tell me, then, what you want? What do these murmurs mean?"

"They mean that we are fighting against our king, and that comes hard to the French soldier."

"So you sigh to be in his Majesty's service?"

"*Dame!* yes."

"And you wish to join your king?"

"Yes," said the soldier, who was deceived by Richon's calm manner, and supposed that the affair would end with his simple exclusion from the garrison.

"Very well," said Richon, seizing the man by his baldric; "but as the gates are closed, you must take the only road that is left open to you."

"What is that?" queried the terrified soldier.

"This," retorted Richon, lifting him with his herculean arm, and tossing him over the parapet.

The soldier, with a yell of terror, dropped into the moat, which, luckily for him, was full of water.

This energetic action was greeted with gloomy silence. Richon believed that he had crushed the sedition, and turned to his men with the air of a gambler who risks everything to gain everything.

"Now," said he, "if there are any partisans of the king here, let them say so, and they will be allowed to go and join him by the same road."

A hundred voices answered:—

"Yes! yes! we are on the king's side, and we want to leave the fort!"

"Oho!" exclaimed Richon, realizing that he had to deal, not with the whim of a single man, but with a general revolt; "oho! that's another matter; I thought that I had simply one malcontent to deal with, but I see that I have five hundred cowards!"

Richon did very wrong to include the whole garrison in his accusation: only a hundred men or thereabouts had spoken; the rest had held their peace, but they began to grumble too, when they were included in the charge of cowardice.

"Come, come," said Richon, "let us not talk all together; if there is an officer who is willing to be false to his oath let him speak for all; I give you my word that he may speak with impunity."

Ferguzon thereupon stepped out from the ranks, and said, saluting his commanding officer with irreproachable courtesy:—

"Commandant, you hear the wish expressed by the garrison. You are fighting against his Majesty our king. Now the greater number of us were not informed that we enlisted to make war upon such a foe. One of these brave fellows, finding this violence done to his opinions, might easily, in the excitement of the assault, have made a mistake in his aim and lodged a bullet in your brain; but we are loyal soldiers, not cowards, as you wrongfully called us. This, then, is our ultimatum, which we make known to you with due respect: send us to the king, or we shall go to him of our own motion."

This speech was received with a universal shout of approval, which proved that the opinion expressed by the lieutenant was shared by the greater part, if not the whole, of the garrison. Richon saw that all was lost.

"I cannot defend the place alone," he said, "and I do not propose to surrender; as my soldiers abandon me, let some one negotiate for them, as he and they think best, but that some one shall not be myself. If the few brave fellows who remain faithful to me, provided that there are any such, are promised their lives, I ask nothing more. Who will be your spokesman?"

"I will be, commandant, if you have no objection, and if my comrades honor me with their confidence."

"Yes, yes, Lieutenant Ferguzon!" cried five hundred voices, among which those of Barrabas and Carrotel could easily be distinguished.

"You are to be the man, monsieur," said Richon. "You are free to go out and in, as you choose."

"And you have no special instructions to give me, commandant?"

"Liberty for my men."

"And for yourself?"

"Nothing."

Such disinterestedness would have brought to their senses men who had been misled simply, but these men were sold.

"Yes! yes! liberty for us!" they cried.

"Have no fear, commandant; I will not forget you in the capitulation."

Richon smiled sadly, shrugged his shoulders, and withdrew to his own apartments, where he shut himself in.

Ferguzon at once visited the royalist camp. Monsieur de La Meilleraie would do nothing, however, without the queen's authorization; and the queen had left Nanon's little house, in order, as she herself said, to avoid witnessing the further humiliation of her army, and had betaken herself to the hôtel de ville at Libourne.

The marshal therefore placed Ferguzon under guard, took horse, and galloped to Libourne, where he found Monsieur de Mazarin, to whom he had, as he supposed, momentous news to announce. But at the marshal's first words, the minister stopped him, to say with his stereotyped smile:—

"We know all that, Monsieur le Maréchal: it was all arranged last evening. Treat with Lieutenant Ferguzon, but make no terms for Monsieur Richon except upon your word."

"What's that?—except upon my word?" exclaimed the marshal; "when my word is given it is as sacred, I trust, as any written engagement."

"Go to, go to, Monsieur le Maréchal; I have received special indulgences from his Holiness, which make it possible for me to relieve people from their oaths."

"That may be," said the marshal, "but those indulgences do not apply to marshals of France."

Mazarin smiled and signified to the marshal that he was at liberty to return to the camp.

The marshal took his leave grumbling, and gave Ferguzon his written guaranty for himself and his men, but simply pledged his word concerning Richon.

Ferguzon returned to the fort, which he and his companions abandoned an hour before dawn, after informing Richon of the marshal's verbal promise. Two hours later, as he was watching from his window the arrival of Ravailly with reinforcements, Richon was arrested in the name of the queen.

At the announcement the gallant commandant's face expressed the liveliest satisfaction. If he were allowed to be at liberty, Madame de Condé might suspect him of treason; a captive, his captivity would justify him in her sight. It was this hope which led him to remain behind, instead of leaving the fort with the others.

They did not content themselves, however, with taking his sword simply, as he expected; but when he was disarmed, four men who were awaiting him at the door threw themselves upon him and bound his hands behind his back.

Richon endured this unworthy treatment with the tranquillity and resignation of a martyr. He was one of the steadfast, stern-tempered souls, who begat the popular heroes of the eighteenth and nineteenth centuries.

He was taken under guard to Libourne and carried before the queen, who eyed him arrogantly; before the king, who, honored him with a ferocious, withering gaze; and before Monsieur de Mazarin, who said to him:—

"You played a bold game, Monsieur Richon."

"And lost, did I not, monseigneur? Now it only remains for me to find out what the stake was."

"I greatly fear that the stake was your head," said Mazarin.

"Inform Monsieur d'Épernon that the king desires his presence," said Anne of Austria. "Let this fellow await his trial here."

With superb disdain in her every movement, she left the room, leading the king by the hand and followed by Monsieur de Mazarin and her courtiers.

Monsieur d'Épernon had arrived an hour before; but like the amorous old fellow he was, his first visit was to Nanon. In the heart of Guyenne he learned of the glorious defence made by Canolles at Île Saint-Georges, and, having always the utmost confidence in his mistress, he congratulated her upon the conduct of her beloved brother, whose countenance, however, he frankly observed, did not give promise of so great nobility of soul, or so great valor.

Nanon had something else to do than laugh in her sleeve at the prolongation of the blunder. At that moment she had to think, not only of her own happiness, but of her lover's liberty. Nanon loved Canolles so devotedly that she could not harbor the thought of his infidelity, although that thought came often to her mind. She had seen naught but affectionate solicitude in the pains he had taken to send her away from him; she believed him to be an unwilling prisoner; she wept and thought of nothing but the moment when, with the powerful assistance of Monsieur d'Épernon, she might obtain his freedom. So it was that she had written again and again to the dear duke, doing everything in her power to hasten his return.

At last he had arrived, and Nanon lost no time in presenting to him her petition touching her pretended brother, whom she was insanely anxious to rescue at the earliest possible moment from the hands of his enemies, or rather from those of Madame de Cambes, for she believed that Canolles in reality was in danger of no worse fate than falling in love with the viscountess.

But that in Nanon's eye was the worst of all dangers. She therefore implored Monsieur d'Épernon, upon her knees, to set her brother at liberty.

"Why, it could not happen better," replied the duke. "I have this moment learned that the governor of Vayres has allowed himself to be taken, and we will exchange him for our brother Canolles."

"Oh!" cried Nanon, "this is a special favor from heaven, my dear duke."

"You love this brother of yours very dearly, do you not, Nanon?"

"Oh, yes! more than my life."

"How strange it is that you never mentioned him to me until that day when I was fool enough—"

"Then Monsieur le Duc, you will—?" said Nanon.

"I will send the governor of Vayres to Madame de Condé, who will send Canolles to us; that is done every day in war-time,—an exchange, pure and simple."

"But will not Madame de Condé deem Monsieur de Canolles of more value than a simple officer?"

"Oh, well, in that case we will send her two or three officers instead of one; in short, we will arrange the matter to your satisfaction, my love; and when our gallant governor of Île Saint-Georges arrives at Libourne, we will give him a triumph."

Nanon's delight was beyond words. To have Canolles once more in her possession was her one burning desire. As for what Monsieur d'Épernon might say when he learned who Canolles really was, she cared but little. Once Canolles was safe beside her, she would tell the duke that he was her lover; she would proclaim it from the housetops, that all the world might hear.

At this juncture the queen's messenger appeared.

"Well, well," said the duke, "this is most fortunate, dear Nanon; I will wait upon her Majesty, and bring back with me the request for the exchange."

"So that my brother may be here?"

"To-morrow, perhaps."

"Go, then, go!" cried Nanon, "and do not lose an instant. Oh! to-morrow, to-morrow," she added, raising her arms with a lovely imploring expression, "to-morrow,—God grant it!"

"Ah! what a loving heart!" muttered Monsieur d'Épernon as he left the room.

When the Duc d'Épernon entered the queen's apartment, Anne of Austria, flushed with wrath, was biting her thick Austrian lips, which were the special admiration of her courtiers, for the very reason that they were her only ugly feature. Monsieur d'Épernon, a famous squire of dames, and accustomed to their smiles, was received like one of the Bordelais rebels.

He looked at the queen in amazement; she did not acknowledge his salutation, but gazed at him, with a threatening frown, from the height of her royal majesty.

"Aha! is it you, Monsieur le Duc?" she said at last after a pause of some duration; "come hither that I may offer you my congratulations upon your selection of officials within your jurisdiction."

"What have I done, madame, I pray to know?" demanded the wondering nobleman; "what has happened?"

"It has happened that you appointed to be governor of Vayres a man who has fired upon the king; that is all."

"I, madame!" cried the duke. "Your Majesty is most certainly in error; I did not appoint the governor of Vayres,—at least, not that I am aware of."

D'Épernon made this reservation because his conscience reproached him with not always making his appointments without assistance.

"Ah! this is interesting," said the queen; "Monsieur Richon was not appointed by you, *perhaps?*" And she emphasized the last word most maliciously.

The duke, who knew Nanon's talent for selecting fit men for the places to be filled, soon recovered his confidence.

"I do not recall the appointment of Monsieur Richon," said he, "but if I did appoint him he must be a faithful servant of the king."

"God's mercy!" retorted the queen; "Monsieur Richon, in your judgment, is a faithful servant of the king!—a faithful servant, in good sooth, who kills five hundred men for us in less than three days!"

"Madame," said the duke, "if such is the case I shall be forced to admit that I am wrong. But before I am convicted, allow me to go and procure the proof that I appointed him."

The queen's first impulse was to detain him, but she thought better of it.

"Go," said she, "and when you have brought me your proof, I will give you mine."

Monsieur d'Épernon hastened from the room, and ran all the way back to Nanon.

"Well," said she, "have you the request for the exchange of prisoners, my dear duke?"

"Oh, yes! of course! it was an excellent time to speak of that," rejoined the duke; "the queen is in a tearing rage."

"What is the cause of that?"

"Because either you or I appointed Monsieur Richon governor of Vayres, and this same governor, who seems to have defended the place like a lion, killed five hundred of our men."

"Monsieur Richon!" repeated Nanon; "I do not know that name."

"The devil take me if I do."

"Then tell the queen boldly that she is mistaken."

"But are you sure that you are not mistaken?"

"Wait a moment; I prefer to have no reason for self-reproach, so I will tell you."

Nanon went to her study, and consulted her register at the letter R. It contained no memorandum of a commission issued to Richon.

"You can go back to the queen," she said, returning, "and tell her fearlessly that she is in error."

Monsieur d'Épernon did not pause to take breath between Nanon's house and the hôtel de ville.

"Madame," said he, proudly, as he entered the queen's apartment, "I am innocent of the crime imputed to me. The appointment of Monsieur Richon was made by your Majesty's ministers."

"In that case my ministers sign themselves D'Épernon," retorted the queen, dryly.

"How so?"

"It must be so, as that signature is written at the foot of Monsieur Richon's commission."

"Impossible, madame!" rejoined the duke, in the hesitating tone of a man who begins to doubt himself.

"Impossible?" said the queen, with a shrug. "Very good! read for yourself." And she took from the table a document upon which her hand was laid.

Monsieur d'Épernon seized the commission, and ran it through eagerly, examining every fold of the paper, every word, every letter; a terrible thought came to his mind, and kept him rooted to his place.

"May I see this Monsieur Richon?" he asked.

"Nothing easier," replied the queen; "I ordered him to be detained in the adjoining room, in order to afford you that satisfaction. Bring in the villain," she added to the guards who were awaiting her orders at the door.

In a moment Richon was led in, with his hands bound behind his back, and his hat on his head. The duke walked up to him, and fastened his eyes upon him in a piercing gaze, which he endured with his wonted dignity.

One of his guards knocked his hat to the floor with the back of his hand; but this insult did not cause the slightest evidence of excitement on the part of the governor of Vayres.

"Throw a cloak over his shoulders, put a mask on his face, and give me a lighted candle," said the duke.

The first two orders were first obeyed. The queen looked on in amazement at these strange preparations.

The duke walked around Richon, scrutinizing him with the greatest care, trying to refresh his memory upon every detail, but evidently still in doubt.

"Bring me the candle I asked for," said he; "that test will set my doubts at rest."

The candle was brought. The duke held the commission close to the flame, and the heat caused a double cross, drawn below the signature with invisible ink, to appear upon the paper.

At the sight the duke's brow cleared, and he cried:

"Madame, this commission is signed by me, it is true; but it was not signed for Monsieur Richon, or for any other person; it was extorted from me by this man in a sort of ambuscade; but before I delivered it to him, signed in blank, I had made this mark on the paper which your Majesty can see, and it furnishes us with overwhelming proof against the culprit. Look."

The queen eagerly seized the paper, and looked at the cross which the duke pointed out to her.

"I do not understand a single word of the charge you make against me," said Richon, simply.

"What's that?" cried the duke; "you were not the masked man to whom I handed this paper upon the Dordogne?"

"I have never spoken to your lordship before this day; I have never been upon the Dordogne, masked," replied Richon, coldly.

"If it was not you it was some man sent by you."

"It would serve no purpose to conceal the truth," said Richon, as calm as ever; "the commission which you hold in your hand, Monsieur le Duc, I received from Madame la Princesse de Condé, by the hands of Monsieur le Duc de La Rochefoucauld; my name had then been inserted by Monsieur Lenet, with whose writing you are perhaps familiar. How the paper came into the hands of Madame la Princesse, or of Monsieur de La Rochefoucauld; when and where my name was written upon that paper by Monsieur Lenet, I have absolutely no idea, nor do I care, for it does not concern me."

"Ah! do you think so?" retorted the duke, in a bantering tone.

Thereupon he drew near the queen and in a low tone told her a long story, to which she listened with close attention; it was the story of his meeting with Cauvignac, and the adventure of the Dordogne.

The queen, being a woman, perfectly appreciated the duke's jealousy. When he had finished, she said: —

"It's an infamous act, to add to the high treason; the man who does not hesitate to fire upon his king, may well be capable of selling a woman's secret."

"What the devil are they saying there?" muttered Richon, with a frown; for while he could not hear enough to follow the conversation, he heard enough to arouse a suspicion that his honor was being brought in question. Moreover, the flashing eyes of the duke and the queen promised nothing agreeable, and, courageous as the governor of Vayres was, he could not avoid a feeling of uneasiness, although it would have been impossible, from the calm, disdainful expression of his features, to guess what was taking place in his heart.

"He must be tried at once," said the queen. "Assemble a court-martial. You will preside, Monsieur le Duc d'Épernon; so select your associates, and lose no time."

"Madame," said Richon, "there is no occasion for assembling a court-martial, or for a trial. I am a prisoner upon the word of Monsieur le Maréchal de La Meilleraie. I am a voluntary prisoner, for I could have gone out of Vayres with my soldiers; I could have made my escape before or after their evacuation, and I did not do it."

"I know nothing of business of this nature," said the queen, rising to go into the adjoining room; "if you have satisfactory explanations to make, you can urge them upon your judges. Will not this room serve your purpose, Monsieur le Duc?"

"Yes, madame," replied D'Épernon, who immediately selected twelve officers from among those in attendance, and constituted the court.

Richon began to understand his situation, as the judges took their places, and the judge-advocate demanded his name and rank.

Richon answered these questions.

"You are accused of high treason in having fired upon the soldiers of the king," said the judge-advocate; "do you admit your guilt?"

"To deny it would be to deny what you all saw; yes, monsieur, I fired upon the king's troops."

"By virtue of what right?"

"By virtue of the laws of war, by virtue of the same right which Monsieur de Conti, Monsieur de Beaufort, Monsieur d'Elbœuf, and so many others, have invoked under the like circumstances."

"That right does not exist, monsieur, for it is nothing more nor less than rebellion."

"But it was by virtue of that right that my lieutenant capitulated. I appeal to the terms of the capitulation."

"Capitulation!" cried Monsieur d'Épernon, ironically, for he felt that the queen was listening, and the feeling dictated the insult; "you, treat with a marshal of France!"

"Why not, when a marshal of France treated with me?"

"Produce your capitulation, then, and we will judge of its value."

"It was a verbal agreement."

"Produce your witnesses."

"I have but one witness to produce."

"Who is that?"

"The marshal himself."

"Let the marshal be called," said the duke.

"It's useless," interposed the queen, opening the door behind which she was listening; "Monsieur le Maréchal set out two hours since with the advance-guard, to march upon Bordeaux."

With that she closed the door once more.

This apparition froze the blood in every heart, for it imposed upon the judges the necessity of convicting Richon.

"Ah!" said he, "that is all the regard Monsieur de La Meilleraie has for his word. You were right, monsieur," he added, turning to the Duc d'Épernon, "I was foolish to treat with a marshal of France."

From that moment Richon maintained a disdainful silence, and refused to reply to any and all questions. This course simplified the proceedings greatly, and the trial lasted little more than an hour. They wrote little and spoke still less. The judge-advocate closed by demanding the imposition of the death penalty, and at a sign from the Duc d'Épernon the judges unanimously voted for death.

Richon listened to the sentence as if he were a simple spectator, and, as impassive and dumb as ever, was turned over on the spot to the provost of the army.

The Duc d'Épernon betook himself to the apartments of the queen, whom he found in a charming humor, and who invited him to dinner. The duke, who believed himself to be in disgrace, accepted, and returned to

Nanon to inform her of his good fortune in retaining his standing in the good graces of his sovereign.

He found her stretched out upon a reclining chair by a window which looked upon the public square of Libourne.

"Well," said she, "have you discovered anything?"

"I have discovered everything, my dear."

"Nonsense!" said Nanon, not without some in-quietude.

"*Mon Dieu!* I mean what I say. You remember that accusation I was idiot enough to believe,—the accusation that you were carrying on an intrigue with your brother?"

"Well?"

"You remember the blank signature that I was required to give the informer?"

"Yes, what then?"

"The informer is in our hands, my dear, taken in the meshes of his blank signature, like a fox in the trap."

"Can it be?" said Nanon, in dismay; for she knew that Cauvignac was the man, and although she had no very deep affection for her real brother, she did not wish that any ill should befall him; moreover, that same brother might, to extricate himself, tell a multitude of things which Nanon preferred to have remain secret.

"Himself, my dear," continued D'Épernon; "what do you say to that? The rascal, with the assistance of my signature, appointed himself governor of Vayres on his own authority; but Vayres is taken and the culprit is in our hands."

All these details were so like Cauvignac's ingenious combinations that Nanon's alarm redoubled.

"What have you done with this man?" she asked in a voice that betrayed her emotion.

"Why," said the duke, "in a moment you can see for yourself what we have done with him. Yes, 'faith," he added, rising, "it couldn't be better; raise the curtain, or rather throw the window open; he's an enemy of the king, and you can see him hanged."

"Hanged!" cried Nanon. "What do you say, Monsieur le Duc? the man of the blank signature is to be hanged?"

"Yes, my love. Look yonder; do you not see the rope dangling from the beam, and the crowd flocking to the square? And see, there are the fusileers coming with the man himself, over at the left. Look! there is the king at his window."

Nanon's heart was in her mouth; one rapid glance, however, was enough to show her that the man in custody was not Cauvignac.

"Well, well," said the duke, "Sieur Richon is to be hanged as high as Haman; that will teach him to slander women."

"But," cried Nanon, seizing the duke's hand, and summoning all her strength for the struggle, "but the poor wretch is not guilty; perhaps he's a gallant soldier; perhaps he's an honorable man; it may be that you are murdering one who is innocent!"

"No, no, you are greatly mistaken, my dear; he is a forger and a slanderer. Besides, if there were nothing against him but his being governor of Vayres, he would still be guilty of high treason, and it seems to me that, even if that were all, it would be quite enough."

"But hadn't he Monsieur de La Meilleraie's word?"

"He said so, but I do not believe him."

"Why did not the marshal enlighten the court-martial on so important a point?"

"He left Libourne two hours before the court convened."

"O *mon Dieu! mon Dieu!*" cried Nanon; "something tells me that he is innocent, and that his death will bring bad luck to us all. Ah! monsieur, you have great influence, and you say there is nothing you would not do for me—in Heaven's name, then, grant me that man's pardon!"

"I cannot, my dear; the queen herself condemned him, and where she is, there is no other power."

Nanon uttered a sigh which much resembled a groan.

At that moment Richon reached the market-place, and, still tranquil and silent, was led beneath the beam to which the rope was attached; a ladder was already in place awaiting his coming. Richon mounted the ladder with unfaltering step, his noble head towering above the crowd, upon which he gazed with cold contempt. The provost passed the noose around his neck, and the crier proclaimed in a loud voice that the king was about to do justice upon the body of Étienne Richon, forger, traitor, and plebeian.

"The day has come," said Richon, "when it is more honorable to be a plebeian as I am than to be a marshal of France."

The words were hardly out of his mouth when the ladder was pulled from under him, and his body hung trembling from the fatal beam.

A universal feeling of horror scattered the crowd, without a single shout of *Vive le roi!* although every one could see the two royal personages at their window. Nanon hid her face in her hands and fled to the farthest corner of the room.

"Whatever you may think, dear Nanon," said the duke, "I believe that this execution will have a good effect. I am curious to know what they will do at Bordeaux when they learn that we are hanging their governors."

As she thought of what they might do, Nanon opened her mouth to speak, but she could only utter a heartrending shriek, raising her hands to heaven as if in entreaty that Richon's death might not be avenged; then, as if all the springs of life were dried up within her, she fell at full length upon the floor.

"Well, well!" cried the duke, "what's the matter Nanon? What does this mean? Is it possible that it puts you in such a state as this to see a mere upstart hanged? Come, dear Nanon, come to your senses! Why, God forgive me, she has fainted!—and the people of Agen say that she has no feeling! Ho there! help! salt! cold water!"

But no one came at his call, so the duke ran from the room to procure himself what he called for in vain from her servants, who probably did not hear him, so engrossed were they by the spectacle with which the royal generosity regaled them, free of charge.

XIX

At the moment that the terrible drama we have described was being enacted at Libourne, Madame de Cambes, seated beside an oaken table, with Pompée at her side making a sort of inventory of her worldly goods, was writing to Canolles the following letter:—

"Still another postponement, my beloved. Just as I was about to pronounce your name to Madame la Princesse, and ask her consent to our union, the news arrived of the capture of Vayres, and froze the words upon my lips. But I know how you must suffer, and I am not strong enough to endure your grief and my own at the same time. The successes or reverses of this fatal war may carry us too far, unless we decide to take matters into our own hands. To-morrow, dear, to-morrow evening at seven o'clock, I will be your wife.

"This is the plan which I beg you to adopt; it is of the utmost importance that you conform to it in every respect.

"Immediately after dinner you will call upon Madame de Lalasne who, as well as her sister, since I presented you to them, has conceived the greatest admiration for you. There will be card-playing, and do you play like the others; but make no engagement for supper; and when night comes, send away your friends if any of them happen to be around you. When you are quite alone you will see a messenger come in,—I cannot say who it will be,—who will call you by your name, as if you were wanted for some business or other. Whoever the messenger may be, follow him without fear, for he will come from me, and his errand will be to guide you to the place where I await you.

"I should like that place to be the Carmelite church, of which I have such pleasant memories; but as yet I dare not hope that it will be the place, unless they will consent to close the doors for us.

"Meanwhile do to my letter what you do to my hand when I forget to withdraw it from yours. To-day I say to you, 'Until to-morrow;' to-morrow I will say, 'Forever!'"

Canolles was in one of his fits of misanthropy when he received this letter. During the whole of the preceding day, and all that morning he had not so much as seen Madame de Cambes, although, in the space of twenty-four hours he had passed before her windows at least ten times. Thereupon the customary reaction took place in the heart of the lovelorn youth. He accused the viscountess of coquetry; he doubted her love; he recurred instinctively to his memories of Nanon,—of Nanon, always kind, devoted, ardent, and glorying in the love of which Claire seemed to be ashamed; and he sighed, poor heart, between the satiated passion which would not die and the hungry passion which had nothing to feed upon. The viscountess's epistle turned the scale in her favor.

Canolles read it again and again: as Claire had foreseen, he kissed it a score of times as he would have kissed her hand. Upon reflection, Canolles could not conceal from himself that his love for Claire was and had been the most serious affair of his life. With other women that sentiment had always assumed a different aspect, and developed in a different direction. Canolles had played his part as a squire of dames, had posed as a lady-killer, and had almost arrogated to himself the right to be inconstant. With Madame de Cambes, on the contrary, he felt that he was himself under the yoke of a superior power, against which he did not even try to struggle, because his present slavery was far sweeter to him than his former dominion. And in those moments of discouragement when he conceived doubts of the reality of Claire's affection, in those moments when the sorrowing heart falls back upon itself, and augments its sorrow with bitter thoughts, he confessed to himself, without a blush for a weakness which a year earlier he would have deemed unworthy a great heart, that to lose Madame de Cambes would be an insupportable calamity.

But to love her, to be beloved by her, to possess her, heart and soul and body; to possess her, without compromising his future independence,—for the viscountess did not even demand that he should sacrifice his opinions to join the faction of Madame la Princesse, and asked for nothing but his love,—to be in the future the happiest and wealthiest officer in the king's army (for, after all, why should not wealth be considered? wealth does no harm); to remain in his Majesty's service if his Majesty should fittingly reward his fidelity; to leave it if, in accordance with the custom of kings, he proved to be ungrateful,—was not all this, in very truth, greater good fortune, a more superb destiny, if we may so say, than any to which he had ever dared aspire in his wildest dreams?

But Nanon?

Ah! Nanon, Nanon! there was the dull, aching remorse, which lies always hidden in the depths of every noble heart. Only in hearts of common clay does the sorrow which they cause fail to find an echo. Nanon, poor Nanon! What would she do, what would she say, what would become of her, when she should learn the terrible tidings that her lover was the husband of another woman? Alas! she would not, revenge herself, although she would certainly have in her hands all the means of doing so, and that was the thought which tortured Canolles most of all. Oh! if Nanon would but try to take vengeance upon him, if she would set about it in any way she might select, the faithless lover might then look upon her as an enemy, and would at least be rid of his remorse.

But Nanon had not answered the letter wherein he bade her not to write to him. How did it happen that she had followed his instructions so scrupulously? Surely, if she had wished to do so, she would have found a way to send him ten letters; so Nanon had not even tried to correspond with him. Ah! what if Nanon no longer loved him! And Canolles' brow grew dark at the thought that that was possible. It is a pitiful thing, thus to encounter selfish pride even in the noblest hearts.

Luckily Canolles had one sure way of forgetting everything else, and that was to read and reread Madame de Cambes' letter; he read it and reread it, and the remedy was effectual. Our lover thus succeeded in making himself oblivious to everything except his own happiness. And to follow out his mistress's instructions from the beginning, he made himself beautiful, which was a matter of no great difficulty for a youth with his personal advantages and good taste, and set out for Madame de Lalasne's as the clock was striking two.

He was so engrossed in his own happiness that as he passed along the quay he did not see his friend Ravailly, who made sign after sign to him from a boat which was coming down stream as fast as oars could drive it through the water. Lovers, in their happy moments, step so lightly that they seem hardly to touch the ground, and Canolles was already far away when Ravailly stepped ashore.

The latter spoke a few words in a sharp tone to the boatman, and hurried away toward Madame de Condé's abode.

The princess was at table when she heard a commotion in the antechamber; she inquired as to its cause, and was told that Baron de Ravailly, her messenger to Monsieur de La Meilleraie, had that moment arrived.

"Madame," said Lenet, "I think it would be well for your Highness to receive him without delay; whatever the tidings he brings, they are important."

The princess made a sign, and Ravailly entered the room, but his face was so pale and grief-stricken that a glance was enough to convince Madame de Condé that she had before her eyes a messenger of evil.

"What is it, captain?" said she: "what news have you?"

"Pardon me, madame, for appearing before your Highness in this plight, but I thought that the tidings I bring should not be delayed."

"Speak: did you see the marshal?"

"The marshal refused to receive me, madame."

"The marshal refused to receive my envoy?" cried the princess.

"Ah! madame, that is not all."

"What else is there? speak! speak! I am waiting."

"Poor Richon—"

"Yes, I know; he is a prisoner—did I not send you to negotiate his ransom!"

"Although I made all possible speed, I arrived too late."

"What! too late?" cried Lenet; "can any harm have come to him?"

"He is dead."

"Dead!" echoed the princess.

"He was tried for high treason, and was condemned and executed."

"Condemned! executed! Ah! you hear, madame," said the horror-stricken Lenet, "I told you how it would he!"

"Who condemned him? who was so bold?

"A court-martial presided over by the Duc d'Épernon, or rather by the queen herself; indeed, they were not content with his death, but decided that it should be infamous."

"What! Richon—"

"Hanged, madame! hanged like a common malefactor, like a thief or an assassin! I saw his body in the market-place at Libourne."

The princess jumped to her feet, as if acted upon by an invisible spring. Lenet uttered an exclamation of grief. Madame de Cambes, who had risen, fell back upon her chair, putting her hand to her heart, as one does when one receives a grievous wound; she had fainted.

"Take the viscountess away," said the Duc de La Rochefoucauld; "we have no leisure now to attend to swooning women."

Two women bore the viscountess from the room.

"This is a brutally frank declaration of war," said the impassive duke.

"It is infamous!" said the princess.

"It is sheer savagery!" said Lenet.

"It is impolitic!" said the duke.

"Oh! but I trust that we shall find a way to be revenged!" cried the princess, "and that right cruelly!"

"I have my plan!" cried Madame de Tourville, who had said nothing thus far,—"reprisals, your Highness, reprisals!"

"One moment, madame," said Lenet; "deuce take me! how fast you go! The affair is of sufficient importance to require reflection."

"No, monsieur, not at all," retorted Madame de Tourville; "as the king has acted quickly, it is of the utmost importance that we retaliate promptly with the same stroke."

"Why, madame," cried Lenet, "you talk of shedding blood as if you were Queen of France, upon my word. Withhold your opinion at least until her Highness requests you to give it."

"Madame is right," said the captain of the guards; "reprisals are in accordance with the laws of war."

"Come," said the Duc de La Rochefoucauld, calm and unmoved as always, "let us not waste time in idle words as we are doing. The news will soon spread through the city, and an hour hence we shall have lost control of events and passions and men. Your Highness's first care should be to adopt an attitude so firm that it will be deemed to be unchangeable."

"Very well," said the princess, "I place the matter in your hands, Monsieur le Duc, and rely entirely upon you to avenge my honor and your own affection; for Richon was in your own service before entering mine; he came to me from you, and you gave him to me rather as one of your friends than as one of your retainers."

"Never fear, madame," said the duke, bowing; "I shall remember what I owe to you, to myself, and to poor dead Richon."

He led the captain of the guards aside, and talked with him a long while in a low tone, while the princess left the room with Madame de Tourville, followed by Lenet beating his breast in his grief.

The viscountess was at the door. On recovering consciousness her first impulse was to return to Madame de Condé; she met her on the way, but with a face so stern that she dared not question her personally.

"*Mon Dieu! mon Dieu!* what is to be done?" she cried timidly, clasping her hands imploringly.

"We are to have our revenge!" replied Madame de Tourville, with a majestic air.

"Revenge? and how?"

"Madame," interposed Lenet, "if you possess any influence over the princess, use it, I pray you, to prevent the commission of some horrible murder under the name of reprisals."

With that he passed on, leaving Claire in deadly terror. For, by one of those strange intuitions which make one believe in presentiments, the thought of Canolles suddenly passed through her mind. She heard a sad voice in her heart speaking of her absent lover, and rushing feverishly upstairs to her room, she began to dress to go to meet him, when she perceived that the appointed time was still three or four hours distant.

Meanwhile Canolles made his appearance at Madame de Lalasne's in accordance with the instructions contained in the viscountess's letter. It was the president's birthday, and a birthday party was in progress. As it was the pleasantest season of the year, all the guests were in the garden, where a game of tennis was in progress upon a vast lawn. Canolles, whose dexterity was remarkable, was the recipient of several challenges as soon as he appeared, and his skill at the game brought success to his side again and again.

The ladies laughed at the awkwardness of Canolles' rivals and his own address; prolonged bravoes followed every new stroke that he made; handkerchiefs waved in the air, and but little more enthusiasm was needed to cause bouquets to rain down at his feet from the loveliest of hands.

His triumph did not avail to banish from his mind the one great thought that filled it, but it helped him to be patient. However great one's haste to reach a goal, one endures delays more patiently when each delay is an ovation.

However, as the appointed hour drew near, the young man's eyes were turned more frequently toward the door through which the guests came and went, and through which the promised messenger would naturally make his appearance.

Suddenly, as Canolles was congratulating himself upon having, in all probability, but a short time to wait, a strange rumor began to circulate through the joyous assemblage. Canolles noticed that groups formed here and there, talking in undertones, and gazing at him with extraordinary interest, in which there seemed to be an admixture of compassion; at first he attributed this interest to his personal appearance and his dexterity, being very, very far from suspecting its true cause.

He began at last to notice that there was, as we have said, an admixture of something like pity in the earnest looks that were bent upon him. He approached one of the groups, with smiling face; the persons who composed the group tried to smile back at him, but were visibly embarrassed, and they to whom he did not directly address himself moved away.

Canolles turned in one direction after another and saw that every one avoided his glance and slunk away. It was as if some fatal tidings had suddenly swept over the assemblage, and struck every one dumb with terror. Behind him Président de Lalasne was pacing gloomily back and forth with one hand under his chin and the other in his breast. His wife, with her sister on her arm, took advantage of a moment when no one seemed to be looking to walk towards Canolles, and said, without directly addressing him, in a tone which aroused his keenest apprehension:—

"If I were a prisoner of war, upon parole, for fear lest the agreement made with me might be violated, I would leap upon a good horse and ride to the river; I would give ten, twenty, a hundred louis, if need be, to a boatman, but I would leave the city."

Canolles gazed at the two women in utter amazement, and they simultaneously made a terrified gesture which he could not comprehend. He walked toward them to seek an explanation of the words he had heard, but they fled like phantoms, one with her finger on her lips to enjoin silence upon him, the other waving her hand to bid him fly.

At that moment he heard his name at the gate.

He shuddered from head to foot; the name must have been pronounced by the viscountess's messenger, and he darted in that direction.

"Is Monsieur le Baron de Canolles here?" a loud voice asked.

"Yes," cried Canolles, forgetting everything else to remember only Claire's promise; "yes, here I am."

"You are Monsieur de Canolles?" said a man in uniform passing through the gate.

"Yes, monsieur."

"Governor of Île Saint-Georges?"

"Yes."

"Formerly captain in the Navailles regiment?"

"Yes."

The sergeant, for such he seemed to be, waved his hand, and four soldiers, hidden from sight by a carriage, at once came forward; the carriage itself drove up so that its step was close to the gate, and the sergeant ordered Canolles to enter.

The young man looked about. He was absolutely alone, except that he could see, among the trees in the distance, Madame de Lalasne and her sister, like two ghosts, gazing at him, as he fancied, with compassion.

"*Pardieu!*" he said to himself, utterly unable to comprehend what was going on; "Madame de Cambes has selected a strange escort for me. However," he added, smiling at his own thought, "we must not be too particular as to the means."

"We are waiting for you, commandant," said the sergeant.

"I beg your pardon, messieurs," Canolles replied, "I am ready;" and he entered the carriage.

The sergeant and two soldiers entered it with him; the other two took their places, one beside the driver, and the other behind, and the lumbering vehicle rolled away as rapidly as two sturdy horses could draw it.

All this was passing strange, and Canolles began to feel decidedly nervous.

"Monsieur," said he to the sergeant, "now that we are by ourselves, can you tell me where you are taking me?"

"Why, to prison in the first place, commandant," was the reply.

Canolles stared at the man in dumb amazement.

"What! to prison!" he exclaimed at last. "Do you not come from a lady?"

"We do, indeed."

"And is not that lady Madame la Vicomtesse de Cambes?"

"No, monsieur, that lady is Madame la Princesse de Condé."

"Madame la Princesse de Condé!" cried Canolles.

"Poor young man!" murmured a woman who was passing; and she made the sign of the cross.

Canolles felt a shudder of fear run through his veins.

A little farther on, a man who was running along the street, pike in hand, stopped when he saw the carriage and the soldiers. Canolles put his head through the window, and the man evidently recognized him, for he shook his fist at him with an angry and threatening expression.

"Good God! people have gone crazy in this city of yours," said Canolles, still trying to smile. "Have I become in one hour an object of pity or of detestation, that some pity me and others threaten me?"

"Ah! monsieur," the sergeant replied, "those who pity you make no mistake, and it may be that those who threaten you are quite right to do so."

"If I only could understand what it all means," said Canolles.

"You will very soon understand, monsieur."

They reached the door of the prison, where Canolles was ordered to alight, amid the crowd which was beginning to collect. Instead of taking him to his usual room, they led him down into a cell filled with guards.

"I must know what I am to expect," he said to himself; and taking two louis from his pocket he went up to a soldier and put them in his hand.

The soldier hesitated about receiving them.

"Take them, my friend," said Canolles, "for the question I am about to ask you cannot compromise you in any way."

"Say on, then, commandant," rejoined the soldier, first pocketing the two louis.

"Very good! I would like to know the reason of my sudden arrest."

"It would seem," said the soldier, "that you have not heard of poor Monsieur Richon's death?"

"Richon dead!" cried Canolles, in a tone of heartfelt sorrow, for the close friendship between the two men will be remembered. "Was he killed when the fortress was taken?"

"No, commandant, he has been hanged since."

"Hanged!" muttered Canolles, with pallid cheeks, looking about at the ominous surroundings and the savage faces of his keepers. "Hanged! the devil! this is likely to postpone my wedding indefinitely!"

XX

Madame de Cambes had finished her toilet,—a toilet all the more charming for its simplicity,—and throwing a light cape over her shoulders, motioned to Pompée to go before her. It was almost dark, and thinking that she would be less likely to be observed on foot than in a carriage, she ordered her carriage to await her at one of the doors of the Carmelite church, near a chapel in which she had obtained permission for the marriage ceremony to take place. Pompée descended the stairs and the viscountess followed. This assumption of the duties of a scout reminded the old soldier of the famous patrol of the night before the battle of Corbie.

At the foot of the staircase, as the viscountess was about to pass the door of the salon, where there was a great commotion, she met Madame de Tourville dragging the Duc de La Rochefoucauld toward the princess's cabinet, and engaged in an earnest discussion with him on the way.

"One word, madame, I entreat," said she; "what decision has been reached?"

"My plan is adopted!" cried Madame de Tourville, triumphantly.

"What is your plan, madame? I do not know."

"Reprisals, my dear, reprisals!"

"Pardon me, madame, but I am so unfortunate as not to be familiar as you are with warlike terms; what do you mean by the word 'reprisals'?"

"Nothing simpler, dear child."

"Pray explain yourself."

"They hanged an officer in the army of Messieurs les Princes, did they not?"

"Yes; what then?"

"Why, we hunt up an officer of the royal army in Bordeaux, and hang him."

"Great God!" cried Claire, in dismay; "what do you say, madame?"

"Monsieur le Duc," continued the dowager, apparently not heeding the viscountess's alarm, "has not the officer who was in command at Saint-Georges already been arrested?"

"Yes, madame," the duke replied.

"Monsieur de Canolles arrested!" cried Claire.

"Yes, madame," rejoined the duke, coldly, "Monsieur de Canolles is arrested, or soon will be; the order was given in my presence, and I saw the men set out to execute it."

"But did they know where he was?" Claire asked with a last ray of hope.

"He was at the house of our host, Monsieur de Lalasne, in the suburbs, where they say he was having great success at tennis."

Claire uttered a cry. Madame de Tourville turned upon her in amazement, and the duke glanced at her with an imperceptible smile.

"Monsieur de Canolles arrested!" the viscountess repeated. "In God's name, what has he done? What connection has he with the horrible occurrence which saddens us all?"

"What connection has he with it? The very closest, my dear. Is not he a governor, as Richon was?"

Claire tried to speak, but the words died upon her lips.

She seized the duke's arm and gazing at him in terror, succeeded at last in uttering these words in a hoarse whisper: —

"Oh! but it's a feint, is it not, Monsieur le Duc? nothing more than a mere demonstration? We can do nothing — at least so it seems to me — to one who is a prisoner on parole."

"Richon also, madame, was a prisoner on parole."

"Monsieur le Duc, I implore you —"

"Spare your supplications, madame, for they are useless. I can do nothing in the matter; it is for the council to decide."

Claire dropped the duke's arm and hurried to Madame de Condé's cabinet, where she found Lenet striding back and forth, pale and agitated, while Madame de Condé talked with the Duc de Bouillon.

Madame de Cambes glided to the princess's side, as white and light of foot as a ghost.

"Oh, madame," said she, "give me one moment, I entreat you!"

"Ah! is it you, little one? I am not at liberty at this moment; but after the council I am at your service."

"Madame, madame, I must speak to you *before* the council!"

The princess was about to accede, when a door, opposite that by which the viscountess had come in, opened, and Monsieur de La Rochefoucauld appeared.

"Madame," said he, "the council has assembled and is impatiently awaiting your Highness."

"You see, little one," said Madame de Condé, "that it is impossible for me to listen to you at this moment; but come with us to the council, and when it is at an end we will return and talk together."

It was out of the question to insist. Dazzled and bewildered by the frightful rapidity with which events were rushing on, the poor woman began to have the vertigo; she gazed wildly into the faces, and watched the gestures of all about her, without seeing anything, unable to understand what was going on, and struggling in vain to shake off the frightful nightmare that oppressed her.

The princess walked toward the salon. Claire followed her mechanically, nor did she notice that Lenet had taken in his the ice-cold hand that hung listlessly at her side like the hand of a corpse.

They entered the council chamber; it was about eight o'clock in the evening.

It was a vast apartment, naturally dark and gloomy, but made even darker by heavy hangings. A sort of platform had been erected between the two doors, and opposite the two windows, through which the last feeble rays of the dying daylight made their way into the room. Upon the platform were two arm-chairs; one for Madame de Condé, the other for the Duc d'Enghien. On either side of these arm-chairs was a row of *tabourets* for the ladies who composed her Highness's privy council. The other judges were to sit upon benches prepared for them. The Duc de Bouillon stood immediately behind Madame de Condé's chair, and the Duc de La Rochefoucauld behind that of the young prince.

Lenet stood opposite the clerk; beside him was Claire, dazed and trembling.

Six officers of the army, six municipal councillors, and six sheriffs were introduced, and took their seats upon the benches.

Two candelabra, each containing three candles, furnished light for the deliberations of this improvised tribunal; they were placed upon a table in front of Madame la Princesse, so that they shed a bright light upon the principal group, while the other persons present were more or less in shadow according as they were near to or at a distance from this feeble centre of light.

The doors were guarded by soldiers of the army of Madame la Princesse, halberd in hand. The roaring of the crowd could be heard without.

The clerk called the roll of the judges, and each one rose in turn and answered to his name.

Thereupon the judge advocate opened the business upon which they were called together; he detailed the capture of Vayres, Monsieur de La Meilleraie's breach of his word, and the infamous death of Richon.

At that point an officer, who had been stationed at a window for that express purpose, and had received his orders in advance, threw the window open, and the voices of the people in the street rolled in in waves: "Vengeance for Richon! Death to the Mazarinists!" Such was the name bestowed upon the royalists.

"You hear," said Monsieur de La Rochefoucauld, "what the voice of the people demands. Two hours hence, either the people will have cast our authority to the winds and taken the law into their own hands, or it will be too late for reprisals. Adjudge this matter, therefore, messieurs, and that without further delay."

The princess rose.

"Why adjudge, I pray to know?" she cried. "What purpose is to be served by a judgment? You have already heard the judgment pronounced by the good people of Bordeaux."

"Indeed," said Madame de Tourville, "it would be impossible to conceive a simpler situation. It's the law of retaliation pure and simple. Such things as this should be done by inspiration, so to speak, between provost and provost."

Lenet could listen to no more; from the place where he stood he rushed into the midst of the circle.

"Oh! not a word more, madame, I beg you," he cried, "for such counsels, were they to prevail, would be too horrible in their consequences. You forget that the royal authorities themselves, although they chose to inflict infamous punishment, nevertheless preserved the forms of law, and that the punishment, whether just or unjust, was ratified by the decree of a court-martial. Do you think that you have the right to do a thing that the king dared not do?"

"Oh! nothing more is needed than for me to express an opinion, to have Monsieur Lenet maintain the opposite!" exclaimed Madame de Tourville. "Unfortunately, my opinion this time agrees with her Highness's."

"Unfortunately, indeed," said Lenet.

"Monsieur!" cried the princess.

"Ah! madame," continued Lenet, "preserve appearances at least. Will you not still be at liberty to condemn?"

"Monsieur Lenet is right," said La Rochefoucauld. "The death of a man is too serious a matter, especially under such circumstances, for us to allow the responsibility to rest upon a single head, even though it be a princely head."

Leaning toward the princess then, so that her immediate neighbors alone could hear, he added:—

"Madame, take the opinion of all, and then retain only those of whom you are sure, to take part in the trial. In that way we shall have no cause for fear that our vengeance will escape us."

"One moment, one moment," interposed Monsieur de Bouillon, leaning upon his cane, and raising his gouty leg. "You have spoken of taking the responsibility off the princess's shoulders. I have no desire to shirk it, but I would be glad to have others share it with me. I ask nothing better than to continue in rebellion, but in company with Madame la Princesse on the one hand and the people on the other. Damnation! I don't choose to be isolated. I lost my sovereignty of Sedan through a pleasantry of this sort. At that time I had a city and a head. Cardinal de Richelieu took my city; to-day I have nothing left but a head, and I'm not anxious that Cardinal Mazarin should take that. I therefore demand that the notables of Bordeaux take part in the proceedings."

"Such signatures beside ours!" murmured the princess; "go to!"

"The mortise holds the timber in place, madame," rejoined Bouillon, whom the conspiracy of Cinq-Mars had rendered prudent for the rest of his life.

"Is that your opinion, messieurs?"

"Yes," said the Duc de La Rochefoucauld.

"And you, Lenet?"

"Fortunately, madame," replied Lenet, "I am neither prince nor duke, nor municipal official, nor sheriff. I am entitled to hold aloof, therefore, and I will do so."

Thereupon the princess rose, and called upon the assemblage to reply in energetic and unmistakable fashion to the royal challenge. Hardly had she finished what she had to say when the window was thrown open again, and again the voices of the people without invaded the hall, crying:—

"Vive Madame la Princesse! Vengeance for Richon! Death to the Épernonists and Mazarinists!"

Madame de Cambes seized Lenet's arm.

"Monsieur Lenet," said she, "I am dying!"

"Madame la Vicomtesse de Cambes," he replied, "request her Highness's permission to retire."

"No, no," said Claire, "I want—"

"Your place is not here, madame," Lenet interrupted. "You can do nothing for him; I will keep you informed of whatever takes place, and together we will try to save him."

"The viscountess may retire," said the princess. "Those ladies who do not care to be present at this function are at liberty to follow her."

Not a woman stirred; one of the never-ending aspirations of that half of the human race whose destiny it is to fascinate is to usurp the rights of the half destined to command. These ladies saw an opportunity to play the part of men for a moment, and proposed to make the most of it.

Madame de Cambes left the room, supported by Lenet. On the stairs she met Pompée whom she had sent in quest of news.

"Well?" said she inquiringly.

"He is arrested!"

"Monsieur Lenet," said Claire, "I have no confidence or hope save in you and God!" and she rushed despairingly into her own room.

"What questions shall I put to him who is about to appear before us?" Madame la Princess asked, as Lenet resumed his place beside the clerk, "and to whose lot shall it fall to die?"

"It's a very simple matter, madame," replied the duke. "We have some three hundred prisoners, ten or twelve of whom are officers. Let us question them simply as to their names and their rank in the royal army, and the first one who turns out to be the governor of a fortress, as Richon was, we will consider to be the one to whom the lot has fallen."

"It is useless to waste our time questioning ten or twelve different officers, messieurs," said the princess, "you have the list, Monsieur le Greffier: just glance over it, and read the names of those who hold equal rank to Richon's."

"There are but two, madame," said the clerk; "the governor of Île Saint-Georges, and the governor of Braune."

"We have two of them, it is true!" cried the princess; "fate is kind to us, you see. Are they under arrest, Labussière?"

"Certainly, madame," the captain of the guards replied, "and both are in the fortress awaiting the order to appear."

"Let them be brought hither," said Madame de Condé.

"Which one shall we bring?" asked Labussière.

"Bring them both: but we will begin with the first in date, Monsieur le Gouverneur de Saint-Georges."

XXI

A terrified silence, broken only by the receding footsteps of the captain of the guards, and by the constantly increasing murmur of the multitude without, followed this order, which gave the rebellion of Messieurs les Princes a more terrible and perilous aspect than any it had as yet assumed. Its inevitable effect was by a single act to place the princess and her advisers, the army and the city, outside the pale of the law; it was to burden an entire population with responsibility for the selfishness and passions of the few; it was to do on a small scale what the Commune of Paris did on the 2d of September. But, as we know, the Commune of Paris acted on a grand scale.

Not a sound could be heard in the hall; all eyes were fixed upon the door through which the prisoner was expected to appear. The princess, in order to act out her part of presiding magistrate, made a pretence of looking over the lists; Monsieur de La Rochefoucauld had assumed a musing expression, and Monsieur de Bouillon was talking with Madame de Tourville about his gout, which caused him much suffering.

Lenet approached the princess to make a last effort; not that he had any hope of success, but he was one of those conscientious men, who fulfil a duty because their conscience imposes upon them the obligation to do so.

"Consider, madame," said he, "that you are risking the future of your house upon a single throw."

"There is no great merit in that," said the princess dryly, "for I am sure to win."

"Monsieur le Duc," said Lenet, turning to La Rochefoucauld, "do not you, who are so superior to commonplace motives and vulgar human passions, advise moderation?"

"Monsieur," retorted the duke, hypocritically, "I am at this moment discussing the point with my reason."

"Discuss it rather with your conscience, Monsieur le Duc," replied Lenet; "that would be much better."

At that moment they heard the sound of the outer door closing. The sound echoed in every heart, for it announced the arrival of one of the two prisoners. Soon steps resounded on the stairway, halberds rang upon the flags, the door opened, and Canolles appeared.

He had never appeared so distinguished, had never been so handsome; his calm, unmoved face had retained the cheerful expression of happy ignorance. He came forward with easy, unaffected bearing, as he might have done in the salon of Monsieur Lavie, or Président Lalasne, and respectfully saluted the princess and the dukes.

The princess was amazed at his perfect ease of manner, and gazed at the young man for a moment without speaking.

At last she broke the silence.

"Come forward, monsieur," said she.

Canolles obeyed and saluted a second time.

"Who are you?"

"I am Baron Louis de Canolles, madame."

"What rank did you hold in the royal army?"

"I was lieutenant-colonel."

"Were you not governor of Île Saint-Georges?"

"I had that honor."

"You have told the truth?"

"In every point, madame."

"Have you taken down the questions and answers, master clerk?"

The clerk bowed.

"Sign, monsieur," said the princess.

Canolles took the pen with the air of a man who does not understand the purpose of a command, but obeys out of deference to the rank of the person who makes it, and signed his name with a smile.

"'Tis well, monsieur," said the princess; "you may now retire."

Canolles saluted his judges once more, and withdrew with the same grace and freedom from constraint, and with no manifestation of surprise or curiosity.

The door was no sooner closed behind him than the princess rose.

"Well, messieurs?" said she with a questioning accent.

"Well, madame, let us vote," said the Duc de La Rochefoucauld.

"Let us vote," echoed the Duc de Bouillon. "Will these gentlemen be kind enough to express their opinion?" he added, turning to the municipal dignitaries.

"After you, monseigneur," replied one of them.

"Nay, nay, before you!" cried a sonorous voice, in which there was such an accent of determination that everybody stared in amazement.

"What does this mean?" demanded the princess, trying to identify the owner of the voice.

"It means," cried a man, rising, so that there should be no doubt as to his identity, "that I, André Lavie, king's advocate and counsellor of parliament, demand in the king's name, and in the name of humanity, for prisoners detained in Bordeaux upon parole, the privileges and guaranties to which they are entitled. Consequently, my conclusion is—"

"Oho! Monsieur l'Avocat," exclaimed the princess with a shrug, "none of your court jargon in my presence, I pray you, for I do not understand it. This is an affair of sentiment that we are engaged upon, and not a paltry pettifogging lawsuit; every one who has a seat upon this tribunal will understand the propriety of this course, I presume."

"Yes, yes," rejoined the sheriffs and the officers in chorus; "vote, messieurs, vote!"

"I said, and I say again," continued Lavie; unabashed by the princess's rebuke, "I demand their privileges and guaranties for prisoners detained on parole. This is no question of lawsuits, but of the law of nations!"

"And I say, furthermore," cried Lenet, "that Richon was heard in his own defence before he met his cruel fate, and that it is no more than fair that we should hear these accused persons."

"And I," said D'Espagnet, the militia officer, who took part in the attack upon Saint-Georges with Monsieur de La Rochefoucauld, "I declare that if any clemency be shown, the city will rise in revolt."

A shout from without seemed to echo and confirm his words.

"Let us make haste," said the princess. "What penalty shall we inflict upon the accused?"

"There are two of them, madame," suggested several voices.

"Is not one enough for you, pray?" retorted Lenet, smiling scornfully at this sanguinary servility.

"Which shall it be, then; which?" demanded the same voices.

"The fattest one, cannibals!" cried Lavie. "Ah! you complain of injustice and shout sacrilege, and yet you propose to reply to an assassination by two murders! A noble combination of philosophers and soldiers melted together into murderers!"

The flashing eyes of the majority of the judges seemed quite ready to blast the courageous king's advocate. Madame de Condé had risen from her chair and was looking inquiringly into the faces of those about her as if to assure herself that the words she had heard had really been uttered, and if there really was a man on earth bold enough to say such things in her presence.

Lavie realized that his continued presence would result in adding to the bitter feeling, and that his manner of defending the accused would destroy instead of saving them. He determined to retire, therefore, but to retire rather as a judge declining to serve than as a soldier taking to his heels.

"In the name of God Almighty," said he, "I protest against what you propose to do; in the king's name, I forbid it!"

With that, he overturned his arm-chair with a wrathful gesture, and stalked out of the room with his head in the air, like a man strong in the consciousness of duty well done, and indifferent to the possible results thereof.

"Insolent!" muttered the princess.

"No matter! no matter! let him have his way," said several; "Master Lavie's turn will come."

"Let us vote!" exclaimed the judges, almost as one man.

"But why vote without hearing the accused?" said Lenet. "Perhaps one of them will seem to you more guilty than the other. Perhaps you will conclude to concentrate upon a single head the vengeance which you now propose to divide between two."

At that moment the outer door was heard a second time.

"Very good!" said the princess, "we will vote upon both at once."

The judges, who had left their seats in disorder, sat down once more. Again the sound of footsteps was heard, accompanied by the ringing of halberds on the flags; the door opened once more and Cauvignac appeared.

The newcomer presented a striking contrast to Canolles; his garments still showed the effects of his encounter with the populace, despite the pains he had taken to efface them; his eyes glanced hastily from the sheriffs to the officers, from the dukes to the princess, embracing the whole tribunal in a sort of circular glance; then, with the air of a fox devising a stratagem, he came forward, feeling the ground at every step, so to speak, with every faculty on the alert, but pale and visibly disturbed.

"Your Highness did me the honor to summon me to your presence," he began, without waiting to be questioned.

"Yes, monsieur, for I desired to be enlightened upon certain points relative to yourself, which cause us some perplexity."

"In that case," rejoined Cauvignac, with a bow, "I am here, madame, ready to requite the honor your Highness is pleased to confer upon me."

He bowed with the most graceful air he could muster, but it was clearly lacking in ease and naturalness.

"That you may do very speedily," said the princess, "if your answers are as definite as our questions."

"Allow me to remind your Highness," said Cauvignac, "that, as the question is always prepared beforehand, and the response never, it is more difficult to respond than to question."

"Oh! our questions will be so clear and precise," said the princess, "that you will be spared any necessity for reflecting upon them. Your name?"

"Ah! madame, there you are! there is a most embarrassing question, first of all."

"How so?"

"It often happens that one has two names, the name one has received from his family, and the name one has received from himself. Take my own case as an example: I thought that I had sufficient reason for laying aside my first name in favor of another less widely known; which of the two names do you require me to give you?"

"That under which you presented yourself at Chantilly, that under which you agreed to raise a company in my interest, that under which you did raise it, and that under which you sold yourself to Monsieur de Mazarin."

"Pardon me, madame," said Cauvignac; "but I have the impression that I had the honor to reply satisfactorily to all these questions during the audience your Highness was graciously pleased to grant me this morning."

"At this time I put but one question to you," said the princess beginning to lose patience. "I simply ask you your name."

"Very true! but that is just what embarrasses me."

"Write Baron de Cauvignac," said the princess.

The accused made no objection, and the clerk wrote as directed.

"Now, your rank?" said the princess; "I trust you will find no difficulty in replying to this question."

"On the contrary, madame, that is one of the most embarrassing questions you could put to me. If you refer to my rank as a scholar, I am a bachelor of letters, licentiate in law, doctor of theology; I reply, as your Highness sees, without hesitation."

"No, monsieur, we refer to your military rank."

"Ah, yes! upon that point it is impossible for me to reply to your Highness."

"How so?"

"Because I have never really known what I was myself."

"Try to make up your mind upon that point, monsieur, for I am anxious to know."

"Very well; in the first place I constituted myself a lieutenant on my own authority; but as I had no power to sign a commission, and as I never had more than six men under my orders while I bore that title, I fancy that I have no right to take advantage of it."

"But I myself made you a captain," said the princess, "and you are therefore a captain."

"Ah! that is just where my embarrassment redoubles, and my conscience cries more loudly than ever. For I have since become convinced that every military grade in the State must emanate from the royal authority in order to have any value. Now, your Highness did, beyond question, desire to make me a captain, but in my opinion you had not the right. That being so, I am no more a captain now than I was a lieutenant before."

"Even so, monsieur; assume that you were not a lieutenant by virtue of your own act, and that you are not a captain by mine, as neither you nor I have the right to sign a commission; at least you are governor of Braune; and as the king himself signed your commission you will not contest its validity."

"In very truth, madame, it is the most contestable of the three."

"How so?" cried the princess.

"I was appointed, I grant you, but I never entered upon my duties. What constitutes the title? Not the bare possession of the title itself, but the performance of the functions attached to the title. Now, I never performed a single one of the functions of the post to which I was promoted; I never set foot in my jurisdiction; there was on my part no entrance upon my duties; therefore I am no more governor of Braune than I was a captain before being governor, or a lieutenant before being a captain."

"But you were taken upon the road to Braune, monsieur."

"True; but a hundred yards beyond the point where I was arrested, the road divides; thence one road leads to Braune, but the other to Isson. Who can say that I was not going to Isson, rather than to Braune?"

"Enough," said the princess; "the tribunal will take under consideration the force of your defence. Clerk, write him down governor of Braune."

"I cannot prevent your Highness from ordering the clerk to write down whatever seems best to you."

"It is done, madame," said the clerk.

"Good. Now, monsieur, sign your deposition."

"It would give me the greatest pleasure, madame," said Cauvignac; "I should be enchanted to do anything that would be agreeable to your Highness; but in the struggle I was forced to wage this morning against the populace of Bordeaux,—a struggle in which your Highness so generously came to my rescue with your musketeers,—I had the misfortune to have my right wrist injured, and it has always been impossible for me to write with my left hand."

"Record the refusal of the accused to sign, monsieur," said the princess to the clerk.

"Impossibility, monsieur; write impossibility," said Cauvignac. "God forbid that I should refuse to do anything in my power at the bidding of so great a princess as your Highness!"

With that, Cauvignac bowed with the utmost respect, and left the room, accompanied by his two guards.

"I think that you were right, Monsieur Lenet," said the Duc de La Rochefoucauld, "and that we were wrong not to make sure of that man."

Lenet was too preoccupied to reply. This time his usual perspicacity was sadly at fault; he hoped that Cauvignac would draw down the wrath of the tribunal upon his single head; but with his everlasting subterfuges he had amused his judges rather than irritated them. Moreover his examination had destroyed all the effect, if any, produced by Canolles; and the noble bearing, the outspokenness and loyalty of the first prisoner had disappeared, if we may say so, beneath the wiles of the second. Cauvignac had effaced Canolles.

And so when the vote was taken, every vote was given for death.

The princess, after the votes were counted, rose and solemnly pronounced the judgment of the court. Then each one in turn signed the record of the sitting. First the Duc d'Enghien, poor child, who knew not what he was signing, and whose first signature was to cost the life of a man; then the princess, then the dukes, then the ladies of the council, then the officers and sheriffs. Thus everybody had a share in the reprisals. Nobility and bourgeoisie, army and parliament, everybody must be punished for the act of vengeance. As everybody knows, when all the world in general must be punished, the result is that nobody at all is punished.

When the last signature had been appended, the princess, who had her vengeance in her grasp at last, and whose pride was satisfied thereby, went herself and opened the window, which had been opened twice before, and, yielding to her consuming thirst for popularity, exclaimed in a loud voice:—

"Men of Bordeaux, Richon will be avenged, and fitly; rely upon us for that."

A shout of joy, like the roar of thunder, welcomed this declaration, and the people scattered through the streets, happy in the anticipation of the spectacle promised by the words of the princess.

But Madame de Condé had no sooner returned to her own room with Lenet, who followed her sadly, still hoping to induce her to change her resolution, than the door was thrown open, and Madame de Cambes, pale as death and weeping bitterly, threw herself at her feet.

"O madame, in Heaven's name, listen to me!" she cried: "in Heaven's name do not turn me away!"

"What's the matter, pray, my child?" inquired the princess. "Why do you weep?"

"I weep, madame, because I have learned that the judges voted for death, and that you ratified their vote; and yet, madame, you cannot put Monsieur de Canolles to death."

"Why not, my dear, I pray to know? they put Richon to death."

"Because, madame, this same Monsieur de Canolles saved your Highness at Chantilly."

"Ought I to thank him for being deceived by our stratagem?"

"Ah! madame, that's where you are in error; Monsieur de Canolles was not for one instant deceived by the substitution. He recognized me at the first glance."

"Recognized you, Claire?"

"Yes, madame. We made a part of the journey together; Monsieur de Canolles—Monsieur de Canolles was in love with me; and under those circumstances—Ah! madame, perhaps he did wrong, but it is not for you to reproach him for it,—under those circumstances he sacrificed his duty to his love."

"So the man whom you love—"

"Yes," said the viscountess.

"The man whom you asked my leave to marry—"

"Yes."

"Was—"

"Was Monsieur de Canolles himself!" cried the viscountess,—"Monsieur de Canolles, who surrendered to me at Saint-Georges, and who, except for me, would have blown up the citadel with himself and your soldiers,— Monsieur de Canolles, who might have escaped, but who surrendered his sword to me rather than be parted from me. You see, therefore, that if he dies, I must die, too, madame; for his death will lie at my door!"

"My dear child," said the princess, deeply moved, "consider, I pray you, that what you ask is impossible. Richon is dead, and Richon must be avenged. The matter has been duly discussed, and the judgment must be executed; if my husband himself should ask what you ask, I would refuse him."

"Oh! wretched creature that I am!" cried Madame de Cambes, throwing herself upon the floor, and sobbing as if her heart would break; "I have destroyed my lover!"

Thereupon Lenet, who had not as yet spoken, approached the princess.

"Madame," said he, "is not one victim enough? Must you have two heads to pay for Monsieur Richon's?"

"Aha!" said the princess, "monsieur the upright man! that means that you ask the life of one and the death of the other. Is that absolutely just? Tell me."

"It is just, madame, when two men are to die, in the first place that one only should die, if possible, assuming that any mouth has the right to blow out the torch lighted by God's hand. In the second place, it is just, if there is anything to choose between the two, that the upright man should be preferred to the schemer. One must needs be a Jew to set Barabbas at liberty and crucify Jesus."

"Oh! Monsieur Lenet! Monsieur Lenet!" cried Claire, "plead for me, I implore you! for you are a man, and mayhap you will be listened to. And do you, madame," she continued, turning to the princess, "remember that I have passed my life in the service of your family."

"And so have I," said Lenet; "and yet I have asked no reward for thirty years of fidelity to your Highness; but at this juncture, if your Highness is without pity, I will ask a single favor in exchange for these thirty years of fidelity."

"What might it be?"

"That you will give me my dismissal, madame, so that I may throw myself at the king's feet, and consecrate to him what remains of the life I had devoted to the honor of your family."

"Ah, well!" exclaimed the princess, vanquished by this combined attack, "do not threaten, my old friend; do not weep, my sweet Claire; be comforted both, for only one shall die, since you will have it so; but do not come and seek pardon for the one who is destined to die."

Claire seized the princess's hand and devoured it with kisses.

"Oh! thanks, madame! thanks!" she sobbed; "from this moment my life and his are at your service."

"In taking this course, madame," said Lenet, "you will be at the same time just and merciful; which, hitherto, has been the prerogative of God alone."

"And now, madame," cried Claire, impatiently, "may I see him? may I set him free?"

"Such a demonstration at this moment is out of the question," said the princess; "it would injure us irreparably. Let us leave them both in prison; we will take them out at the same time, one to be set at liberty, the other to go to his death."

"But may I not at least see him, to set his mind at rest, to comfort him?"

"To set his mind at rest?" said the princess; "my dear child, I think that you have not the right; the reversal of the judgment would be discovered and commented upon. No, it cannot be; be content to know that he is safe. I will make known my decision to the two dukes."

"I will be patient, madame. Thanks! thanks!" cried Claire; and she fled from the room, to weep at her ease, and thank God from the bottom of her heart, which was overflowing with joy and gratitude.

XXII

The two prisoners of war occupied two adjoining rooms in the same fortress. The rooms were located on the ground-floor, which in most prisons might properly be called the third floor; for prisons do not as a general rule begin at the ground like houses, but have two stories of underground dungeons.

Each door of the prison was guarded by a detachment of men selected from among the princess's guards; but the crowd, having taken note of the preparations which satisfied its thirst for vengeance, gradually melted away from the neighborhood of the prison, whither it had hurried upon learning that Canolles and Cauvignac had been taken there. Whereupon the guards who were stationed in the inner corridor, rather to protect the prisoners from the popular fury than from any fear of their escaping, left their posts, and thenceforth the ordinary sentries were simply doubled.

The people, finding that there was nothing more to be seen where they were, naturally betook themselves to the spot where executions generally took place,—the Esplanade, to wit. The words tossed down to them from the council-hall were instantly circulated throughout the city, and every one drew his own conclusions from them. But the one thing about which there could be no doubt was that there would be a spectacle of horrible interest that same night, or on the following day at latest; it was an additional fascination for them not to know precisely what to look forward to.

Artisans, tradesmen, women, and children hurried toward the ramparts, and as it was quite dark and the moon would not rise until about midnight, many carried torches in their hands. Almost all the windows were open, too, and many people had placed torches or lamps on the window-sills, as they were accustomed to do on fête-days. But the ominous muttering of the crowd, the terrified glances of the sightseers, and the frequent passage of patrols on foot and mounted, afforded sufficient evidence that it was no ordinary fête for which such lugubrious preparations were being made.

From time to time cries of rage arose from the groups, which formed and dissolved with a rapidity characteristic of the effect of a certain class of occurrences. These cries always resembled those which penetrated to the council-hall on several occasions:—

"Death to the prisoners! vengeance for Richon!"

The cries, the bright light, the tread of many horses interrupted Madame de Cambes' devotions. She went to her window and looked out in dismay at all the men and women with eyes flashing fiercely, who seemed like wild beasts let loose in the arena, roaring for the human victims they were to devour. She asked herself how it could be that all these human beings, whom the two prisoners had never injured in any way, could so savagely demand the death of two of their fellow-creatures; and she could find no reply to her question, poor woman, for of all the passions of mankind she knew only those which soften the heart.

From the window at which she stood, Madame de Cambes could see the summit of the high, frowning towers of the fortress above the roofs of the houses and the tree-tops. That was where Canolles was, and her eyes wandered most frequently to them. But she could not avoid turning them from time to time into the street, and then she would see those threatening faces and hear those blood-curdling cries of vengeance, and an icy shudder would run through her veins.

"Ah!" she said to herself, "in vain do they forbid my seeing him; I must find a way to get to him! These horrible noises may reach his ear; he may think that I have forgotten him; he may accuse me; he may curse me. Oh! every moment that passes without my trying to find a way to comfort him seems to me like treachery to him; it is impossible for me to continue inactive, when perhaps he is calling me to his rescue. Oh! I must see him. Yes, but, *mon Dieu!* how to get to see him?—who will take me to the prison? what power have I to order the doors opened? Madame la Princesse has refused to give me a pass, and she had just granted so much in answer to my prayers that she was quite right to refuse. There are guards, there are enemies of his around the fortress; the whole population has scented blood, and doesn't propose to be cheated of its prey; they will think that I mean to help him escape, rescue him; oh! yes: and I would rescue him if he had not already the safeguard of her Highness's word. If I tell them that I simply want to see him they won't believe me, and will turn me away; and again, do I not run the risk of losing what I have already gained if I take this step against Madame la Princesse's will? Will she not be likely to retract the promise she gave me? And yet to leave him to pass the long hours of the night in anguish and torture! Oh! I feel that it is impossible, for myself even more than for him! I will pray God for help, and perhaps he will inspire me."

Thereupon Madame de Cambes for the second time knelt before her crucifix, and began to pray with a fervor which might have touched Madame la Princesse's heart could she have heard her.

"Oh! I will not go, I will not go," said she; "for I understand that it is indeed impossible for me to go thither. All night he will perhaps accuse me of abandoning him. But to-morrow, to-morrow, my God, will set me right in his sight, will it not?"

Meanwhile the uproar, the constantly increasing excitement of the crowd, the sinister glare, which shone into her room, where there was no light, and at times illuminated it as by lightning, caused her such intense terror that she placed her hands over her ears, and pressed her closed eyes against the cushion of her prie-Dieu.

At that moment the door opened, and, unheard by her, a man entered; after pausing a moment upon the threshold, with an expression of affectionate compassion, when he saw how her whole body was shaken by her sobbing, he approached with a sigh, and laid his hand upon her arm.

Claire rose to her feet in dismay.

"Monsieur Lenet!" she exclaimed: "Monsieur Lenet: ah! you have not abandoned me?"

"No," was the reply: "I feared that you were but partly reassured, and I ventured to come to you to ask if I can be of service to you in any way."

"Oh, my dear Monsieur Lenet," cried Claire, "how good you are, and how grateful I am to you!"

"It seems that I was not mistaken," said Lenet. "One rarely is mistaken, God knows, when one fancies that one's fellow-creatures are suffering," he added with a sad smile.

"Ah! monsieur," cried Claire, "you say truly; I am indeed suffering!"

"Did you not obtain all that you desired, madame, and more, I confess, than I myself dared hope?"

"Yes, of course; but—"

"But—I understand; you are terrified, are you not, to see the fierce joy of this mob in its thirst for blood; and you are moved to pity for the fate of the other poor wretch who is to die in your lover's place?"

Claire was silent for a moment with pale cheeks and her eyes fixed upon Lenet's; then she put her hand to her sweat-bedewed brow.

"Oh! forgive me, or rather curse me!" said she; "for, selfish brute that I am, I have not even thought of him. No, Lenet, no; in all possible humility I confess that these fears, these prayers, these tears of mine are for him who is to live; for, absorbed as I am by my love, I had forgotten him who is to die!"

Lenet smiled sadly.

"Yes," said he, "that may well be, for it is human nature; it may be that the selfishness of individuals is the salvation of the masses. Every one cuts a circle about himself and his own people with a sword. Come, madame," he continued, "pursue your confession to the end. Confess frankly that you are in haste to have the poor wretch undergo his fate; for his death will ensure the safety of your *fiancé!*"

"Oh! I hadn't thought of that as yet, Lenet; upon my word I hadn't. But do not turn my thoughts in that direction, for I love him so dearly that I do not know what I may be capable of wishing in the intensity of my love."

"Poor child!" said Lenet, in a most compassionate tone, "why did you not say all this sooner?"

"Oh! *mon Dieu!* you terrify me. Is it too late? Is he not really safe?"

"He is, since Madame la Princesse has given her word; but—"

"But what?"

"Alas! can one be sure of anything in this world, and do not you yourself, who believe as I do that he is safe, weep instead of rejoicing?"

"I weep because I cannot visit him, my friend," Claire replied. "Consider, that he must hear these fearful noises, and believe that he is in imminent danger; consider, that he may accuse me of lukewarmness, of forgetfulness, of treachery! Oh Lenet, Lenet, what torture! Really, if the princess knew how I suffer, she would have pity on me."

"Very well, viscountess, you must see him."

"See him! impossible. You are well aware that I asked leave of her Highness to see him, and that her Highness refused."

"I know, and I approve her refusal with all my heart; and yet—"

"And yet you advise me to disobey!" cried Claire in surprise, gazing earnestly at Lenet, who lowered his eyes in confusion.

"I am old, dear viscountess, and suspicious just because I am old,—not in this matter, for the princess's word is sacred. She has said that only one of the prisoners shall die; but, accustomed as I have become in the course of a long life to see fortune turn against the one who seems most secure of her favor, my rule is always to seize any opportunity that presents itself. See your *fiancé*, viscountess; take my advice and see him."

"Oh! Lenet, you terrify me beyond words; really you do!"

"I have no such intention; moreover, would you prefer that I advise you not to see him? You would not, would you? And you would scold me even more severely, I know, if I had said the opposite of what I do say."

"Yes, yes, I admit it. But you tell me to see him; that was my one desire; I was praying when you arrived that I might be allowed to see him. But isn't it impossible?"

"Is anything impossible to the woman who took Saint-Georges?" asked Lenet, with a smile.

"Alas!" said Claire, "for two hours I have been trying to think of some way of obtaining admission to the fortress, but I cannot."

"What would you give me if I were to show you a way?"

"I would give you—I would give you my hand on the day that I go to the altar with him."

"Thanks, my child," said Lenet; "indeed, you could do nothing more acceptable to me, for I love you like a father; thanks."

"Tell me the way! Tell me the way!" said Claire.

"It is this. I asked Madame la Princesse for a pass to allow me to talk with the prisoners; for if there were any way of saving Captain Cauvignac I would be glad to enroll him in our party; but the pass is useless to me now, as you have condemned him to death with your prayers for Monsieur de Canolles."

Claire could not repress a shudder.

"So take this paper," continued Lenet; "there is no name mentioned in it, you see."

Claire took it and read:—

> "The keeper of the fortress will permit the bearer of this to converse for half an hour with either of the two prisoners of war, as he may choose.

> "CLAIRE-CLÉMENCE DE CONDÉ."

"You have a suit of man's clothes," said Lenet; "put it on. You have the permit; use it."

"Poor fellow!" murmured Claire, unable to banish from her mind the thought of Cauvignac to be executed in place of Canolles.

"He undergoes the common fate," said Lenet. "Being weak, he is devoured by the strong; having no protector, he pays for him who has; he is an intelligent fellow."

Claire meanwhile was turning the paper over and over in her hands.

"Do you know," said she, "that you tempt me cruelly with this permit? Do you know that if I once hold my poor friend in my arms I am quite capable of taking him with me to the ends of the world?"

"I would advise you to do it, madame, if it were possible; but this permit does not give you *carte-blanche,* and you can use it for no other purpose than that for which it was intended."

"True," said Claire, reading it once more; "and yet they have given me Monsieur de Canolles; he is mine; they cannot take him from me again!"

"Nor does any one think of doing so. Come, come, madame, waste no time; don your male costume, and begone. This permit gives you half an hour; I know that half an hour is very little; but after the half-hour will come your whole life. You are young, and have many years before you; God grant that they be happy years."

Claire seized Lenet's hand, drew him to her side, and kissed his forehead as she might have done to the most affectionate of fathers.

"Go, go," said Lenet, pushing her gently toward the door, "do not lose time; the man who truly loves is never resigned."

As he watched her pass into another room, where Pompée, at her bidding, was waiting to assist in her transformation, —

"Alas!" he muttered, "who knows?"

XXIII

The threatening shouts of the excited crowd had not, in fact, escaped Canolles' attention. Through the bars at his window he was able to feast his eyes upon the animated, changing picture which was presented to his view, and which varied little from one end of the city to the other.

"*Pardieu!*" said he, "this is an annoying mischance, Richon's death. Poor Richon! he was a gallant fellow! His death will redouble the severity of our captivity; they will not allow me to go about the city as before; no more meetings, and no marriage, unless Claire can resign herself to the chapel of a prison. She will be content with that, I know. One can be married as well in one chapel as another. But it's an evil omen, none the less. Why the deuce could they not have received the news to-morrow instead of to-day?"

He went to the window and looked out.

"What a strict watch they are keeping!" he continued; "two sentries! When I think that I shall be mewèd up here a week, a fortnight perhaps, until something new occurs to make them forget this! Fortunately, events follow rapidly on one another's heels just now, and the Bordelais are fickle-minded; meanwhile I shall have passed some very unpleasant hours all the same. Poor Claire! she must be in despair; luckily she knows that I have been arrested. Yes, she knows it and so knows that I am not at fault— Good lack! where are all those people going? They seem to be bound for the Esplanade!—but there can be no parade there, nor an execution, at this hour. They are all going in the same direction. Upon my word one would say that they know I am here, like a bear, behind my bars."

Canolles began to pace up and down with folded arms; finding himself within the walls of a real prison, his mind turned for a moment to philosophical ideas, with which he commonly bothered his head but little.

"What an idiotic thing war is!" he muttered. "Here is poor Richon, with whom I dined hardly a month ago, dead! He ought to have made sure of death by a cannon-ball, as I would have done—as I would have done if any other than the viscountess had besieged me. This war of women is, in good sooth, the most to be dreaded of all wars. At least, I have had no share in the death of a friend. Thank God, I haven't drawn my sword against my brother! that is a consolation to me. And it is to my little feminine good genius that I owe that, too. Take it for all in all, I owe her many things."

At that moment an officer entered, and interrupted Canolles' soliloquy.

"Do you wish for supper, monsieur?" he asked. "If so, give your orders; the jailer is instructed to furnish you with whatever you desire."

"Well, well," said Canolles, "it would seem that they propose at least to treat me honorably while I remain here. I feared something different for an instant, when I saw the stern face of the princess, and the repellent bearing of all her judges."

"I am waiting," rejoined the officer, bowing.

"Ah! to be sure; I beg your pardon. The extreme courtesy of your question led to certain reflections. Let us return to the matter in hand. Yes, monsieur, I will sup, for I am very hungry; but I am of sober habits, and a soldier's supper will content me."

"Now," said the officer, drawing nearer to him with evident interest, "have you no commissions,—in the city? Do you expect nothing? You say that you are a soldier; so am I; look upon me, therefore, as a comrade."

Canolles stared at him in amazement.

"No, monsieur," said he; "no, I have no commissions in the city; no, I expect nothing, unless it be a certain person whom I may not name. As for looking upon you as a comrade, I thank you for the suggestion. Here is my hand, monsieur, and later, if I need anything, I will remember what you say."

It was the officer's turn to stare at Canolles in amazement.

"Very well, monsieur," said he, "you will be served at once;" and he withdrew.

A moment later two soldiers entered with the supper; it was more elaborate than Canolles had asked for, and he sat down at the table and ate heartily.

The soldiers in their turn gazed wonderingly at him. Canolles mistook their amazement for envy, and as the wine was excellent Guyenne, he said to them:—

"My friends, order two glasses."

One of the soldiers smiled, and procured the articles in question. Canolles filled them; then poured a few drops of wine into his own.

"Your health, my friends!" said he.

The two soldiers took their glasses, mechanically touched them to Canolles', and drank without reciprocating his toast.

"They are not very polite," thought Canolles, "but they drink well; one cannot have everything."

He continued his supper, and brought it triumphantly to a close. When he had finished he rose, and the soldiers removed the table.

The officer returned.

"*Pardieu!* monsieur," said Canolles, "you should have supped with me; the supper was excellent."

"I could not enjoy that honor, monsieur, for I have just left the table myself. I return—"

"To bear me company?" said Canolles. "If so, accept my warmest thanks, monsieur, for it is very kind of you."

"No, monsieur, my errand is less agreeable. I come to inform you that there is no minister in the prison, and that the chaplain is a Catholic; I know you to be a Protestant, and this fact may annoy you somewhat—"

"Annoy me, monsieur? how so?" demanded Canolles, innocently.

"Why," said the embarrassed officer, "in the matter of your devotions."

"My devotions! Nonsense!" laughed Canolles. "I will think of that to-morrow. I pray only in the morning."

The officer stared at Canolles in open-mouthed astonishment, which gradually changed to profound compassion. He bowed and left the room.

"Damnation!" said Canolles, "why, every one is crazy! Since poor Richon's death everybody I meet has the aspect of an idiot or a madman. *Sarpejeu!* shall I never see a sensible face again?"

The words were hardly out of his mouth when the door opened once more, and before he had time to see who had opened it, some one threw herself into his arms, and winding her arms around his neck deluged his face with tears.

"God's mercy!" cried the prisoner, extricating himself from the embrace; "another lunatic! Upon my soul, I believe I am in an asylum!"

But the gesture that he made in stepping back knocked the new-comer's hat to the floor, and the lovely blond tresses of Madame de Cambes fell down about her shoulders.

"You here!" he cried, rushing to her, and taking her in his arms once more. "You! oh! forgive me for not recognizing you, or rather for not divining your presence."

"Hush!" said she, picking up her hat and hastily replacing it on her head; "hush! for if they knew it was I, perhaps they would turn me out. At last I am permitted to see you once more! Oh, *mon Dieu! mon Dieu!* how happy I am!"

Her bosom heaved, and she sobbed as if her heart would break.

"*Once more!*" said Canolles; "you are permitted to see me *once more,* you say? In Heaven's name, are you not to see me more than this once?" he added, with a laugh.

"Oh! do not laugh!" said Claire; "my dear love, your gayety distresses me. Do not laugh, I implore you! I have had such difficulty in procuring admission,—if you knew!—and I was so near not being able to come at all! Except, for Lenet, the best of men—But let us talk of yourself, my poor dear. *Mon Dieu /* it is really you, is it not? It is really you whom I can press to my heart again?"

"Why, yes, it is I, it is really I," said Canolles, smiling.

"Oh! do not affect this cheerful demeanor,—it is useless, I know all. They did not know that I loved you, so they hid nothing from me—"

"What is it that you know, pray?" queried Canolles.

"You expected me, didn't you?" the viscountess continued. "You were displeased by my silence? Were you not already blaming me?"

"Unhappy and dissatisfied I was, beyond question, but I did not blame you. I suspected that circumstances stronger than your will kept you from my side; and the main cause of my unhappiness, through it all, has been the necessary postponement of our marriage for a week,—perhaps for two weeks."

Claire stared at Canolles in like amazement to that exhibited by the officer a moment before.

"Are you speaking seriously?" said she; "are you not really any more alarmed than you seem to be?"

"Alarmed?" said Canolles, "alarmed at what? Can it be," he added with a laugh, "that I am exposed to some danger of which I know nothing?"

"Oh! the poor fellow!" cried Claire; "he knew nothing of it!"

Dreading, doubtless, to reveal the whole truth without warning to him whose life was imperilled thereby, she checked, by a violent effort, the words that had risen from her heart to her lips.

"No, I know nothing," said Canolles, gravely. "But you will tell me, won't you? I am a man! Speak, Claire, speak."

"You know that Richon is dead?" said she.

"Yes, I know it."

"But do you know how he died?"

"No, but I suspect. He was killed at his post, was he not, in the breach at Vayres?"

Claire was silent for a moment; then, in a tone as solemn as that of a bell tolling for the dead, she replied:

"He was hanged in the market place at Libourne!"

Canolles started back.

"Hanged!" he cried; "Richon,—a soldier!"

Suddenly the color fled from his cheeks, and he drew his trembling hand across his brow.

"Ah! now I understand it all," said he; "I understand my arrest, my examination, the officer's words, and the silence of the soldiers; I understand the step you have taken, your tears when you found me so cheerful; I understand the crowds, the cries, and the threats. Richon was murdered! and they will revenge Richon upon me!"

"No, no, my beloved! no, beloved of my heart!" cried Claire, beaming with joy, seizing both Canolles' hands, and gazing with all her soul into his eyes. "No, they will not sacrifice you, dear prisoner! You were not mistaken,—you were marked out for the sacrifice; you were condemned; you were doomed to die; death was very near to you, my darling *fiancé*. But have no fear; you may speak of happiness and of the future, for she whose whole life is consecrated to you has saved your life! Be joyous and happy, but beneath your breath; for you may awake your ill-fated companion, upon whose head the storm will break, who is to die in your place!"

"Oh! hush, hush, dear love! you freeze my blood with horror," said Canolles, hardly recovered, despite Claire's ardent caresses, from the terrible blow he had received. "I, so calm and confident, so idiotically happy, was in imminent danger of death! And when? at what moment of all others? Just Heaven! at the moment when I was to become your husband! Upon my soul, it would have been a double murder!"

"They call that 'reprisal,'" said Claire.

"Yes, yes,—it is true; they are right."

"Now you are frowning and pensive again."

"Oh!" cried Canolles, "it isn't that I fear death; but death would part us—"

"If you had died, my love, I should have died too. But, instead of giving way to sadness, rejoice with me. Look you, to-night—perhaps within an hour—you will leave the prison. Either I will come here myself for you, or I will await you at the outer door. Then, without losing a moment, a second, we will fly—oh! instantly! I cannot wait! this accursed city terrifies me. To-day I have succeeded in saving you; but to-morrow some other unforeseen mischance may take you from me again!"

"Ah! Claire, my best beloved, do you know that this is almost too great happiness at a single stroke; yes, in very truth, too great happiness! I shall die of it—"

"Well, then," said Claire, "be joyous and cheerful, as you naturally are."

"Why do not you do the same?"

"See, I am laughing."

"And that sigh?"

"The sigh, my dearest, is for the poor wretch who pays for our joy with his life."

"Yes, yes, you are right! Oh! why can you not take me away with you at this moment? Come, my good angel, open your wings and fly away with me!"

"Patience, patience! my beloved husband! To-morrow I will carry you—where? I neither know nor care—to the paradise of our love. Meanwhile I am here."

Canolles took her in his arms and strained her to his breast. She threw her arms around his neck and lay unresistingly, trembling with agitation, against that heart, which was scarcely beating, so oppressed was it by conflicting emotions.

Suddenly, for the second time, a heart-breaking sob shook her frame, and happy as she was, her tears fell thick and fast upon Canolles' face.

"Well, well!" said he, "is this your cheerfulness, my poor dear angel?"

"It is the last remnant of my sorrow."

As she spoke the door opened, and the same officer announced that the half-hour had expired.

"Adieu!" whispered Canolles; "or rather hide me in the folds of your cloak, and take me with you!"

"Hush, dear love!" she replied, in a low tone, "for you break my heart! Do you not see that I am dying with longing to do it? Be patient for your own sake, and for mine. In a few hours we shall meet again never to part."

"I am patient," said Canolles, joyfully, completely comforted by this assurance; "but we must part now. Courage, my dear, and let us say adieu. Adieu, Claire, adieu!"

"Adieu!" said she, trying to smile; "ad—"

But she could not complete the cruel word. For the third time her voice was stifled with sobs.

"Adieu! adieu!" cried Canolles, seizing her in his arms anew, and covering her brow with burning kisses, "adieu!"

"The devil!" muttered the officer, "luckily I know that the poor fellow has no great reason to fear, or this scene would break my heart!"

He escorted Claire to the door and then returned.

"Now, monsieur," said he to Canolles, who had fallen back upon a chair, exhausted by his emotion, "it's not enough for you to be happy, you must be compassionate too. Your neighbor, your unfortunate fellow-prisoner, who is to die, is entirely alone; no one is interested in him, and he has no one to comfort him. He desires to see you. I have taken it upon myself to allow him to do so, but your consent also is necessary."

"My consent!" cried Canolles, "oh! I give it willingly. Poor devil! I await him with open arms! I do not know him, but that makes no difference."

"He seems to know you, however."

"Is he aware of the fate in store for him?"

"No, I think not. You understand that he must be left in ignorance of it."

"Oh! never fear."

"Listen, then: eleven o'clock will soon strike, and I shall return to the guard-house; after eleven o'clock the jailers are supreme in the interior of the prison. Your jailer has been warned that your neighbor will be with you, and he will come here for him when it is time for him to return to his own cell. If he knows nothing, tell him nothing; if he does know, tell him from us that we soldiers all pity him from the bottom of our hearts. To die is nothing, but *sacrebleu!* to be hanged is to die twice over."

"Is it decided that he is to die?"

"By the same death as Richon, in order that the reprisal may be complete. But we are chattering here, while he is awaiting your reply, anxiously no doubt."

"Go to him, monsieur, and believe that I am deeply grateful to you, both for him and myself."

The officer opened the door of the adjoining cell, and Cauvignac, somewhat pale, but with a jaunty air and with head erect, entered the cell of Canolles, who walked forward several steps to meet him.

Thereupon the officer waved his hand to Canolles, cast a pitying glance at Cauvignac, and took his leave, taking with him his soldiers, whose heavy footfalls could be heard for some time in the corridors.

Soon the jailer made his round; they heard the clashing of his keys in the different doors.

Cauvignac was not depressed, because there was in the man an unalterable confidence in himself, an inextinguishable hope in the future. But, beneath his calm exterior and his mask of cheerfulness, a bitter grief was biting at his heart like a serpent. That sceptical soul, which had always doubted everything, had come at last to doubt its very doubts.

Since Richon's death Cauvignac had not eaten or slept.

Accustomed as he was to make light of the misfortunes of others because he took his own so gayly, our philosopher had not once thought of laughing at an event which led to so terrible a result as that, and, despite himself, he saw, in all the mysterious threads which led up to his responsibility for Richon's death, the unswerving hand of Providence, and he began to believe, if not in the reward of good deeds, at least in the punishment of evil deeds.

He resigned himself to his fate, therefore, and gave himself over to thought; but, as we have said, the result of his resignation was that he no longer ate or slept.

It was a strange and mysterious fact that his own death, which he anticipated, moved him much less than the death of the comrade in misfortune, whom he knew to be within two yards of him, awaiting the fatal decree, or execution without the formality of a decree. All this turned his thoughts once more to Richon, his avenging spectre, and the twofold catastrophe resulting from what had seemed to him a charming piece of mischief.

His first idea had been to escape; for, although he was a prisoner on parole, he thought that he might without scruple disregard his engagements, as his captors had disregarded theirs by putting him in prison. But he was shrewd enough to realize that escape was impossible, despite his ingenuity. Thereupon he became more firmly convinced than ever that he was fast in the clutches of inexorable fatality; and he had but one desire,—namely, to talk for a few moments with his companion, whose name had caused him a feeling of sad surprise, and to effect a reconciliation in his person with the whole human race he had outraged so shamefully.

We do not affirm that all these reflections of his were the results of remorse,—no, Cauvignac was too much of a philosopher to suffer from remorse,—but it was something that closely resembled it, namely violent self-reproach for having done evil for nothing. With time, and a combination of circumstances suited to maintain him in this frame of mind, this sentiment might perhaps have had the same result as remorse; but time was lacking.

Upon entering Canolles' cell, Cauvignac waited first of all, with his ordinary prudence, until the officer who showed him in had withdrawn; then, when he saw that the door was securely fastened, and the wicket hermetically closed, he walked up to Canolles, who, as we have said, had taken some steps to meet him, and warmly pressed his hand.

Notwithstanding the gravity of his situation, Cauvignac could not forbear a smile as his eye fell upon the handsome, refined young man, of venturesome and joyous disposition, whom he had twice before surprised in very different situations, once when his mission was to send him to Nantes, and again to take him to Île Saint-Georges. Furthermore, he recalled his momentary usurpation of his name, and the amusing mystification of the duke resulting therefrom; and gloomy and forbidding as the prison was, the souvenir was so mirth-provoking that, for a moment, the present was forgotten.

For his part, Canolles recognized him at the first glance as the person with whom he had come in contact on the two occasions we have mentioned; and as Cauvignac, on those two occasions had been, all things considered, a messenger of good tidings, his compassion for the poor fellow's sad fate increased tenfold, especially as he knew that it was his own safety that made Cauvignac's death inevitable; and in so sensitive a mind as his such a thought caused infinitely deeper remorse than a downright crime would have caused his companion.

He welcomed him therefore with the greatest kindness of manner.

"Well, baron," Cauvignac began; "what do you say to our present situation? It is a little too precarious to be comfortable, it seems to me."

"Yes, here we are in prison, and God knows when we shall get away from here," rejoined Canolles, trying to put a good face on the matter, in order to lighten his companion's agony with a ray of hope.

"When we shall get away from here!" repeated Cauvignac. "May God, whom you invoke, vouchsafe, in his mercy, to postpone it as long as possible! But I do not think he is disposed to respite us for long. I saw from my window, as you must have seen from yours, an excited crowd rushing in a certain direction,—toward the Esplanade, unless I am much mistaken. You know the Esplanade, my dear baron, and you know to what uses it is put?"

"Oh, nonsense! You exaggerate the danger, I am sure. The crowd were heading for the Esplanade, it is true, but it was to see some military punishment, no doubt. To make us pay for Richon's death would be frightful; for, after all, we are both entirely innocent of his death."

Cauvignac started and fastened his eyes upon Canolles' face with, a gloomy expression which gradually softened to one of pity.

"Well, well," he said to himself, "here's a poor fellow who deceives himself as to the situation. But I must tell him how it really stands; for where would be the use of encouraging him in his error only to make the blow more crushing at the last? whereas, when one has time to prepare, the fall always seems a little easier."

After a pause of some duration, he took both Candles' hands in his, and gazing into his face with an intentness which greatly embarrassed him, he said:—

"Monsieur, my dear monsieur, let us send for a bottle or two of the excellent Braune wine you know of. Alas! I might have drunk my fill of it if I had been governor a little longer, and I will even go so far as to admit that my predilection for that vintage led me to apply for that position in preference to any other. God punishes me for my gluttony."

"I shall be glad to join you," said Canolles.

"Very good, and as we drink we will talk; if what I have to tell you is not very pleasant, the wine will be good at least, and one will make up for the other."

Canolles knocked on the door, but there was no response; he knocked still louder, and a child, who was playing in the corridor, came to the door.

"What do you want?" he asked.

"Wine," said Canolles; "tell your papa to bring two bottles."

The child ran off, and a moment later returned to say:

"Papa is busy talking with a gentleman just now; he will come very soon."

"Will you let me ask you a question, my dear?" said Cauvignac.

"What is it?"

"What gentleman is your papa talking with?" he asked in his most insinuating tone.

"With a tall gentleman."

"This is a charming child," said Cauvignac; "wait a moment and we shall learn something. How is the gentleman dressed?"

"All in black."

"The devil! Do you hear? all in black! What is the name of this tall gentleman dressed all in black? Do you happen to know that, my dear?"

"His name is Monsieur La Vie."

"Aha!" said Cauvignac; "the king's advocate! I fancy that we have no reason to be apprehensive of anything he is likely to do. Let us take advantage of their conversation to converse ourselves. Here, my little fellow" he added, slipping a piece of money under the door, "here's something to buy marbles with. It's a good thing to make friends everywhere," he continued, as he stood erect once more.

The child joyfully seized the coin, and thanked the donor.

"Well, monsieur," said Canolles, "you were saying—"

"Oh, yes! I was saying that you seem to me to be sadly astray as to the fate that awaits us when we leave the prison; you speak of the Esplanade, of military punishments; but I am inclined to think that we are the objects of the public attention, and that there is something more than mere flogging in the wind."

"Nonsense!" said Canolles.

"Zounds! monsieur, you look at things in rather a more cheerful light than I am able to do; perhaps because you haven't the same reasons for alarm that I have. But don't boast too much of your prospects, for they 're not over-flattering. Yours are nothing, however, compared to mine, and mine,—I must say it because I am firmly convinced that it is so,—are most infernally dark. Do you know who I am, monsieur?"

"That's a strange question surely. You are Captain Cauvignac, Governor of Braune, I suppose."

"Yes, for the moment; but I have not always borne that name or that title. I have changed my name very often, and have tried many different titles. For instance, one day I called myself Baron de Canolles, just as you call yourself."

Canolles looked him in the eye.

"Yes, I understand," pursued Cauvignac, "you are wondering whether I am insane, are you not? Have no fears on that score, for I am in full possession of all my mental faculties, and have never been more completely sane."

"Explain yourself, then," said Canolles.

"Nothing easier. Monsieur le Duc d'Épernon—You know Monsieur le Duc d'Épernon, do you not?"

"By name only; I never saw him."

"Luckily for me. Monsieur d'Épernon, I say, surprised me one day at a certain house where I knew that you were a favored guest, so I took the liberty of borrowing your name."

"Monsieur, what mean you?"

"There, there, softly! Don't be selfish enough to be jealous of one woman just as you are on the point of marrying another! And even if you should be,—and it would be quite consistent with human nature, for man is a vile brute,—you will forgive me in a moment. I am too closely connected with you for you to quarrel with me."

"I do not understand a word that you are saying, monsieur."

"I say that I have a right to be treated by you as a brother, or at least as a brother-in-law."

"You speak in enigmas, and I am still all at sea."

"Very good; I will enlighten you with a single word. My true name is Roland de Lartigues, and Nanon is my sister."

Canolles' suspicions gave way before a sudden swelling of the heart.

"You, Nanon's brother!" he cried. "Oh, poor fellow!"

"Yes, poor fellow, indeed!" rejoined Cauvignac; "you have hit the point exactly; for in addition to a multitude of other disagreeable circumstances connected with my encounter with the authorities here, is that of bearing the name of Roland de Lartigues, and of being Nanon's brother. You are aware that my dear sister is not in the odor of sanctity in the nostrils of Messieurs les Bordelais. Once let it be known that I am Nanon's brother, and

I am thrice lost. Now there is one La Rochefoucauld here, and one Lenet, who know everything."

"Ah!" said Canolles, in whose mind Cauvignac's Words awoke certain memories; "ah! I understand now why poor Nanon called me her brother in that letter. Dear girl!"

"Yes," said Cauvignac, "she was indeed a dear girl, and I much regret that I did not always follow her instructions to the letter; but what would you have? if one could foretell the future there would be no need of God."

"What has become of her?" Canolles asked.

"Who can say? Poor child! She is in despair, no doubt,—not on my account, for she doesn't know of my arrest, but for you, whose fate it is more than likely that she has learned."

"Have no fear," said Canolles. "Lenet will not disclose the fact that you are Nanon's brother, and Monsieur de La Rochefoucauld has no reason to wish you ill; so no one will know anything about it."

"If they know nothing about that, they will know enough else, believe me; for instance, they will know that it was I who provided a certain document signed in blank, and that that blank signature—but, damnation! let us forget, if we can. What a pity that the wine doesn't come!" he continued, looking toward the door. "There's nothing like wine to make a fellow forget."

"Come, come," said Canolles, "courage!"

"*Pardieu!* do you think that I lack it? Wait until you see me at the critical moment when we go for a turn on the Esplanade. But there is one thing that worries me; shall we be shot, beheaded, or hanged?"

"Hanged!" cried Canolles. "Great God! we are noblemen, and they will not inflict such an outrage on the nobility."

"Oh! you will see that they are quite capable of picking flaws in my genealogy; then, too—"

"What now?"

"Will you or I be the one to go first?"

"For God's sake! my dear friend," said Canolles, "don't get such ideas in your head! Nothing is less certain than this death that you anticipate so confidently; people are not tried, condemned, and executed in a night."

"Hark ye," rejoined Cauvignac; "I was over yonder when they tried poor Richon, God rest his soul! Trial, judgment, hanging, all together, lasted hardly more than three or four hours; let us allow for somewhat less activity in this case,—for Madame Anne d'Autriche is Queen of France, and Madame de Condé is only a princess of the blood,—and that gives us four or five hours. As it is three hours since we were arrested, and two since we appeared before our judges, we can count upon an hour or two more to live; that's but a short time."

"In any event," said Canolles, "they will wait till daybreak before executing us."

"Ah! that is not at all certain; an execution by torch-light is a very fine spectacle; it costs more, to be sure, but as Madame la Princesse is much in need of the assistance of the Bordelais, it may well be that she will decide to incur the extra expense."

"Hush!" said Canolles, "I hear footsteps."

"The devil!" exclaimed Cauvignac, turning a shade paler.

"It's the wine, no doubt," said Canolles.

"Ah, yes!" said Cauvignac, gazing more than earnestly at the door, "it may be that. If the jailer enters with the bottles, all is well; if on the other hand—"

The door opened, and the jailer entered without the bottles.

Canolles and Cauvignac exchanged a significant glance, but the jailer took no note of it,—he seemed to be in such haste, the time was so short, and it was so dark in the cell.

He entered and closed the door.

Then he walked up to the prisoners and said, drawing a paper from his pocket:—

"Which of you is Baron de Canolles?"

"The devil!" they exclaimed with one voice, exchanging a second glance.

Canolles hesitated before replying, and Cauvignac did the same; the former had borne the name too long to doubt that the question was meant for him; but the other had borne it sufficiently long to fear that his falsehood was coming home to him.

However, Canolles understood that he must reply, so at last he said:—

"I am he."

The jailer drew nearer to him.

"You were the governor of a fortress?" he inquired.

"Yes."

"But so was I governor of a fortress; I, too, have borne the name of Canolles," said Cauvignac. "Come, explain yourself, and let there be no mistake. Mischief enough has come out of my transactions with regard to poor Richon, without my being the cause of another man's death."

"So your name is Canolles now?" said the jailer to Canolles.

"Yes."

"And your name was formerly Canolles?" he said to Cauvignac.

"Yes," was the reply, "for a single day, and I begin to think that I made a great fool of myself that day."

"You were both governors of fortresses?"

"Yes," they replied, in the same breath.

"Now for one more question, which will clear up the whole matter."

The two prisoners waited in absolute silence.

"Which of you," said the jailer, "is the brother of Madame Nanon de Lartigues?"

Cauvignac made a grimace which would have been comical at a less solemn moment.

"Did I not tell you," he said to Canolles, "did I not tell you, my dear fellow, that that was where they would attack me? If I should tell you," he added, turning to the jailer, "that I am Madame Nanon de Lartigues' brother, what would you say to me, my friend?"

"I should tell you to follow me instantly."

"Damnation!" ejaculated Cauvignac.

"But she has also called me her brother," said Canolles, trying in some degree to avert the storm that was evidently gathering over the head of his unfortunate companion.

"One moment, one moment," said Cauvignac, passing in front of the jailer, and taking Canolles aside; "one moment, my young friend; it isn't fair that you should be Nanon's brother under such circumstances. I have made others pay my debts enough, and it's no more than fair that I should take my turn at paying them."

"What do you mean?" demanded Canolles.

"Oh! it would take too long to tell you, and you see our jailer is losing patience, and tapping his foot on the floor. It's all right, my friend, all right; never fear, I will go with you. Adieu, my dear fellow; my doubts are set at rest on one point at least, for I know that I am to go first. God grant that you do not follow me too quickly. Now it remains to know what sort of death it is to be. The devil! if only it isn't hanging! Oh! I am coming, *pardieu!* I am coming. You're in a terrible hurry, my good man. Well then, my dear brother, my dear brother-in-law, my dear friend,—a last adieu, and good-night!"

With that Cauvignac stepped toward Canolles and held out his hand, which Canolles grasped in both of his own and pressed affectionately.

Meanwhile Cauvignac was looking at him with a strange expression.

"What do you want?" said Canolles; "have you any request to make?"

"Yes."

"Then make it boldly."

"Do you sometimes pray?

"Yes."

"Well, then, when you pray, say a word for me." He turned to the jailer, whose impatience was visibly increasing.

"I am Madame Nanon de Lartigues' brother," said he; "come, my friend—"

The jailer did not wait for him to say it a second time, but hastily left the room, followed by Cauvignac, who waved a last farewell to Canolles from the threshold.

The door closed behind them, their steps receded rapidly, and everything relapsed into absolute silence, which seemed to him who was left behind like the silence of death.

Canolles fell into a melancholy frame of mind, which resembled terror. This fashion of spiriting a man away by night, without commotion, without guards, was more alarming than the preparations for the infliction of the death penalty when made in broad daylight. All his fear, however, was on his companion's behalf, for his confidence in Madame de Cambes was so great that since he had seen her he was absolutely without fear for himself, notwithstanding the alarming nature of the news she brought.

So it was that the sole subject of his absorption at that moment was the fate in store for the comrade who was taken from him. Thereupon Cauvignac's last request came to his mind; he fell upon his knees and prayed.

In a few moments he rose, feeling comforted and strong, and awaiting calmly the arrival of the succor promised by Madame de Cambes, or her own presence.

Meanwhile Cauvignac followed the jailer through the dark corridor without a word, and reflecting as deeply as his nature allowed him to do.

At the end of the corridor, the jailer closed the door with the least possible noise, and after listening for a moment to certain ill-defined sounds which came up from the lower floors, turned sharply to Cauvignac, and said:

"Come! my gentleman, off we go."

"I am ready," rejoined Cauvignac, majestically.

"Don't speak so loud," said the jailer, "and walk faster;" and he started down a stairway leading to the underground dungeons.

"Oho!" said Cauvignac to himself, "do they propose to cut my throat in some dark corner, or consign me to a dungeon? I have heard it said that they sometimes content themselves with exhibiting the four limbs on a public square, as Cæsar Borgia did with Ramiro d'Orco. This jailer is all alone, and his keys are at his belt. The keys must open some door or other. He is short, I am tall; he is weak, I am strong; he is in front, I am behind; I can very soon choke the life out of him if I choose. Do I choose?"

Cauvignac, having decided that he did choose, had already extended his muscular hands to put his plan in execution, when the jailer suddenly turned about in a great fright.

"Hush!" said he, "do you hear nothing?"

"Upon my word," said Cauvignac, still speaking to himself, "there is something decidedly mysterious in all this; and so much caution ought to alarm me greatly, if it doesn't reassure me."

He stopped abruptly, and demanded:—

"Whither are you taking me?"

"Don't you see?" said the jailer; "into the vaults."

"Deuce take me!" said Cauvignac: "do they propose to bury me alive?"

The jailer shrugged his shoulders, and led the way through a labyrinth of winding corridors, until they came to a low arched door, on which the moisture stood in great drops; from the other side came a strange roaring sound.

The jailer opened the door.

"The river!" cried Cauvignac, starting back in dismay-as his eyes fell upon a swiftly flowing stream as black and forbidding as Acheron.

"Yes, the river; do you know how to swim?"

"Yes—no—that is to say—Why the devil do you ask me that?"

"Because if you can't swim, we shall have to wait for a boat that is stationed over yonder, and that means a loss of quarter of an hour, to say nothing of the danger that some one may hear the signal I shall have to give, and so discover us."

"Discover us!" cried Cauvignac. "In God's name, my dear fellow, are we escaping?"

"*Pardieu!* of course we are."

"Where are we going?"

"Where you please."

"I am free, then?"

"As free as the air."

"Oh, my God!" cried Cauvignac.

Without adding a word to that eloquent exclamation, without looking to right or left, without thought as to whether his companion was following him, he darted to the river, and plunged in more rapidly than a hunted otter. The jailer imitated him, and after a quarter of an hour of silent efforts to stem the current, they both were within hailing distance of the boat. The jailer whistled three times; the oarsmen, recognizing the pre-concerted signal, rowed toward them, promptly lifted them into the boat, bent to their oars without a word, and in less than five minutes set them both ashore upon the other bank.

"Ouf!" said Cauvignac, who had not uttered a single word from the moment that he threw himself into the stream. "Ouf! I am really saved! Dear jailer of my heart, God will reward you!"

"I have already received forty thousand livres," said the jailer, "which will help me to wait patiently for the reward God has in store for me."

"Forty thousand livres!" cried Cauvignac in utter stupefaction. "Who the devil can have put out forty thousand livres for me?"

THE ABBEY OF PEYSSAC

I

A word of explanation becomes necessary at this point, after which we will resume the thread of our narrative.

Indeed, it is high time for us to return to Nanon de Lartigues, who, at the sight of poor ill-fated Richon expiring on the market-place at Libourne, uttered a shriek and fell in a swoon.

Nanon, however, as our readers must ere this have discovered, was not a woman of a weak and shrinking temperament. Despite her slender stature she had borne long and bitter sorrows, had endured crushing fatigue, and defied danger of the most appalling kind; and her sturdy, loving heart, of more than ordinary steadfastness, could bend as circumstances required, and rebound more stanch and courageous than ever after every fillip of destiny.

The Duc d'Épernon, who knew her, or who thought that he knew her, was naturally amazed therefore to see her so completely crushed by the sight of mere physical suffering,—the same woman who, when her palace at Agen was destroyed by fire, never uttered a cry (although she was within an ace of being burned alive) lest she should give pleasure to her enemies, who were thirsty for a sight of the torture which one of them, more vindictive than the others, sought to inflict upon the mistress of the detested governor; and who had looked on without winking while two of her women were murdered by mistake for her.

Nanon's swoon lasted two hours, and was followed by a frightful attack of hysteria, during which she could not speak, but could simply utter inarticulate shrieks. It became so serious that the queen, who had sent message upon message to her, paid her a visit in person, and Monsieur de Mazarin insisted upon taking his place at her bedside to prescribe for her as her physician. Apropos, he made great pretensions to skill in the administration of medicine for the suffering body, as well as of theology for the imperilled soul.

But Nanon did not recover consciousness until well into the night. It was some time after that before she could collect her thoughts; but at last, pressing her hands against her temples, she cried in a heart-rending tone:

"I am lost! they have killed him!"

Luckily these words were so incomprehensible that those who heard charged them to the account of delirium.

They left an impression on their minds, however, and when the Duc d'Épernon returned the next morning from an expedition which had taken him away from Libourne on the preceding afternoon, he learned at the same time of her protracted swoon, and of the words she uttered when she came to her senses. The duke was well acquainted with her sensitive, excitable nature. He realized that there was something more than delirium in her words, and hastened to her side.

"My dear girl," he said to her as soon as they were left alone, "I know all that you have suffered in connection with the death of Richon, whom they were so ill-advised as to hang in front of your windows."

"Oh yes! it was fearful! it was infamous!"

"Another time," said the duke, "now that I know the effect it has upon you, I will see to it that rebels are hanged on the Place du Cours, and not on the Place du Marché. But of whom were you speaking when you said that they had killed him? It couldn't have been Richon, I fancy; for Richon was never anything to you, not even a simple acquaintance."

"Ah! is it you, Monsieur le Duc?" said Nanon, supporting herself on her elbow and seizing his arm.

"Yes, it is I; and I am very glad that you recognize me, for that proves that you are getting better. But of whom were you speaking?"

"Of him, Monsieur le Duc, of him!" cried Nanon; "you have killed him! Oh, the poor, poor boy!."

"Dear heart, you frighten me! what do you mean?"

"I mean that you have killed him. Do you not understand, Monsieur le Duc?"

"No, my dear," replied D'Épernon, trying to induce Nanon to speak by entering into the ideas her delirium suggested to her; "how can I have killed him, when I do not know him?"

"Do you not know that he is a prisoner of war, that he was a captain, that *he* was commandant of a fortress, that he had the same titles and the same rank as this unhappy Richon, and that the Bordelais will avenge upon him the murder of the man whose murder you were responsible for? For it's of no use for you to pretend that it was done according to law, Monsieur le Duc; it was a downright murder!"

The duke, completely unhorsed by this apostrophe, by the fire of her flashing eyes, and by her nervous, energetic gestures, turned pale, and beat his breast.

"Oh! 't is true!" he cried, "'t is true! poor Canolles! I had forgotten him!"

"My poor brother! my poor brother!" cried Nanon, happy to be at liberty to give vent to her emotion, and bestowing upon her lover the title under which Monsieur d'Épernon knew him.

"*Mordieu!* you are right," said the duke, "and I have lost my wits. How in God's name could I have forgotten the poor fellow? But nothing is lost; they can hardly have heard the news at Bordeaux as yet; and it will take time to assemble the court-martial, and to try him. Besides, they will hesitate."

"Did the queen hesitate?" Nanon retorted.

"But the queen is the queen; she has the power of life and death. They are rebels."

"Alas!" said Nanon, "that's an additional reason why they should not stand on ceremony; but what do you mean to do? Tell me."

"I don't know yet, but rely on me."

"Oh!" cried Nanon, trying to rise, "if I have to go to Bordeaux myself, and surrender myself in his place, he shall not die."

"Never fear, dear heart, this is my affair. I have caused the evil and I will repair it, on the honor of a gentleman. The queen still has some friends in the city, so do not you be disturbed."

The duke made her this promise from the bottom of his heart.

Nanon read in his eyes determination, sincerity, and good-will, and her joy was so overpowering that she seized his hands, and said as she pressed them to her burning lips:—

"Oh, Monseigneur, if you succeed, how I will love you!"

The duke was moved to tears; it was the first time that Nanon had ever spoken to him so expansively or made him such a promise.

He at once rushed from the room, renewing his assurances to Nanon that she had nothing to fear. Sending for one of his retainers, whose shrewdness and trust-worthiness were well known to him, he bade him go at once to Bordeaux, make his way into the city, even if he had to scale the ramparts, and hand to Lavie, the advocate-general, the following note, written from beginning to end by his own hand: —

> "See to it that no harm comes to Monsieur de Canolles, captain and commandant in his Majesty's service.

> "If he has been arrested, as is probable, use all possible means to set him free; bribe his keepers with whatever sum they demand, —a million if need be, —and pledge the word of Monsieur le Duc d'Épernon for the governorship of a royal château.

> "If bribery is unavailing, use force; stop at nothing; violence, fire, murder will be overlooked.

> "Description: tall, brown eye, hooked nose. If in doubt, ask him this question: —

> "'Are you Nanon's brother?'"

> "Above all things *haste* there is not a moment to lose."

The messenger set out and was at Bordeaux within three hours. He went to a farm-house, exchanged his coat for a peasant's smock-frock, and entered the city driving a load of meal.

Lavie received the letter quarter of an hour after the decision of the court-martial. He went at once to the fortress, talked with the jailer-in-chief, offered him twenty thousand livres, —which he refused, then thirty thousand, which he also refused, and finally forty thousand, which he accepted.

We know how Cauvignac, misled by the question which Monsieur d'Épernon relied upon as a safeguard against mistake, "Are you Nanon's brother?" yielded to what was perhaps the only generous impulse he had ever felt during his life, and answered, "Yes," and thus, to his unbounded amazement, regained his freedom.

A swift horse bore him to the village of Saint-Loubes, which was in the hands of the royalists. There they found a messenger from the duke, come to meet the fugitive on the duke's own horse, a Spanish mare of inestimable value.

"Is he saved?" he demanded of the leader of Cauvignac's escort.

"Yes," was the reply, "we have him here."

That was all that the messenger sought to learn; he turned his horse about, and darted away like a flash in the direction of Libourne. An hour and a half later, the horse fell exhausted at the city gate, and sent his rider headlong to the ground at the feet of Monsieur d'Épernon, who was fuming with impatience to hear the one word, "yes." The messenger, half-dead as he was, had sufficient strength to pronounce that word which cost so dear, and the duke hurried away, without losing a second, to Nanon's lodgings, where she lay upon her bed, gazing wildly at the door, which was surrounded by servants.

"Yes!" cried D'Épernon; "yes, he is saved, dear love; he is at my heels, you will see him in a moment."

Nanon fairly leaped for joy; these few words removed from her breast the weight that was stifling her. She raised her hands to heaven, and, with her face wet with the tears this unhoped for happiness drew from her eyes, which despair had made dry, cried in an indescribable tone:—

"Oh! my God, my God! I thank thee!"

As she brought her eyes back to earth, she saw at her side the Duc d'Épernon, so happy in her happiness that one would have said his interest in the dear prisoner was no less deep than hers. Not until then did this disturbing thought come to her mind:—

"How will the duke be recompensed for his kindness, his solicitude, when he sees the stranger in the brother's place, an almost adulterous passion substituted for the pure sentiment of sisterly affection?"

Her reply to her own question was short and to the point.

"No matter!" she thought, "I will deceive him no longer; I will tell him the whole story; he will turn me Out and curse me; then I will throw myself at his feet to thank him for all he has done for me these three years past, and that done, I will go hence poor and humble, but rich in my love, and happy in the anticipation of the new life that awaits us."

In the midst of this dream of self-denial, of ambition sacrificed to love, the throng of servants opened to give passage to a man who rushed into the room where Nanon lay, crying:—

"My sister! my dear sister!"

Nanon sat up in bed, opened her startled eyes to their fullest extent, turned paler than the belaced pillow behind her head, and for the second time fell back in consternation, muttering:—

"Cauvignac! my God! Cauvignac!"

"Cauvignac!" the duke repeated, looking wonderingly about, evidently in search of the man to whom that exclamation was addressed. "Cauvignac! is any one here named Cauvignac?"

Cauvignac was careful not to reply; he was not as yet sufficiently sure of his safety to justify a frankness which even under ordinary circumstances would have sat strangely upon him. He realized that by answering to the name he would ruin his sister, and would infallibly ruin himself at the same time; he held his peace therefore, and allowed Nanon to speak, reserving the right to correct her mistakes.

"What of Monsieur de Canolles?" she cried in a tone of angry reproach, darting a flaming glance at Cauvignac.

The duke frowned and began to bite his moustache. All those present, save Francinette, who was very pale, and Cauvignac, who did his utmost not to turn pale, knew not what to think of this burst of wrath, and gazed at one another in amazement.

"Poor sister!" whispered Cauvignac in the duke's ear, "she was so alarmed for me that her brain is turned and she doesn't know me."

"I am the one to whom you must reply, villain!" cried Nanon. "Where is Monsieur de Canolles? What has become of Him? Answer, answer, I tell you!"

Cauvignac formed a desperate resolution; it was necessary to risk everything to win everything, and to rely upon his impudence to carry him through; for to seek safety in confession, to inform the Duc d'Épernon of the fact that the false Canolles, whose fortune he had made his care, was identical with the Cauvignac who had levied troops against the queen, and had then sold those same troops to the queen, was equivalent to going voluntarily to join Richon on the gallows. He therefore went close to the Duc d'Épernon, and said to him with tears in his eyes:—

"Monsieur, this is no mere delirium, but downright madness; grief has turned her brain so that she does not recognize those who are nearest to her. If any one can restore her lost reason, you understand that it is myself; I beg you therefore to send away all the servants, except Francinette, who may remain at hand to look to her wants; for it would be as disagreeable to you as to myself, to see strangers laughing at the expense of my poor sister."

Perhaps the duke would not have yielded so readily to this specious reasoning,—for, credulous as he was, he began to be suspicious of Cauvignac,—had he not received a summons to wait upon the queen, Monsieur de Mazarin having convoked an extraordinary session of the council.

While the messenger was delivering his message, Cauvignac leaned over Nanon, and said in her ear:—

"In Heaven's name, sister, be calm! If we can exchange a few words in private, all will be well."

Nanon fell back upon the bed, more self-controlled at all events, if no calmer; for hope, however small the dose, is a balm which allays the heart-ache.

The duke, having decided to play the part of Orgon and Géronte to the end, returned to Nanon and kissed her hand, saying:—

"The crisis has passed, I trust, my dear; I leave you with the brother who is so dear to you, for the queen has sent for me. Believe me, nothing less than her Majesty's commands would induce me to leave your side at such a moment."

Nanon felt that her strength was failing her. She could not answer the duke, but simply looked at Cauvignac and pressed his hand as if to say:—

"Have you not deceived me, brother? May I really hope?"

Cauvignac answered her pressure, and said to Monsieur d'Épernon:—

"Yes, Monsieur le Duc, the crisis seems to have passed, and my sister will soon realize that she has by her side a faithful and devoted heart, ready to undertake anything to make her happy."

Nanon could restrain herself no longer; she burst out sobbing as if her heart would break, for so many things had combined to break her spirit that she was no longer anything more than an ordinary woman,—weak, that is to say, and dependent upon tears to give vent to her emotion.

The duke left the room, shaking his head, and commending Nanon to Cauvignac's care with an eloquent look.

"Oh! how that man tortures me!" cried Nanon, as soon as his back was turned; "if he had remained a moment longer, I believe I should have died."

Cauvignac raised his hand to bid her be silent; then he put his ear to the door to make sure that the duke had really gone.

"Oh! what care I," cried Nanon, "whether he listens or does not listen? You whispered two words in my ear to give me comfort; tell me what you think, what you hope!"

"Sister," replied Cauvignac, assuming a grave demeanor, which was by no means habitual with him, "I will not tell you that I am sure of success, but I will repeat what I said before, that I will do everything in the world to succeed."

"To succeed in what?" demanded Nanon; "we understand one another this time, do we not; there is no ghastly practical joke between us?"

"To succeed in saving the unfortunate Canolles."

Nanon gazed at him with terrifying intensity.

"He is lost, is he not?"

"Alas!" was the reply; "if you ask me for my honest, outspoken opinion, I admit that the prospect is dark."

"How indifferently he says it!" cried Nanon. "Do you know, wretch, what that man is to me?"

"I know that he is a man whom you prefer to your brother, since you would have saved him rather than me, and when you saw me you welcomed me with a curse."

Nanon made an impatient gesture.

"*Pardieu!* you are right," said Cauvignac; "I do not say that by way of reproach, but as a simple observation; for look you, with my hand upon my heart—I do not say upon my conscience, for fear I have none—I declare that if we were together once more in the cell in Château-Trompette, knowing what I know, I would say to Monsieur de Canolles, 'Monsieur, Nanon calls you her brother; it is you they seek, not I,'—and he would come to you in my place, and I would die in his."

"Then he is to die!" cried Nanon in a burst of grief, which proves that in the best organized minds death never presents itself as a certainty, but always as a fear simply; "then he is to die!"

"Sister," Cauvignac replied, "this is all that I can tell you, and upon it we must base all that we do. In the two hours since I left Bordeaux many things may have happened; but do not despair, for it is equally true that absolutely nothing at all may have happened. Here is an idea that has come into my head."

"Tell it me, quickly."

"I have a hundred men and my lieutenant within a league of Bordeaux."

"A sure man?"

"Ferguzon."

"Well?"

"Well, sister, whatever Monsieur de Bouillon may say, whatever Monsieur de La Rochefoucauld may do, whatever Madame la Princesse may think, who deems herself a far greater captain than her two generals, I have an idea that, with my hundred men, half of whom I will sacrifice, I can make my way to Monsieur de Canolles."

"Oh! you deceive yourself, brother; you will never get to him; you will never get to him!"

"But I will, *morbleu!* or I will die in the attempt!"

"Alas! your death would prove your good-will, but it would not save him. He is lost! he is lost!"

"But I tell you no, even if I have to give myself up in his place," cried Cauvignac, in a burst of quasi-generosity that surprised himself.

"Give yourself up!"

"Yes, to be sure; for no one has any reason to hate Monsieur de Canolles; on the other hand, every one loves him, while I am universally detested."

"Why should you be detested?"

"For the simplest of reasons; because I have the honor to be bound to you by the closest ties of blood. Forgive me, my dear sister, but what I say is extremely flattering to a good royalist."

"Wait a moment," said Nanon, putting her finger on her lips.

"I am listening."

"You say that I am bitterly detested by the people of Bordeaux?"

"Why, they fairly execrate you."

"Is it so?" said Nanon, with a smile, half-pensive, half-joyous.

"I did not think I was telling you something that would be so agreeable to you to hear."

"Yes, yes," said Nanon, "it is very sensible at all events, if not exactly agreeable. Yes, you are right," she continued, speaking rather to herself than to her brother; "they do not hate Monsieur de Canolles, nor do they hate you. Wait, wait!"

She rose, threw a long silk cloak about her lithe and graceful form, and, sitting at her table, hastily wrote a few lines, which Cauvignac, as he watched the flush that mounted to her brow, and the heaving of her bosom, judged to be of great moment.

"Take this," said she, sealing the letter, "and ride alone to Bordeaux, without soldiers or escort. There is a mare in the stable that can do the distance in an hour. Bide as fast as she will carry you, deliver this letter to Madame la Princesse, and Monsieur de Canolles is saved!"

Cauvignac looked at his sister in open-mouthed amazement; but he knew how clear-sighted she was, and wasted no time criticising her instructions. He hurried to the stable, leaped upon the horse she had described, and half an hour thereafter was more than half-way to Bordeaux.

Nanon, as soon as she saw him from her window galloping away, knelt, atheist as she was, and repeated a short prayer; after which she bestowed her money and jewels in a casket, ordered a carriage, and bade Francinette array her in her most splendid garments.

II

Save the neighborhood of the Esplanade, whither everybody was hurrying, the city of Bordeaux seemed deserted. In the streets which lay at a distance from that favored-quarter there was no sound save the tread of the patrol, or the terrified voice of some old woman as she closed and locked her door.

But in the direction of the Esplanade there was a dull, continuous murmur as of waves beating upon a distant shore.

Madame la Princesse had finished her correspondence, and had sent word to Monsieur le Duc de La Rochefoucauld that she would receive him.

At the princess's feet, crouching upon a rug, and studying with the keenest anxiety her face and her humor, was Claire, evidently awaiting a moment when she might speak without annoying her; but her enforced patience, her studied calmness were belied by the nervous movements of the fingers with which she was folding and crumpling a handkerchief.

"Seventy-seven signatures!" cried the princess; "it's not all pleasure you see, Claire, to play at being queen."

"Indeed it is, madame; for in taking the queen's place you assumed her most gracious prerogative, that of being merciful."

"And that of punishing, Claire," rejoined the princess proudly, "for one of the seventy-seven signatures was written at the foot of a death-warrant."

"And the seventy-eighth will be at the foot of a pardon, will it not, madame?" pleaded Claire.

"What do you say, little one?"

"I say, madame, that I think it is quite time for me to go and set my prisoner free; may I not spare him the frightful spectacle of his companion led forth to his death? Ah! madame, as you consent to pardon him, pray, let it be a full and complete pardon!"

"I' faith, yes! you are quite right, little one; but, in very truth I had forgotten my promise amid all this serious business, and you have done well to remind me of it."

"Then—" cried Claire, beaming with joy.

"Do what you choose."

"One more signature, then, madame," said Claire, with a smile which would have melted the hardest heart, a smile which no painter's brush could reproduce, because it belongs only to the woman who loves, that is to say, to life in its divinest essence.

She placed a paper upon Madame la Princesse's table, and held it while she wrote:—

> "The governor of Château-Trompette is ordered to allow Madame la Vicomtesse de Cambes access to Monsieur le Baron de Canolles, to whom we restore his liberty without reservation or condition."

"Is that right?" the princess asked.

"Oh! yes, madame!"

"And I must sign it?"

"Most assuredly."

"Ah! little one," said Madame de Condé, with her most gracious smile, "I seem compelled to do whatever you want."

And she wrote her name.

Claire pounced upon the paper like an eagle upon its prey. She hardly took time to thank her Highness, and rushed from the room pressing the paper against her heart.

On the stairway she met Monsieur de La Rochefoucauld, who was always followed wherever he went by a number of officers and admiring citizens.

Claire greeted him with a happy little smile. Monsieur de La Rochefoucauld, surprised beyond measure, stopped for an instant upon the landing, and followed her with his eyes to the bottom of the stairs before entering Madame de Condé's apartment.

"All is ready, madame," he said, when he was in her Highness's presence.

"Where?"

"Over yonder."

The princess seemed to be trying to make out his meaning.

"On the Esplanade," said the duke.

"Ah yes! very good," rejoined the princess, affecting great calmness of manner, for she felt that he was looking at her, and so, notwithstanding her woman's nature which inclined her to shudder, she listened to the voice of her dignity as leader of a great party, which bade her show no sign of weakness. "If everything is ready, let the affair proceed."

The duke hesitated.

"Do you think it advisable that I should be present?" inquired the princess, with a tremor in her voice which she could not entirely repress, notwithstanding her self-control.

"Why, that is as you please, madame," replied the duke, who was at that moment engaged in one of his physiological studies.

"We will see, duke, we will see; you know that I have pardoned one of the condemned men."

"Yes, madame."

"And what do you say to that step?"

"I say that whatever your Highness does is well done."

"Yes, I thought it better so. It will be more befitting our dignity to show the Épernonists that while we do not fear to resort to reprisals, and to treat with her Majesty as one power with another, we have confidence in the strength of our cause, and return evil for evil without excitement or exaggeration."

"It is very politic."

"Is it not, duke?" rejoined the princess, seeking to gather La Rochefoucauld's real meaning from his tone and manner.

"But," he continued, "it is still your opinion, is it not, that one of the two should expiate Richon's death? For if it remains unavenged, the impression may gain ground that your Highness sets but little store by the gallant men who devote their lives to your service."

"Oh! assuredly! and one of the two shall die, on my honor as a princess! never fear."

"May I know which of the two your Highness has deigned to pardon?"

"Monsieur de Canolles."

"Ah!"

This *ah!* was pronounced in a most significant tone.

"Can it be that you have any particular ground for wishing that gentleman ill, Monsieur le Duc?"

"I! Madame, was I ever known to wish anybody well or ill? I divide all men into two categories: obstacles, and supporters. The former must be overthrown, and the latter supported,—so long as they support us; that is my policy, madame, and I might almost say my whole moral code."

"What infernal scheme is he concocting, and what is he driving at?" muttered Lenet; "he acted as if he detested poor Canolles."

"Well," the duke continued, "if your Highness has no other orders to give me—"

"No, Monsieur le Duc."

"I will take leave of your Highness."

"Is it to be tonight?"

"In quarter of an hour."

Lenet made ready to follow the duke.

"Are you going to see the spectacle, Lenet?" the princess asked him.

"Oh! no, madame; I am not addicted to violent emotion, as you know; I will content myself with going half way, that is to say, as far as the prison, to witness the touching picture of poor Canolles restored to freedom by the woman he loves."

The duke made a wry face. Lenet shrugged his shoulders, and the solemn procession left the palace to go to the prison.

Madame de Cambes had traversed the distance in less than five minutes; she showed the order to the sentinel at the drawbridge, then to the doorkeeper at the prison, and asked to see the governor.

The governor scrutinized the order with the inexpressive eye characteristic of prison-governors, which never lights up at sight of a death-warrant or pardon, recognized the signature and seal of Madame de Condé, saluted the messenger, and said, turning to the door:

"Call the lieutenant."

Then he motioned to Madame de Cambes to be seated; but her excitement and impatience were too intense to allow her to be at rest, and she remained on her feet.

The governor thought it incumbent upon him to speak to her.

"You know Monsieur de Canolles?" he said in the same tone in which he would have asked what the weather was.

"Oh! yes, monsieur," was the reply.

"He is your brother, mayhap, madame?"

"No, monsieur."

"A friend?"

"He is—my *fiancé*," said Madame de Cambes, hoping that this confession would induce the governor to hasten the discharge of the prisoner.

"Ah!" he rejoined in the same tone, "I congratulate you, madame."

Having no further questions to ask, he relapsed into immobility and silence.

The lieutenant entered.

"Monsieur d'Orgemont," said the governor, "call the chief turnkey, and see that Monsieur de Canolles is set at liberty; here is the order for his discharge."

The lieutenant bowed and took the paper.

"Do you wish to wait here?" the governor asked.

"Am I not permitted to accompany monsieur?"

"Yes, madame."

"Then I will do so; you understand,—I wish to be the first to tell him that his life is saved."

"Go then, madame, and receive the assurance of my respect."

Madame de Cambes made a hasty courtesy to the governor and followed the lieutenant. He was the same officer who had talked with Canolles and with Cauvignac, and he went about the duty assigned him with the zeal born of sympathy. In a moment he and Madame de Cambes were in the court-yard.

"The chief turnkey!" cried the lieutenant. "He will be here in an instant, madame; have no fear," he added.

The second turnkey appeared.

"Monsieur le lieutenant," said he, "the turnkey in chief cannot be found; we have sought in vain for him."

"Oh, monsieur," cried Claire; "does this mean further delay?"

"No, madame, the order is explicit; be calm."

Madame de Cambes thanked him with one of those glances which none but women and angels have to give.

"You have duplicate keys to all the cells?" asked Monsieur d'Orgemont.

"Yes, monsieur."

"Open Monsieur de Canolles' door."

"Monsieur de Canolles in number two?"

"Yes, number two; open at once."

"By the way, I believe they are both together in there," said the turnkey; "you can choose the best-looking."

Jailers in all ages have been facetious. But Madame de Cambes was too happy to take offence at the heartless pleasantry. On the contrary she smiled at it, and would have embraced the man if need be to induce him to hasten so that she might be with Canolles a second earlier.

At last the door was opened. Canolles who had heard steps in the corridor, and recognized the viscountess's voice, threw himself into her arms, and she, forgetting that he was neither her husband or her lover, strained him to her heart with all her strength. The peril that had threatened him, the eternal separation to which they had come so close, purified everything.

"Well, my dear," said she, radiant with joy and pride, "you see that I have kept my word: I have obtained your pardon as I promised; I have come to fetch you, and we are going away."

Even as she spoke she was dragging him toward the corridor.

"Monsieur," said the lieutenant, "you may well devote your whole life to madame, for you certainly owe it to her."

Canolles made no reply; but his eyes gazed fondly at the saving angel, and his hand pressed the hand of the loving woman.

"Oh! do not hasten so," said the lieutenant, with a smile; "it is all over, and you are free, so take time to open your wings."

But Madame de Cambes, paying no heed to these words of good cheer, continued to drag Canolles through the corridors. Canolles let her have her will, exchanging friendly signs with the lieutenant. They reached the staircase, and descended the stairs as if they were provided with the wings of which the lieutenant had spoken. At last they stood in the court-yard; one more door, and the atmosphere of the prison would cease to oppress their long-suffering hearts.

That last door was finally thrown open. But on the other side, the drawbridge was thronged with a troop of gentlemen, archers and guards; they were Monsieur de La Rochefoucauld and his acolytes.

Without knowing why, Madame de Cambes shuddered. Some evil thing had befallen her every time that that man had come in her path.

As to Canolles, if he experienced any emotion whatever, no trace of it appeared upon his features.

The duke saluted Madame de Cambes and Canolles, and even paused to offer his congratulations. Then he made a sign to his followers, and they made way for the lovers to pass.

Suddenly a voice was heard at the far end of the court-yard, inside the prison:—

"Number one is empty; the other prisoner is not in his cell; I have searched everywhere and cannot find him!"

These words sent a thrill of excitement through all who heard them; the Duc de La Rochefoucauld started, and unable to restrain his first impulse, put out his hand as if to stop Canolles.

Claire saw the movement and every vestige of color fled from her cheeks.

"Come, come," said she, "let us make haste!"

"Pardon me, madame," said the duke, "but I must ask you to be patient for a moment. Give us time, if you please, to clear up this mistake; it will be a matter of a moment only, I promise you."

He made another sign to his followers and the passage was closed.

Canolles looked at Claire, at the duke, at the point whence the voice came, and he too turned pale.

"But why should I wait, monsieur?" demanded Claire. "Madame la Princesse de Condé signed the order for Monsieur de Canolles to be set free; here is the order, and his name is specifically mentioned; look, I beg you."

"Certainly, madame, it is as you say, and I do not assume to deny the validity of the order; it will be as effectual a moment hence as now; be patient therefore; I have sent a person to investigate who will very soon return."

"But how does that concern us?" Claire persisted. "What connection is there between Monsieur de Canolles and the prisoner in number one?"

"Monsieur le Duc," said the captain of the guards, whom the duke had sent to make inquiries, "we have searched for the other prisoner to no purpose; he cannot be found, and the chief turnkey has also disappeared; his child, whom we questioned, says that his father and the prisoner went out together by the secret door that opens on the river."

"Oho!" ejaculated the duke, "do you know anything of this, Monsieur de Canolles? An escape!"

At these words the whole truth flashed upon Canolles in an instant. He understood that it was Nanon who was watching over him; that it was he whom the jailer had come to seek; that it was he for whom the designation of Madame de Lartigues' brother was intended; that Cauvignac had unwittingly taken his place, and found freedom where he thought to find death. All these thoughts rushed into his mind at the same moment; he put his hands to his head and staggered, and only recovered himself when he saw that the viscountess was trembling and gasping for breath at his side.

Not one of these involuntary tokens of alarm escaped the duke.

"Close the doors!" he shouted. "Monsieur de Canolles, be kind enough to remain; this affair must be investigated, as you will understand."

"But, Monsieur le Duc," cried poor Claire, "you do not presume, I trust, to act in opposition to an order of Madame la Princesse!"

"No, madame," said the duke, "but I conceive it to be most important that she should be informed of what has taken place. I will not say to you, 'I will go to her myself;' you might believe it to be my purpose to influence our august mistress; but I will say, 'Do you go, madame;' for you know better than any one how to solicit Madame de Condé's clemency."

Lenet made an almost imperceptible sign to Claire.

"Oh! I will not leave him!" she cried, convulsively pressing the young man's arm.

"I will go to her Highness," said Lenet; "do you come with me, captain; or come yourself, Monsieur le Duc."

"So be it, I will go with you. Monsieur le capitaine will remain here and continue the search in our absence; perhaps the other prisoner may be found."

As if to enforce the latter portion of his sentence, La Rochefoucauld said a few words in the officer's ear, then took his departure with Lenet.

At the same time the viscountess and Canolles were forced back into the court-yard by the crowd of horsemen in attendance upon Monsieur de La Rochefoucauld, and the door clanged behind them.

During the last ten minutes the scene had taken on a character of such gravity and solemnity that all those who witnessed it stood by, pale-faced and silent, exchanging glances of deep meaning, and gazing at Canolles and Claire as if to read in their eyes which of the two was suffering the more. Canolles realized that it was for him to find courage for both; his demeanor was grave but most affectionate to his weeping companion, who clung to him, red-eyed and hardly able to stand, drew him closer to her side, smiled upon him with an expression of heart-breaking affection, and shuddered as she looked about upon that throng of men, seeking in vain one friendly face.

The captain, who had received his instructions from the duke, spoke in a low tone to his officers. Canolles, whose glance was keen, and whose ear was quick to hear the slightest hint that tended to change his suspicion to certainty, heard him, despite the care he took to speak as low as possible, utter these words: —

"We must devise some means of sending away that poor woman."

He tried thereupon to release his arm from the caressing grasp that detained it. Claire divined his purpose and clung to him with all her strength.

"You must continue your search," she cried; "perhaps they have not searched thoroughly, and the man will yet be found. Let us all search; it is not possible that he has escaped. Why should not Monsieur de Canolles have escaped with him? Come, Monsieur le Capitaine, order them to continue the search, I entreat you."

"They have searched, madame, and are searching at this moment. The jailer is well aware that his head will pay the penalty if he doesn't produce his prisoner; so that his interest alone would lead him to make a most thorough search."

"*Mon Dieu!*" murmured Claire, "and Monsieur Lenet does not return!"

"Patience, dear heart, patience," said Canolles, in the soothing tone in which one speaks to children; "Monsieur Lenet has but just gone; he has barely had time to reach Madame la Princesse; give him time to explain matters to her and then to return with her reply." He gently pressed her hand as he spoke; then, noticing that the captain of the guards was gazing at him intently and with evident impatience, he said to him: —

"Do you wish to speak with me, captain?"

"Yes, monsieur," he replied, for the unremitting scrutiny of the viscountess kept him on the rack.

"Monsieur," she cried, "take us to Madame la Princesse, I implore you. What difference can it make to you? As well take us to her as leave us here in suspense; she will see him, monsieur, she will see me, I will speak to her, and she will renew her promise."

"That is an excellent idea of yours, madame," said the officer, seizing hastily upon the suggestion; "go to her yourself, go! you have every chance of success."

"What do you say to it, baron?" the viscountess asked. "Do you think it would be well? You would not deceive me; what ought I to do?"

"Go, madame," said Canolles, with a mighty effort.

The viscountess dropped his arm, walked away a few steps, then ran back to him.

"Oh! no! no!" said she, "I will not leave him."

At that moment the outer door opened.

"Ah! God be praised!" she cried; "here are Monsieur Lenet and Monsieur le Duc!"

Behind Monsieur de La Rochefoucauld with his sphinx-like face, came Lenet with sorrowful countenance and trembling hands. At the first glance he exchanged with the counsellor, Canolles saw that there was no hope for him, that his doom was sealed.

"What have you to tell?" demanded Claire, rushing impetuously to meet Lenet, and dragging Canolles with her.

"Madame la Princesse is much embarrassed —" stammered Lenet.

"Embarrassed!" cried Claire, "what does that mean?"

"It means that she asks for you," interposed the duke, "that she wishes to speak with you."

"Is that true, Monsieur Lenet," demanded Claire, without pausing to reflect that the question was an insult to the duke.

"Yes, madame," faltered Lenet.

"But what of him?" she asked.

"Of whom?"

"Monsieur de Canolles."

"Oh! Monsieur de Canolles will return to his cell, and you will bring back the princess's reply to him."

"Will you remain with him, Monsieur Lenet?"

"Madame—"

"Will you remain with him?" she repeated.

"I will not leave him."

"You will not leave him, you swear that you will not?"

"My God!" muttered Lenet, gazing from the man who awaited his sentence to the woman whose death one word from his mouth might cause. "My God! since one of the two is doomed, give me strength to save the other."

"You will not swear, Monsieur Lenet!"

"I swear," replied the counsellor, putting his hand to his heart.

"Thanks, monsieur," said Canolles beneath his breath, "I understand you.—Go, madame," he added, turning to the viscountess; "you see that between Monsieur Lenet and Monsieur le Duc I am in no danger."

"Do not let her go without embracing her," said Lenet.

Canolles' brow was bedewed with icy sweat; a sort of mist came before his eyes; he detained Claire, as she was about to leave him, and pretending that he had something to whisper to her, drew her to his heart, and said in her ear:—

"Entreat without servility; I wish to live for you, but you should wish me to live honored."

"I will entreat in such fashion as to save you," she replied; "are you not my husband in God's sight?"

Canolles, as he released her, found a way to touch her neck with his lips, but so cautiously that she did not feel it, and the poor creature, mad with apprehension, left him without returning his last kiss. As she was about to leave the court-yard she turned, but there was a line of guards between her and the prisoner.

"Where are you, my friend? I cannot see you; one word, one word I pray, so that I may go with your voice in my ears."

"Go, Claire," said Canolles. "I await your return."

"Go, go, madame," said a kind-hearted officer; "the sooner you go, the sooner you will return."

"Monsieur Lenet, dear Monsieur Lenet," cried Claire's voice in the distance, "I rely upon you; you will answer to me for him."

And the door closed behind her.

"Good!" muttered the philosophical duke; "that was not over pleasant; but at last we are in the realm of the possible once more."

III

As soon as the viscountess had disappeared, and her voice had died away in the distance, the gate having been closed behind her, the circle of officers drew closer around Canolles, and two men of sinister mien, suddenly appearing as if they had sprung from the ground, approached the duke and humbly awaited his commands.

The duke simply pointed to the prisoner. He himself drew near to him, and said, with his customary glacial courtesy: —

"Monsieur, you doubtless understand that the departure of your companion in misfortune renders you liable to the penalty which was to be inflicted upon him."

"Yes, monsieur," replied Canolles, "I suspected as much; but there is one thing of which I am perfectly certain, that Madame la Princesse granted a pardon to me by name. I saw, and you yourself might have seen just now, the order for my release in the hands of Madame la Vicomtesse de Cambes."

"It is true, monsieur," said the duke, "but Madame la Princesse could not have anticipated the present state of affairs."

"I am to understand, then, that Madame la Princesse recalls her signature?"

"Yes," replied the duke.

"A princess of the blood is false to her word?"

The duke maintained his impassive demeanor.

Canolles looked about him.

"Has the time arrived?" he asked.

"Yes, monsieur."

"I thought that you would await the return of Madame la Vicomtesse de Cambes; you promised her that nothing should be done in her absence. It seems that nobody has any regard for his word to-day."

And the prisoner gazed reproachfully, not at the Duc de La Rochefoucauld, but at Lenet.

"Alas! monsieur," cried the latter, with tears in his eyes, "forgive us. Madame la Princesse positively refused to show mercy to you. I begged very earnestly none the less; Monsieur le Duc will bear witness to that, and God as well. But she deems it imperative that Richon's death should be paid for in kind, and she was as immovable as stone. Now do you yourself pass judgment on my conduct, Monsieur le Baron; instead of allowing the burden of your horrible situation to fall partly upon the viscountess, I ventured,—pray forgive me, for I feel that I stand in great need of your forgiveness,—I ventured to cause it to fall upon you alone, for you are a soldier and of gentle birth."

"In that case," faltered Canolles, whose voice was choked with emotion, "in that case I shall not see her again! When you bade me embrace her, it was for the last time!"

A sob stronger than stoicism or pride shook Lenet's frame. He stepped back and wept bitterly. Canolles thereupon fixed his piercing gaze upon the men who stood about him, but could see on every side none but faces rendered stern and pitiless by Richon's cruel death, and among them a very few timid creatures, who were stiffening their muscles to conceal their emotion and help them to swallow their tears and sighs.

"Oh! it is terrible to think upon," murmured the youth, in a moment of superhuman clearness of vision which opens before the soul a boundless field of view over what men call life,—that is to say, a few brief instants of happiness scattered here and there like islands in the midst of an ocean of tears and suffering,—"terrible to think upon! I had in my arms the woman I adore, who had just told me for the first time that she loved me; I had before me a long and blissful life, the realization of my fondest dream; and lo! in a moment, in a second, death takes the place of it all!"

He felt a tightness at his heart, and a pricking sensation in his eyes as if he were going to weep; but he remembered in time that he was, as Lenet said, a soldier and a gentleman.

"O pride," he said to himself, "the only form of courage that has any real existence, come to my aid! Should I bewail the loss of so vain and futile a thing as life? How they would laugh if they could say: 'On learning that he was to die, Canolles wept!' How did I bear myself on the day I was besieged at Saint-Georges, when the Bordelais showed the same eagerness for my death as to-day? I fought, I jested, I laughed. Very good! by the heaven above, which hears my words and is mayhap dealing wrongfully with me; by the devil who is struggling at this moment with my good angel, I will bear myself to-day as I bore myself on that day, and if I no longer fight, I will at least continue to jest, and will laugh on to the end."

At once his face became calm, as if all emotion had vanished from his heart; he passed his hand through his beautiful black hair, and walked up to Monsieur de La Rochefoucauld and Lenet with a smile upon his lips.

"Messieurs," said he, "as you know, one requires time to become accustomed to everything in this world, which is so filled with strange and unexpected events; I have taken, and I did wrong not to ask your leave to take, a moment to accustom myself to the thought of death; if it was too long a time, I ask your pardon for compelling you to wait."

Profound astonishment was depicted on the faces of all the bystanders, and the prisoner was aware that that feeling soon gave place to admiration; his strength was increased tenfold by his consciousness of that sentiment, so honorable to him.

"Whenever you are ready, messieurs," said he; "I am waiting for you now."

The duke, dumbfounded for an instant, at once resumed his usual phlegmatic demeanor, and gave the signal. Thereupon the gates were opened and the procession made ready to set out.

"One moment," cried Lenet, to gain time; "one moment, Monsieur le Duc! We are escorting Monsieur de Canolles to his death, are we not?"

The duke made a gesture of surprise, and Canolles looked wonderingly at Lenet.

"Why, yes," said the duke.

"Very good!" rejoined Lenet, "in that case the gallant gentleman cannot do without a confessor."

"Pardon me, pardon me, monsieur," interposed Canolles; "I can do without one perfectly well."

"How so?" Lenet asked, making signs to the prisoner which he would not understand.

"Because I am a Huguenot," replied Canolles, "and a zealous Huguenot, too, I promise you. If you wish to confer one last favor upon me, I pray you let me die as I am."

Even as he repelled the suggestion, the young man made a gesture of gratitude, which proved that he perfectly understood Lenet's purpose.

"If there is no further cause for delay, let us be off," said the duke.

"Make him confess! make him confess!" cried a few of the more vindictive bystanders.

Canolles drew himself up to his full height, looked about him on all sides with a calm and confident glance, and said sternly to the duke:—

"Are we going to act like cowards, monsieur? Me-thinks that if any person has the right to follow out his desires, I, who am the hero of the fête, have that right, I refuse to see a confessor, but I demand the scaffold, and that at the earliest possible moment; 'tis my turn to be weary of waiting."

"Silence!" cried the duke, turning to the crowd. When silence was restored in obedience to his potent voice and glance, he said to Canolles:—

"Monsieur you may do as you choose."

"Thanks, monsieur. In that case, let us go, and quickly; may we not?"

Lenet took Canolles' arm.

"On the contrary, let us go slowly," said he. "Who knows? A reprieve, an occurrence that we cannot fore-see, are among the possibilities. Go slowly, I implore you in the name of her who loves you, and who will weep so bitterly if we go too fast."

"Oh! do not speak to me of her, I entreat; all my courage vanishes at the thought that I am to be parted forever from her. But what am I saying? On the other hand, Monsieur Lenet, do speak of her, tell me again and again that she loves me, and will always love me, and above all, that she will weep for me!"

"Come, come, my dear, unfortunate child," said Lenet, "do not give way to your feelings; remember that these men are looking at you, and that they know not of whom we are speaking."

Canolles proudly raised his head, and his hair fell in wavy black curls about his neck. By this time they were in the street; the light of many torches shone upon his calm and smiling face.

He could hear women weeping, and there were some who said:—

"Poor baron, so young and so fair!"

They marched along for some time in silence; suddenly he exclaimed:—

"Oh! Monsieur Lenet, I would that I might see her once more!"

"Do you wish me to go in search of her, and bring her to you?" asked Lenet, who had no longer any will of his own.

"Oh! yes," whispered Canolles.

"Very well! I will go; but you will kill her."

"So much the better!" whispered selfishness to the young man's heart; "if you kill her, she will never belong to another."

But he overcame this last weakness as suddenly as it assailed him.

"No, no," said he, seizing Lenet's hand; "you promised to remain with me, so remain."

"What does he say?" the duke inquired of the captain of the guards.

Canolles overheard the question.

"I was saying, Monsieur le Duc," said he, "that I thought it was not so far from the prison to the Esplanade."

"Alas!" interposed Lenet, "do not complain of the distance, my poor boy, for we have arrived."

As he spoke the torch-bearers and the head of the procession disappeared around a street-corner.

Lenet pressed the young man's hand, then went up to the duke, determined to make one last effort before they actually reached the place of execution.

"Monsieur," said he, "once more I implore you for mercy! you will ruin our cause by executing Monsieur de Canolles."

"On the contrary," retorted the duke, "we prove that we deem it a just cause, as we do not fear to make reprisals."

"But reprisals can only be made between equals, Monsieur le Duc, and whatever you may say, the queen will still be queen, and we her subjects."

"Let us not discuss such matters before Monsieur de Canolles," rejoined the duke aloud; "surely you can see the impropriety."

"Do not speak of mercy before Monsieur le Duc;" retorted Canolles; "surely you can see that his *coup d'État* is in process of accomplishment; do not annoy him for so small a matter."

The duke made no reply; but his compressed lips and his ironical glance showed that the blow had struck home. Meanwhile they had not ceased to go forward, and Canolles now found himself at the entrance to the Esplanade. In the distance, that is, at the other side of the square, could be seen the crowd, in a vast circle formed by the glittering musket-barrels. In the centre arose a shapeless black something, which Canolles could not clearly distinguish in the shadow, and he thought that it was an ordinary scaffold. But when the torches reached the centre of the square, their light fell full upon that black object, at first unrecognizable, and revealed the hideous silhouette of a gibbet.

"A gibbet!" cried Canolles, halting, and pointing to the structure. "Is not that a gibbet that I see yonder, Monsieur le Duc?"

"It is; you are not mistaken," he replied, coldly.

A wrathful flush reddened the young man's brow; he threw aside the two soldiers who were marching on either hand, and at one bound found himself face to face with Monsieur de La Rochefoucauld.

"Monsieur," he cried, "do you forget that I am of gentle blood? All the world knows, even the executioner himself, that a nobleman is entitled to be beheaded."

"Monsieur, there are circumstances—"

"It is not in my own name that I speak," Canolles interrupted, "but in the name of all the nobility, in which you hold so high a place, who have been prince and are now duke; it will be a lasting shame, not for me, who am innocent, but for one and all of you, that one of your caste should die upon the gallows."

"Monsieur, Richon was hanged by order of the king."

"Richon, monsieur, was a gallant soldier, and at heart as noble as any man in this wide world, but he was not of noble birth; I am."

"You forget," said the duke, "that this is a matter of reprisals; were you a prince of the blood, we would hang you."

Canolles instinctively put his hand to his side for his sword, but when he failed to find it there, the realization of his situation came over him once more in all its force; his wrath vanished, and he remembered that his real superiority lay in his very weakness.

"Monsieur philosopher," said he, "woe to those who resort to reprisals, and woe thrice over to those who, when they resort to them, lay aside all humanity! I did not plead for mercy, but justice. There are those who love me, monsieur; I emphasize the word, because I am aware that you yourself do not appreciate how one can love. Upon the hearts of those who love me you are about to impress forever, with the memory of my death, the dishonoring image of the gibbet. A sword-thrust, I beseech you, or a musket-ball! Give me your dagger that I may kill myself, and then you may hang my dead body if it will give you any pleasure."

"Richon was hanged alive, monsieur," was the cold reply.

"Be it so! Now, listen to what I say. Some day some frightful misfortune will overtake you; when that day comes, you will remember that it is punishment from on high: for my own part, I die with the firm conviction that my death is your work."

Thereupon Canolles, shuddering and pale, but filled with exalted courage, approached the gallows and stood, proud and disdainful, facing the populace, with his foot upon the first step of the ladder.

"Now, executioner," said he, "do your duty."

"There is only one!" cried the crowd in amazement; "the other! where is the other? we were promised two!"

"Ah! that is one thing that consoles me in a measure," said Canolles, with a smile; "this amiable populace is not content with what you are doing for it; do you hear what it says, Monsieur le Duc?"

"Death! death! vengeance for Richon!" roared ten thousand voices.

"If I irritate them," thought Canolles, "they are quite capable of tearing me in pieces; in that case I shall not be hanged, and Monsieur le Duc will go insane with rage.

"You are cowards!" he cried; "I see some among you who took part in the attack on Saint-Georges, when I made you all run away! You are venting your spite on me to-day because I whipped you."

A roar of rage was the only reply.

"You are cowards!" he repeated; "rebels, villains!"

A thousand knives gleamed in the air, and stones began to fall at the gallows foot.

"Good!" muttered Canolles. "The king hanged Richon," he added aloud, "and he did well; when he takes Bordeaux, he will hang many another—"

At these words the crowd rushed like a torrent toward the gallows, broke through the guards, overturned the palisades, and threw themselves, roaring like wild beasts, upon the prisoner.

At a gesture from the duke, one of the executioners raised Canolles by taking him under the arms, while the other adjusted a noose around his neck.

Canolles felt the cord and redoubled his taunts and insults; if he wished to be killed in time he had not a moment to lose.

At that supreme moment he looked around for the last time; he could see naught but naming eyes and threatening arms. One man, however, a mounted soldier, pointed to his musket.

"Cauvignac! 'tis Cauvignac!" cried Canolles, clinging to the ladder with both his hands, which were not bound.

Cauvignac made a motion indicating that he had been unable to save him, and levelled his weapon at him. Canolles understood him.

"Yes, yes!" he cried, emphasizing his words with his head.

Now let us see how Cauvignac happened to be at hand.

IV

We saw Cauvignac taking his departure from Libourne, and we know the object of his journey.

When he reached the spot where his men, under Ferguzon's command, lay in camp, he paused an instant, not to take breath, but to put in execution a plan which his inventive genius had formed in half an hour and while he was riding like the wind.

In the first place he said to himself, with infinite good sense, that if he made his appearance before Madame la Princesse after what had happened, Madame la Princesse, who was about to hang Canolles, against whom she had nothing, would not fail to hang him, of whom she had good reason to complain; and so his mission, which might be successful in so far that Canolles would be saved, would assuredly fail in that he would be hanged. He lost no time therefore in changing coats with one of his soldiers, ordered Barrabas, whose face was less familiar to Madame la Princesse, to don his most elaborate costume, and started off again at a gallop for Bordeaux in that worthy's company. He was disturbed about one thing, namely, the contents of the letter of which he was the bearer, and which his sister had written with such absolute confidence that he had but to hand it to Madame la Princesse to ensure Canolles' safety. His uneasiness on this point increased to such a degree that he resolved to read the letter and set his mind at rest, remarking to himself that a shrewd negotiator could never succeed in his negotiation unless he knew all the ins and outs of the matter in hand; and then, too, if it must be said, Cauvignac never sinned in the direction of having too great confidence in his neighbor, and Nanon, though she was his sister,— indeed, for the very reason that she was his sister,—might very well bear her brother a grudge, in the first place because of the adventure of Jaulnay, and again because of his unforeseen escape from Château-Trompette, and might be trusting to chance to restore everything to its proper place.

He therefore unsealed the letter,—a very simple task, as it was sealed with a bit of wax only, and experienced a very strange and painful sensation as he read what follows:—

MADAME LA PRINCESSE,—It seems that you must have an expiatory victim for poor Richon's death; do not, I pray you, take an innocent man, but take the real culprit. I do not wish that Monsieur de Canolles should die, for to put him to death would be to avenge assassination by murder. As you read this letter I shall be within a league of Bordeaux, with all that I possess. You will deliver me to the populace, who detest me, for they have already tried twice to take my life, and you will keep for yourself my wealth, which amounts to two millions. Oh! madame, I ask this favor of you upon my knees; I am in part the cause of this war; with my death the province will be pacified and your Highness will be triumphant. Madame, a reprieve for quarter of an hour! You need not release Canolles until you have me in your power; but then, upon your soul, you will let him go, will you not?

And I shall be respectfully and gratefully yours,

NANON DE LARTIGUES.

Having read the letter Cauvignac was amazed beyond expression to find his heart swollen with emotion and his eyes moist.

He sat motionless and silent as if he could not believe his eyes. Suddenly he cried:—

"It is true, then, that there are in the world hearts that are generous for the mere pleasure of being generous! *Morbleu!* she shall see that I am as capable as another of being generous when the need arises."

As they were at the gates of the city, he handed the letter to Barrabas, with these instructions simply:—

"To whatever is said to you, reply: 'On the king's business!' nothing more, and deliver this letter into no hands but Madame la Princesse's own."

While Barrabas galloped away toward the princess's temporary domicile, Cauvignac rode in the direction of Château-Trompette.

Barrabas met with no obstacle; the streets were empty, the city seemed deserted, for everybody had gone to the Esplanade.

At the palace gate the sentries undertook to forbid his passage, but, as Cauvignac bade him do, he waved his letter, crying:—

"On the king's business! On the king's business!"

The sentries took him for a messenger from the court, and raised their halberds, and Barrabas entered the palace without further hindrance.

If the reader will take the trouble to remember, this was not the first time that Master Cauvignac's worthy lieutenant had had the honor of appearing in Madame de Condé's presence. He alighted, and as he knew the road, darted rapidly up the staircase, passed through the crowd of startled servants, and made his way into the princess's suite. There he halted, for he found himself face to face with a woman at whose feet another woman was kneeling.

"Oh! madame, mercy, in the name of Heaven!" the latter was saying.

"Leave me, Claire," replied the princess; "be reasonable; remember that we have laid aside the emotions of womankind as well as the garments; we are Monsieur le Prince's lieutenants, and reasons of State control our actions."

"Oh! madame, there are no such things as reasons of State for me," cried Claire; "nor political parties; nor opinions. For me there is nothing and nobody in the world but the man who is to leave it, and when he has left it there will be naught for me but death!"

"Claire, my child, I have already told you that it is impossible; they put Richon to death, and if we do not return like for like we shall be dishonored."

"Ah! madame, one is never dishonored for having pardoned; one is never dishonored for having made use of the prerogative which belongs only to the King of Heaven, and the kings of earth; one word, madame, a single word; the poor boy is waiting!"

"Why, Claire, you are mad! I tell you it is impossible!"

"But I told him that he was safe; I showed him his pardon signed by your own hand; I told him that I would return with your ratification of the pardon!"

"I signed it on condition that the other was to die; why did he allow the other to escape?"

"He had absolutely no part in the escape, I give you my solemn word; besides, the other may not have escaped; he may yet be found."

"Very true! beware!" interposed Barrabas, who arrived at that moment.

"Madame, they will take him away; the time is flying, madame; they will grow weary of waiting."

"You are right, Claire," said the princess, "for I ordered that it should be all over at eleven, and the clock is just striking eleven; it must be all over."

The viscountess uttered a shriek of despair, and rose to her feet, to find herself face to face with Barrabas.

"Who are you? what do you want?" she cried. "Have you come so soon to tell me of his death?"

"No, madame," replied Barrabas, assuming his most affable expression, "on the contrary, I come to save him."

"How so?" cried Claire; "speak at once!"

"By handing this letter to Madame la Princesse."

Claire put out her hand, snatched the letter from the messenger, and handed it to the princess.

"I have no idea what there may be in this letter," said she, "but in Heaven's name read it!"

The princess opened the letter and read it aloud, while Madame de Cambes, turning paler at every line, devoured the words as they fell from her Highness's lips.

"From Nanon?" cried the princess when she had read it through. "Nanon is close by! Nanon gives herself up! Where is Lenet? Where is the duke? Call a messenger, a messenger!"

"I am here, madame," said Barrabas, "ready to go wherever your Highness would have me."

"Go to the Esplanade, to the place of execution, and bid them suspend operations, — but no, they would not believe you," she added, and seizing her pen, wrote at the bottom of the letter, "Suspend!" and handed it open to Barrabas, who rushed from the room.

"Ah!" murmured the viscountess, "she loves him more dearly than I; and he will owe his life to her, wretched creature that I am!"

Stunned by that thought, she fell helplessly upon a chair, although she had received upon her feet all the crushing blows of that terrible day.

Meanwhile Barrabas did not lose a second; he flew down the stairs as if he had wings, leaped upon his horse, and rode furiously away toward the Esplanade.

While he was on his way to the palace, Cauvignac had ridden straight to Château-Trompette. There, favored by the darkness, and rendered unrecognizable by the broad brim of his hat being pulled down over his eyes, he had questioned the bystanders and learned the whole story of his escape in all its details, and that Canolles was to pay the penalty for him. Instinctively, hardly aware of what he was doing, he thereupon hurried away to the Esplanade, driving the spurs into his horse, galloping madly through the crowd, upsetting and riding over every one who came in his way.

When he reached the Esplanade he spied the gallows, and uttered a yell, which was drowned by the howling of the populace, upon whom Canolles was heaping insults in order to excite them to tear him to pieces. It was then that Canolles saw him, divined his purpose, and motioned to him that he was welcome.

Cauvignac stood up in his stirrups and looked in every direction, hoping to see Barrabas or some messenger from the princess, and listening to hear the word: *"Reprieve!"* but he could see nobody and could hear nobody save Canolles, whom the executioner was just about to push from the ladder into eternity, and who pointed to his heart.

Thereupon Cauvignac raised his musket, pointed it toward the young man, took careful aim, and fired.

"Thanks!" said Canolles, opening his arms; "at least I die the death of a soldier."

The ball pierced his breast.

The executioner pushed the body from the ladder, and it swung at the end of the infamous rope; but it was nothing more than a corpse.

It was as if the report of the musket was a signal, so quickly was it followed by a thousand others.

Suddenly a voice cried:—

"Stop! stop! cut the rope!"

But the voice was drowned in the yelling of the mob; moreover, the rope was cut by a bullet. In vain did the guard resist; they were overborne by the huge waves of people; the gallows was overthrown and demolished; the executioners took flight; the crowd overflowed the square, seized upon the body, tore it limb from limb, and dragged the pieces about through the streets.

Stupid in its hatred, it believed that it was adding to the young nobleman's punishment, whereas it was really saving him from the infamy he dreaded so deeply.

During this scene Barrabas accosted the duke, and handed him the letter of which he was the bearer, although he could see for himself that he had arrived too late.

The duke, notwithstanding the brisk discharge of firearms, simply drew a little aside,—for his courage was as calm and cool as every other of his qualities,—and read the letter.

"It's a pity," he said, turning to his officers; "the plan that this Nanon suggests would have been preferable perhaps; but what's done is done.—By the way," he added after reflecting a moment, "as she is to await our reply on the other side of the river, we may even yet be able to gratify her."

Without further thought for the messenger, he put spurs to his horse, and rode back with his escort to the princess.

At that moment the storm which had been gathering for some time, burst over Bordeaux, and a heavy rain, accompanied with vivid lightning, deluged the Esplanade as if to wash it clean of innocent blood.

V

While these things were taking place at Bordeaux, while the people were dragging the body of poor Canolles through the street, while the Duc de La Rochefoucauld was returning to flatter the pride of Madame la Princesse by pointing out to her that her power to do evil was as great as any queen's, while Cauvignac was spurring toward the city gates with Barrabas, deeming it useless to pursue their mission farther, a carriage drawn by four breathless, foam-flecked horses, came to a standstill upon the shore of the Garonne opposite Bordeaux, and between the villages of Belcroix and La Bastide.

Eleven o'clock had just struck.

A mounted courier, who followed the carriage, leaped hastily to the ground as it stopped, and opened the door.

A woman hurriedly alighted, looked up at the sky, which was all ablaze with a bright red light, and listened to the distant shouts and noises.

"You are sure," said she to the maid who alighted after her, "that we have not been followed?"

"No, madame; the two outriders who remained behind at madame's command, have just come up with the carriage, and they have not seen or heard anything."

"Do not you hear anything in the direction of the city?"

"It seems to me that I hear shouting in the distance."

"Do you see nothing?"

"I see something like the reflection of a fire."

"Those are torches."

"Yes, madame, yes, for they move about and dance up and down like wills o' the wisp; do you hear how much louder and more distinct the shouts seem to grow, madame?"

"*Mon Dieu!*" faltered the young woman, falling on her knees upon the damp soil; "*mon Dieu! mon Dieu!*"

It was her only prayer. A single word presented itself to her mind; her lips could pronounce no other; it was the name of him who alone could perform a miracle in her favor.

The maid was not mistaken. Torches were waving and the cries seemed to be coming nearer; a musket-shot rang out, followed by fifty others and by a tremendous uproar; then the torches vanished and the shouts receded; a storm was rumbling overhead, the rain began to fall; but what cared Nanon for that? It was not the lightning of which she was afraid.

Her eyes were constantly fixed upon the spot where she had heard so great a tumult. She could no longer see or hear anything at that spot, and it seemed to her in the glare of the lightning that the square was empty.

"Oh! I haven't the strength to wait here any longer," she cried. "To Bordeaux! take me to Bordeaux!"

Suddenly she heard the sound of horses' footsteps rapidly approaching.

"Ah! they are coming at last," she cried. "Here they are! Adieu, Finette, I must go alone; take her up behind you, Lombard, and leave in the carriage everything that I brought."

"But what do you mean to do, madame, in God's name?" cried the terrified maid.

"Adieu, Finette; adieu!"

"But why, adieu, madame? Where are you going?"

"I am going to Bordeaux."

"Oh! don't do that, madame, in heaven's name! they will kill you."

"Very good! for what purpose do you suppose that I am going thither?"

"Oh! madame! Help, Lombard! help me prevent madame—"

"Hush! leave me, Finette. I have remembered you, never fear: go; I do not wish that any harm should befall you. Obey me! They are coming nearer, here they are."

As she spoke a man galloped up to the carriage, followed at some little distance by another horseman; his horse was roaring rather than breathing.

"Sister! sister!" he cried. "Ah! I come in time!"

"Cauvignac!" cried Nanon. "Well, is it all arranged? Is he awaiting me? Shall we go?"

But, instead of replying, Cauvignac leaped down from his horse, and seized Nanon in his arms. She allowed him to do as he pleased, with the stiff inertness of ghosts and fools. He placed her in the carriage, bade Lombard and Francinette take their places beside her, closed the door, and leaped upon his horse. In vain did poor Nanon, once more in possession of her faculties, shriek and struggle.

"Do not release her," said Cauvignac: "whatever happens do not release her. Keep the other door, Barrabas, and do you, coachman, keep your horses on the gallop or I'll blow your brains out."

These orders followed one another so rapidly that there was a moment's delay in putting them in execution; the carriage was slow to move, the servants were trembling with apprehension, even the horses seemed to hesitate.

"Look alive there, ten thousand devils!" shouted Cauvignac; "they are coming! they are coming!"

In the distance could be heard the hoof-beats of many horses, approaching rapidly with a noise like thunder.

Fear is contagious. The coachman, at Cauvignac's threat, realized that some great danger was impending, and seized the reins.

"Where are we going?" he faltered.

"To Bordeaux! to Bordeaux!" cried Nanon from within the carriage.

"To Libourne, ten thousand furies!" cried Cauvignac.

"Monsieur, the horses will fall before they have gone two leagues."

"I don't ask them to go so far!" retorted Cauvignac, spurring them with his sword. "Let them hold out as far as Ferguzon's camp, that's all I ask."

The heavy vehicle thereupon set forth at a terrifying pace. Men and horses, sweating, gasping, bleeding, urged one another on, the first by their shouts, the others by their loud neighing.

Nanon tried to resist, to free herself, to leap down from the carriage, but she exhausted her strength in the struggle, and soon fell back utterly worn out; she was no longer conscious of what was taking place. By dint of seeking to distinguish Cauvignac amid the hurly-burly of fleeing shadows, her head went round and round; she closed her eyes with a despairing cry, and lay cold and motionless in her maid's arms.

Cauvignac rode forward to the horses' heads. His horse left a trail of fire along the road.

"Help, Ferguzon! help!" he cried.

His call was answered by a cheer in the distance.

"Demons of hell," cried Cauvignac, "you are playing against me, but I believe, upon my soul, that you will lose again to-day. Ferguzon! Ferguzon! help!"

Two or three musket shots rang out in their rear, and were answered by a general discharge from in front.

The carriage came to a stand-still; two of the horses fell from exhaustion, and a third was struck by a bullet.

Ferguzon and his men fell upon the troops of Monsieur de La Rochefoucauld; as they outnumbered them three to one, the Bordelais soon found it hopeless to continue the struggle; they turned tail and fled, and victors and vanquished, pursuers and pursued, vanished in the darkness like a cloud driven by the wind.

Cauvignac remained with the footmen and Francinette beside the insensible Nanon. Luckily they were within a hundred yards of the village of Carbonblanc. Cauvignac carried Nanon in his arms as far as the first house; and there, having given orders to bring up the carriage, placed his sister upon a bed, and, taking from his breast an object which Francinette could not distinguish, slipped it into the poor woman's clenched hand.

The next morning, on awaking from what she thought at first was a frightful dream, Nanon put her hand to her face, and felt something soft and silky caress her pale cheeks. It was a lock of Canolles' hair which Cauvignac had heroically rescued, at the peril of his life, from the Bordelais tigers.

VI

For eight days and nights Madame de Cambes lay tossing in delirium upon the bed to which she was carried, unconscious, upon learning the terrible news.

Her women took care of her, but Pompée kept the door; no other than the old servant, as he knelt beside his unhappy mistress's bed, could awake in her a glimmer of reason.

Numerous visitors besieged the door; but the faithful squire, as inflexible in carrying out his orders as an old soldier should be, courageously denied admission to all comers, at first from the conviction that any visitor whatsoever would annoy his mistress, and subsequently by order of the physician, who feared the effect of too great excitement.

Every morning Lenet presented himself at the door, but it was closed to him as to all others. Madame la Princesse herself appeared there with a large retinue, one day when she had been to call upon poor Richon's mother, who lived in a suburb of the city. It was her purpose, aside from her interest in the viscountess, to show perfect impartiality. She came therefore, intending to play the gracious sovereign; but Pompée informed her with the utmost respect that he had strict orders from which he could not depart; that all men, even dukes and generals, and all women, even princesses, were included in the terms of his orders, and Madame de Condé above all others, inasmuch as a visit from her, after what had happened, would be likely to cause a terrible paroxysm.

The princess, who was fulfilling, or thought she was fulfilling, a duty, and asked nothing better than to avoid the interview, did not wait to be told twice, but took her leave with her suite.

On the ninth day Claire recovered consciousness; it was noticed that, during her delirium, which lasted eight times twenty-four hours, she wept incessantly; although fever ordinarily dries up the source of tears, hers had ploughed a furrow, so to speak, beneath her eyes, which were surrounded by a circle of red and pale blue, like those of the sublime Virgin of Rubens.

On the ninth day, as we have said, when it was least expected, and when her attendants were beginning to lose hope, her reason suddenly returned, as if by enchantment; her tears ceased to flow; her eyes gazed about upon her surroundings, and rested with a sad smile upon the maids who had cared for her so zealously, and upon Pompée who had so faithfully stood guard at her door. Then she lay for some hours, with her head resting on her hand, without speaking, dry-eyed, dwelling upon the same thought, which recurred to her mind again and again with ever-increasing force.

Suddenly, without considering whether her strength was commensurate with her determination, she exclaimed:

"Dress me."

Her women drew near, dumbfounded, and undertook to remonstrate; Pompée stepped a short distance into the room and clasped his hands imploringly.

But the viscountess repeated, gently, but firmly:—

"I bade you dress me."

The women made ready to obey. Pompée bowed and backed out of the room.

Alas! the plump, rosy cheeks were now as pale and thin as those of the dying; her hand, as beautiful as ever, and of as lovely shape, was almost transparent, and lay as white as ivory upon her breast, which put to shame the snowy linen wherein it was enveloped. Beneath her skin could be seen the violet veins which told of the exhaustion caused by great suffering. The clothes she had laid aside the day before, so to speak, and which then fitted closely to her slender, graceful form, now fell about her in loose folds.

They dressed her as she wished, but it was a long operation, for she was so weak that thrice she nearly fainted. When she was dressed she walked to the window, but turning sharply away, as if the sight of the sky and the city terrified her, she seated herself at a table, asked for pen and ink, and wrote a note to Madame la Princesse, soliciting the favor of an audience.

Ten minutes after the letter had been despatched by the hand of Pompée to its destination, a carriage stopped at the door, and almost immediately Madame de Tourville was announced.

"Was it really you," she cried, "who wrote to Madame la Princesse requesting an audience."

"Yes, madame; will she refuse me?"

"Oh! far from it, my dear child; I came hither at once to say to you from her that you know perfectly well that you have no need to request an audience, for you are welcome at any hour of the day or night."

"Thanks, madame," said Claire, "I will avail myself of the privilege."

"How so?" cried Madame de Tourville. "Do you mean to go out in your present condition?"

"Have no fear, madame," replied the viscountess; "I feel perfectly well."

"And you will come?"

"Instantly."

"I will go and tell Madame la Princesse of your purpose."

And Madame de Tourville went out as she came in, with a ceremonious reverence to the viscountess.

The prospect of this unexpected visit produced, as will readily be understood, great excitement in the little court. The viscountess's plight had aroused an interest as keen as it was widespread, for it was by no means true that Madame La Princesse's conduct in the late affair was universally approved. Curiosity was at its height, therefore; officers, maids of honor, courtiers, thronged to Madame de Condé's cabinet, hardly able to believe in the promised visit, for it was but the day before that Claire's condition was represented to be almost hopeless.

Suddenly Madame la Vicomtesse de Cambes was announced.

At the sight of those pallid features, as cold and motionless as marble, the hollow, black-ringed eyes, from which all the life and fire had fled, a murmur of compassion made itself heard in the princess's circle.

Claire did not seem to notice it.

Lenet, deeply moved, walked forward to meet her, and timidly put out his hand. But Claire, without accepting it, walked past him toward Madame de Condé, whom she saluted with noble dignity. She walked the whole length of the apartment with firm step, although she was so pale that she thought every moment that she would fall.

The princess, herself intensely excited and deathly pale, watched Claire's approach with a feeling resembling terror; nor had she the strength to conceal the feeling, which was plainly depicted on her face.

"Madame," said the viscountess in a grave voice, "I have requested this audience which your Highness is pleased to grant me, in order to ask you, in the face of all, if you have been content with my fidelity and devotion since I have had the honor to serve you."

The princess put her handkerchief to her lips, and faltered:—

"Most assuredly, my dear viscountess, I have had reason to praise your conduct on all occasions, and I have expressed my gratitude to you more than once."

"That statement is very precious to me, madame, for it permits me to solicit your Highness to relieve me from further attendance upon you."

"What!" cried the princess, "you wish to leave me, Claire?"

Claire bowed respectfully, but made no reply. Shame, remorse, or sorrow could be detected upon every face. A deathlike silence pervaded the assembly.

"But why do you leave me?" continued the princess at last.

"I have but a few days to live, madame," replied the viscountess, "and those few days I desire to pass in caring for the welfare of my soul."

"Claire, dear Claire!" cried the princess, "pray reflect—"

"Madame," the viscountess interrupted, "I have two favors to ask at your hands; may I hope that you will grant them?"

"Oh! speak, speak!" cried Madame de Condé, "for I shall be only too happy if I can do aught for you."

"You can, madame."

"What are the favors you wish to ask me?"

"The first is the gift of the abbacy of Sainte-Radegonde, vacant since the death of Madame de Montivy."

"You an abbess, my dear child! surely you cannot think of it!"

"The second, madame," continued Claire, with a slight trembling in her voice, "is that I may be permitted to inter on my estate at Cambes the body of my *fiancé*, Monsieur le Baron Raoul de Canolles, murdered by the the people of Bordeaux."

The princess turned away and pressed a trembling hand to her heart. The Duc de La Rochefoucauld turned pale and lost countenance. Lenet opened the door and fled incontinently.

"Your Highness does not deign to reply," said Claire; "do you refuse? Perhaps I have asked too much."

Madame de Condé had only enough strength to nod her head in token of assent, before she fell back in a swoon upon her chair.

Claire turned away as unmoved as if she were of stone, and passed majestically from the room through the lane of courtiers, standing with heads bent; not until the door had closed behind her, did they realize that no one had thought of going to Madame de Condé's assistance.

Five minutes later a carriage rolled slowly out of the court-yard; Madame de Cambes was taking leave of Bordeaux.

"What is your Highness's decision?" Madame de Tourville inquired of Madame de Condé when she came to herself.

"Comply with the wishes of Madame la Vicomtesse de Cambes in respect to both the petitions she addressed to us just now, and implore her to forgive us."

EPILOGUE

I

THE ABBESS OF SAINTE-RADEGONDE DE PEYSSAC

A month had passed away since the events we have described. One Sunday evening, after vespers, the Abbess of Sainte-Radegonde de Peyssac came forth last from the church at the end of the convent garden, now and then turning her tear-reddened eyes toward a dark thicket of yews and fir-trees, with such an expression of longing and regret that one would have said that her heart was in that spot and seeking to detain her there.

Before her, the nuns, veiled and silent, walking in single file along the path to the convent, seemed like a long procession of phantoms returning to the tomb, followed by another phantom who left the earth behind regretfully.

One by one the nuns disappeared beneath the sombre arches of the cloister; the superior followed them with her eyes until the last one had entered, then let them fall upon the capital of a Gothic column half buried in the grass, with an indescribable expression of hopeless despair.

"Oh, my God! my God!" said she, placing her hand on her heart, "thou art my witness that I cannot endure this life, of which I did not realize the true nature. I sought solitude and obscurity in the cloister, and not the constant scrutiny of all these curious eyes."

With that she raised her head, and took a step toward the little clump of firs.

"After all," said she, "what matters the world to me, since I have denied it? The world has done me naught but injury; society has been pitiless to me, and why should I concern myself with its opinions,—I, who have sought shelter with God, and depend upon him alone? But perhaps God frowns upon this love which lives on in my heart and consumes it. In that case, may he either tear it from my heart, or tear my heart from my body!"

But no sooner had the poor desperate creature pronounced these words than, casting her eyes upon the gown she wore, she was horrified at the thought of the blasphemy of which she had been guilty, so out of harmony was it with her saintly costume. With her thin white hand she wiped away the tears that glistened on her eyelids, and, raising her eyes to heaven, consecrated her life to everlasting suffering in a single look.

At that moment she heard a voice at her ear; it was the voice of the sister who kept the door of the convent.

"Madame," said she, "there is a woman in the parlor who wishes to be allowed to speak to you."

"Her name?"

"She refuses to tell it except to you."

"To what class in life does she seem to belong?99

"She seems a person of distinction."

"Still society, society!" murmured the abbess.

"What answer shall I give her?"

"That I await her coming."

"Where, madame?"

"Bring her hither; I will listen to her here in the garden, sitting upon this bench. I need the air; I stifle when I am indoors."

The portress withdrew, to reappear a moment later, followed by a woman whom it was easy to recognize as a woman of distinction by her garments, which were handsome, although of sombre hue.

She was rather below the average height; her rapid gait lacked something of nobility perhaps, but her presence exhaled an indescribable charm. She carried under her arm a little ivory casket, whose polished whiteness contrasted sharply with the black satin of her jet-trimmed dress.

"Madame," said the portress, "this is Madame la Supérieure."

The abbess lowered her veil, and turned toward the stranger, and as she saw that she kept her eyes turned upon the ground, and that she was deadly pale and trembling with emotion, she bestowed a kindly glance upon her, and said:—

"You expressed a wish to speak with me, and I am ready to listen to you, my sister."

"Madame," replied the stranger, "I have been so happy that in my pride I have thought that not even God himself could destroy my happiness. To-day God has breathed upon it, and I feel that I must weep and repent I have come to seek shelter here, so that my sobs may be stifled by the thick walls of your convent, and that my tears, which trace a furrow upon my cheeks, may not make me a laughing-stock to the world; so that God, who might seek me amid scenes of merry-making, would find me weeping in the sanctuary, and praying contritely at its altar."

"Your heart is deeply wounded, I can see, for I too know what it is to suffer," replied the young superior; "and in its agony the heart cannot clearly distinguish between what really is, and what it desires. If solitude, mortification of the flesh, and to do penance are what you need, my sister, come to us, and suffer with us; but if you seek a place where you can give vent freely to your grief and your despair, where no curious gaze will be fastened upon you, oh, madame! madame! fly from this place, and take refuge in your own room, where the world will see you much less than you will be seen here, and the hangings of your oratory will absorb the sound of your sobs much more effectively than the planks of our cells. And God, unless the enormity of your crimes has compelled him to turn his eyes away from you, will see you wherever you are."

The stranger raised her head, and gazed in profound amazement at the young abbess who talked in such an extraordinary strain.

"Why, madame," said she, "should not all who suffer seek the Lord's help; and is not your establishment a consecrated station upon the way to heaven?"

"There is but one path that leads to God, my sister," replied the nun, carried away by her despair. "What do you regret? For what do you weep? What do you desire? Society has turned a cold shoulder upon you, your friends are false to you, you lack money, or some transitory sorrow has made you a believer in everlasting misery; am I not right? You are suffering at this moment, and you fancy that you will suffer always thus, even as, when one sees an open wound, one fancies that it will never close. But you are mistaken; every wound that is not mortal will heal; so suffer on, and let your sorrow take its course; you will be cured, and then, if you are bound to us, suffering of another sort will begin; and that suffering will be in very truth unending, implacable, and past endurance. You will look out, through a barrier of brass, upon the world, to which you cannot return; then you will curse the day when the door of this holy hostelry, which you take for a station on the road to heaven, closed upon you. This that I say to you is not in strict accordance with our rules perhaps,—I have not been abbess long enough to know them thoroughly,—but 't is in strict accord with the feelings of my heart, and it is what I see every hour, not, in my own case, thank God! but all about me."

"Oh! no, no!" cried the stranger, "the world is at an end for me; I have lost everything that made the world attractive to me. No, madame, have no fear; I shall never regret it, never,—I am sure I shall never regret it!"

"Then the sorrow that afflicts you has a deeper source? Instead of an illusion have you lost a reality? Have you been separated forever from a husband, or child—or from a friend? Ah! then I pity you with all my heart, madame, for your heart is pierced from side to side and your wound is incurable. In that case, come to us, madame; the Lord will comfort you; he will replace the friends or kindred you may have lost with us, who form one large family, a flock of which he is the shepherd; and," added the abbess in a lower tone, "if he does not comfort you, which is quite possible, there will remain to you the last poor consolation of weeping with me, who came hither like yourself, in quest of comfort, but have not yet found it here."

"Alas!" cried the stranger, "was it such words as these that I hoped to hear? Is it thus that the unhappy are consoled?"

"Madame," said the superior, putting out her hand as if to ward off the rebuke, "do not speak of unhappiness before me; I know not who you may be, I know not what has happened to you, but you know nothing of unhappiness."

"Oh!" cried the stranger, in an agonized tone which made the superior shudder, "you do not know me, madame, for if you did know me, you would not speak so to me; besides, you cannot fairly judge my suffering, for to do that you must have suffered what I suffer; meanwhile, receive me, make me welcome, open the gates of God's house to me; and by my tears and cries and agony you will know if I am truly unhappy."

"Yes," said the superior, "I realize from your accent and from your words that you have lost the man you love, have you not?"

The stranger sobbed, and wrung her hands.

"Oh! yes, yes!" said she.

"Very well; since it is your desire, be one of our community; but first let me tell you what awaits you here, if your sufferings are equal to mine: two everlasting, pitiless walls, which, instead of turning our thoughts toward heaven, whither they should rise, constantly confine them to the earth, from which you will be separated; for while the blood flows, and the pulses beat, and the heart loves, none of the faculties are extinct; isolated as we are, and hidden from sight as we believe ourselves to be, the dead call to us from the depths of the tomb: 'Why do you leave the place where your dead are buried?'"

"Because all that I have loved in the world is here," replied the stranger, in a choking voice, throwing herself at the feet of the superior, who gazed at her in profound astonishment. "Now you have my secret, my sister; now you can understand my grief, my mother. I implore you on my knees—you see my tears—to accept the sacrifice I make to God, or rather to grant the favor I ask at your hands. He is buried in the church of Peyssac; let me weep upon his tomb, which is here."

"What tomb? Of whom are you speaking? What do you mean?" cried the superior, drawing back from the kneeling woman, at whom she gazed with something very like terror.

"When I was happy," continued the penitent, in a voice so low that it was drowned by the sighing of the wind among the branches, "when I was happy—and I have been very happy—I was called Nanon de Lartigues. Do you recognize me now, and do you know what it is that I implore?"

The superior sprang to her feet as if released by a spring, and stood for a moment, motionless and pale, with uplifted eyes and clasped hands.

"Oh, madame!" she said at last in a voice which she struggled to render calm, but which trembled with emotion, "oh, madame, is it true that you, who come here to weep beside a tomb, have no knowledge who I am? You do not know that I have purchased with my freedom, with my happiness in this world, and with all the tears of my heart the melancholy pleasure of which you now claim an equal portion. You are Nanon de Lartigues; I, when I had a name, was the Vicomtesse de Cambes."

Nanon, with a sharp cry, walked up to the superior, and, raising the hood which shaded the nun's dull eyes, recognized her rival.

"'T is she!" murmured Nanon. "And she was so lovely when she came to Saint-Georges! Poor woman!"

She stepped back, with her eyes still fixed on the viscountess, and shaking her head.

"Oh!" cried the viscountess with a touch of the pride that all men feel to know that their capacity for suffering is greater than their fellows'; "it is kind of you to say that, and it has done me good. I must have suffered cruelly to have undergone so cruel a change; I must have wept bitterly; I am more unhappy than you, therefore, for you are lovely still."

And the viscountess raised her eyes, beaming with the first ray of joy that had shone in them for a month past, as if seeking Canolles in the sky above her head.

Nanon, still on her knees, hid her face in her hands and burst into tears.

"Alas! madame," said she, "I did not know to whom my petition was addressed; for the last month I have known nothing of what was taking place, and that ignorance has preserved my beauty; beyond all question I have been mad. Now I am at your command. I have no desire to make you jealous of the dead. I ask to be admitted here as the humblest of your nuns; you can do with me as you please, and if I disobey you can subject me to the severest discipline,—you have the dungeon and the *impace*. But," she added in a trembling voice, "you will at least let me from time to time see the place where the man we both loved so dearly is buried?"

She fell, sobbing and almost unconscious, upon the turf.

The viscountess made no reply; leaning against the trunk of a sycamore, she seemed ready to expire at her side.

"Oh! madame," cried Nanon, "you do not answer; you refuse! Be it so; I have a single treasure in my possession, and you perhaps have nothing that was his; grant my request and that treasure is yours."

As she spoke she took from her breast a large locket which was attached to a gold chain about her neck, and, offered it to Madame de Cambes, holding it open in her hand.

Claire pounced upon the relic, and kissed the cold, life-less hair with such vehemence that it seemed as if her heart came to her lips to share the kiss.

"Do you think," said Nanon, still kneeling at her feet, "that you have ever suffered more than I suffer at this moment?"

"Ah! you carry the day, madame," said Claire, lifting her up and taking her to her arms; "come, come, my sister, for I love you better than all the world for having shared this treasure with me."

She leaned over Nanon, as she gently raised her, and lightly kissed her cheek who had been her rival.

"Yes, you shall be my sister and my dearest friend," said she; "yes, we will live and die together, talking of him and praying for him. He sleeps near by in our church; it was the only favor I could obtain from her to whom I devoted my life. May God forgive her!"

With that, Claire took Nanon's hand, and side by side, stepping so lightly that they scarcely bent the blades of grass beneath their feet, they walked to the clump of yew-trees behind which the church was hidden.

The viscountess led Nanon to a chapel, in the centre of which a simple stone stood up some four inches above the ground; a cross was carved upon the stone.

The viscountess pointed to it without speaking.

Nanon knelt and kissed the cold marble. Claire leaned against the altar, kissing the lock of hair. The one was trying to accustom herself to the thought of death, the other to dream for the last time of life.

A quarter of an hour after, the two women returned together to the house. Except to pray, they had not for an instant broken their woebegone silence.

"Madame," said the viscountess, "from this hour you have your cell in this convent; would you like the one adjoining mine?—we shall be separated less."

"I thank you very humbly, madame," said Nanon, "for the offer, and I gratefully accept it. But before I leave the world forever let me say farewell for the last time to my brother, who is waiting at the gate; he also is overcome with sorrow."

"Alas!" said Claire, to whose mind the thought came instinctively that Cauvignac's safety caused the death of his companion in captivity; "go, my sister."

Nanon left the room.

II
THE BROTHER AND SISTER

As Nanon said, Cauvignac was waiting, sitting upon a stone a few steps from his horse, at whom he was gazing sadly, while the horse himself browsing upon the dry grass so far as the length of his rein permitted, raised his head from time to time to gaze intelligently into his master's face.

Before the adventurer was the dusty road, which, as it passed out of sight a short distance away among the elms which covered a slight elevation, seemed to start from the convent to lose itself in space.

One might have said, and it may have occurred to the adventurer, although his mind was little given to philosophical turns of thought, that over yonder was the world, and that its tumult died at that cross-surmounted iron gate.

In fact, Cauvignac had arrived at that stage of introspection when we might fairly expect him to have thought upon such subjects.

But he had already forgotten himself in this sentimental reverie over long for a man of his character. He appealed therefore to his consciousness of what his manly dignity required of him, and, ashamed of having been so weak, said to himself:—

"What! should not I, who am so superior in mind to all these men of courage, be at least their equal in courage, or rather in lack of courage? Damnation! Richon is dead, beyond question; Canolles is dead, that is equally true; but I am still alive, and after all, that, it seems to me, is the principal thing.

"Very good; but for the very reason that I am alive, I think, and when I think, I remember, and when I remember, I am sad. Poor Richon! such a gallant officer! Poor Canolles! such a handsome fellow!—both hanged, and that by my fault, ten thousand devils! by the fault of Roland Cauvignac! Ouf! 't is a sorry affair; I am choking.

"And with all the rest, my sister, who has not always had reason to applaud my acts, as she has no farther motive for humoring me, now that

Canolles is dead and she has been fool enough to break with Monsieur d'Épernon,—my sister has probably a deadly grudge against me, and as soon as she has a moment to herself will take advantage of it to disinherit me during her lifetime.

"Sure it is that that is the real source of my misfortunes, and not these infernal memories that haunt me. Canolles, Richon; Richon, Canolles! In God's name, have I not seen men die by hundreds, and were they anything more than men? But there are times all the same when, upon my honor, I believe I regret that I was not hanged with him; I should have died in good company at least, but who can say in what company I shall die now?"

At that moment the monastery clock struck seven. The sound recalled Cauvignac to himself, for he remembered that his sister bade him wait until seven o'clock, and the bell announced that Nanon would soon appear, and he would be called upon to resume his rôle of comforter.

The door opened immediately, in fact, and Nanon did appear. She walked across the little court-yard where Cauvignac might have waited had he chosen, strangers being privileged to enter there; for it had not yet become hallowed ground, although it could hardly be called a profane spot.

But the adventurer preferred not to go so far, saying that the proximity of convents, especially of convents of women, gave him always unpleasant thoughts, and so he remained, as we have said, outside the gate upon the road.

As he heard steps upon the sand Cauvignac turned and saw Nanon, still separated from him by the barred gate.

"Ah!" said he, with a tremendous sigh, "here you are at last, little sister. When I see one of these ghastly gates close upon a poor woman, I always think of the door of the tomb closing upon a dead man, and I no more expect to see the one again without her novice's frock, than the other without his winding-sheet."

Nanon smiled sadly.

"Good!" said Cauvignac, "you have ceased to weep; that's a point gained."

"True," said Nanon, "I can weep no more."

"But you can still smile, and that's much better; by your leave we'll go now, shall we not? I don't know why it is, but this place awakens all sorts of thoughts in my mind."

"Salutary?"

"Salutary indeed! is that what you call them? However, we won't discuss the matter, and I am delighted that you think them so. You have laid in a goodly store of the same kind, I trust, dear sister, and will have no occasion to come hither in search of more for a long while."

Nanon did not reply; she was thinking.

"Among these salutary thoughts," Cauvignac ventured to suggest, "I trust that you have cultivated forgetfulness of injuries done you?"

"Forgiveness, at least, if not forgetfulness."

"I should prefer the other, but no matter; one must not be too exacting when one is in the wrong. You forgive the wrong I have done you, little sister?"

"It is all forgiven."

"Ah! you delight me beyond expression; henceforth, then, you will feel no repugnance at the sight of me?"

"Not only no repugnance, but great pleasure."

"Pleasure?"

"Yes, my friend."

"Your friend! Ah! Nanon, that is a title that pleases me, for you are under no compulsion to bestow it on me, while you are compelled to call me your brother; so you can endure to have me near you?"

"Oh! I do not say that," replied Nanon; "certain things are impossible, we must both recognize that."

"I understand," said Cauvignac, with a sigh of greater proportions than the first. "Exiled! you exile me, isn't that what it amounts to? I am to see you no more. Very well! although it's a very painful thing for me to see you no more, upon my honor, Nanon, still I know that I deserve it, and I have brought it upon myself. Moreover, what is there for me to do in France, now that peace is made, Guyenne pacified, and the queen and Madame de Condé are the best friends in the world? You see, I am no such fool as to fancy that I am in the good graces of either of the two princesses. So the best thing I can do is to go into exile, as you say. Bid farewell to the wanderer, little sister. There is war in Africa; Monsieur de Beaufort is going to fight the heathen, and I will go with him. To tell the truth, it's not that the heathen do not seem to me to be a thousand times nearer right than the faithful; but that's for kings to decide, not for us. I may be killed over yonder, and that's all I ask. I will go; you will hate me less, when you know I am dead."

Nanon, who had listened to this flow of words with lowered head, raised her great eyes to Cauvignac's face.

"Do you mean this?" she asked.

"What?"

"This that you say you are contemplating, brother."

Cauvignac had allowed himself to be drawn into this long harangue, like a man accustomed to warm himself up with the sound of his own voice in default of real feeling. Nanon's question called him back to the actual, and he bethought himself how he could descend from that fine frenzy to something more commonplace, but more business-like.

"Well, yes, little sister," said he, "I swear—by what? I know not. Look you, I swear, *foi de Cauvignac,* that I am really sad and unhappy since Richon's death and—In fact, sitting there on that stone just now, I used numberless arguments to harden my heart, which I had never heard of until now, but which now is not content to beat, but talks and cries and weeps. Tell me, Nanon, is that what you call remorse?"

The appeal was so natural and pitiful, despite its burlesque savagery, that Nanon realized that it came from the bottom of the heart.

"Yes," said she, "it is remorse, and you are a better man than I thought."

"Very well, if it is remorse here goes for the African campaign; you will give me a trifle to cover the expense of the journey and my equipment, won't you, little sister? Would I could carry away all your grief with my own!"

"You will not go away, my friend," said Nanon, "but you will live henceforth as prosperously as those most favored by destiny. For ten years you have straggled with poverty; I say nothing of the risks you have run, for they are incident to the life of a soldier. On this last occasion your life was saved where another's life was lost; it must have been God's will that you should live, and it is my desire, quite in accord with his will, that your life from this day on shall be happy."

"What a way you have of saying that, little sister! Pray what do you mean by it?"

"I mean that you are to go to my house at Libourne before it is pillaged; there you will find in the secret cupboard behind my Venetian mirror—"

"In the secret cupboard?" queried Cauvignac.

"Yes, you know it well, do you not?" said Nanon, with a feeble smile; "you took two hundred pistoles from it last month, didn't you?"

"Nanon, do me the justice to admit that I might have taken more had I wished, for the cupboard was filled with gold; but I took no more than the sum that I actually needed."

"That is true," said Nanon, "and I am only too glad to bear witness to it, if it excuses you in your own eyes."

Cauvignac blushed and hung his head.

"*Mon Dieu!*" said Nanon, "think no more about it; you know that I forgive you."

"What proof have I?"

"This: you will go to Libourne, you will open the cupboard, and you will find there all of my fortune that I was able to turn into money,—twenty thousand crowns in gold."

"What shall I do with them?"

"Take them."

"But to whom are the twenty thousand crowns to belong?"

"To you, my brother; it is all that I have to give, for, as you know, when I left Monsieur d'Épernon I asked nothing for myself, and my houses and lands were seized."

"What do you say, sister?" cried Cauvignac, in dismay.

"What idea have you in your head now?"

"Simply, Roland, that you are to take the twenty thousand crowns."

"That's very well for me, but what about yourself?"

"I have no use for that money now."

"Ah! I understand,—you have other funds; so much the better. But it's an enormous sum, sister; think of it! It's too much for me, at least at one stroke."

"I have no other funds; I keep nothing but my jewels. I would be glad to give you them as well, but I must use them to pay for the privilege of entering this convent."

Cauvignac leaped into the air in his surprise.

"This convent!" he cried; "you, my dear sister, propose to enter a convent?"

"Yes, dear brother."

"Oh! in Heaven's name, don't do that, little sister. A convent! you have no idea what a fearful bore it will be. I can tell you something of it, having been at the seminary. A convent! Nanon, don't do it; it will kill you."

"I hope so," said Nanon.

"Sister, I will not have your money at that price, do you hear? *Cordieu!* it would burn me."

"Roland," rejoined Nanon, "my purpose in entering here, is not to make you rich, but to secure happiness for myself."

"But it's stark madness," said Cauvignac; "I am your brother, Nanon, and I won't allow it."

"My heart is already here, Roland; what would my body do elsewhere?"

"It's frightful to think of; oh! Nanon, dear sister, in pity's name!"

"Not a word more, Roland. You understand me? The money is yours; make good use of it, for your poor Nanon will no longer be at hand to give you more, perforce or willingly."

"But what have I ever done for you that you should be so kind to me?"

"The only thing I could expect, the only thing I could have asked you to do, in bringing me what you did from Bordeaux the night that he died and I could not die."

"Ah! yes, I remember,—the lock of hair."

The adventurer hung his head; he felt an unfamiliar sensation in his eye, and put his hand to it.

"Another would weep," said he; "I do not know how to weep, but upon my soul, I suffer as much, if not more."

"Adieu, brother," said Nanon, offering him her hand.

"No, no, no!" said Cauvignac, "I will never say adieu to you of my free will. Is it fear that drives you into the convent? If so, we will leave Guyenne, and travel the world over together. I too have an arrow in my heart, which I shall carry with me wherever I go, and the pain it causes me will help me to sympathize with your pain. You will talk to me of him, and I will talk to you of Richon; you will weep, and perhaps I shall succeed in weeping too, and it will do me good. Would you like to go to some desert island? I will serve you, faithfully and with deep respect, for you are a saint. Would you like me to be a monk? I confess that I can't do that. But do not enter the convent, do not say adieu to me."

"Adieu, dear brother."

"Would you like to remain in Guyenne, despite the Bordelais, despite the Gascons, despite the whole world? I no longer have my company, but I still have Ferguzon, Barrabas, and Carrotel. We four can do many things. We will be your body-guard, and the queen herself will not be so well guarded. And if they ever get at you, if ever a hair of your head is injured, you can safely say, 'They are all four dead; *requiescant in pace!*'"

"Adieu," said Nanon.

Cauvignac was about to resort to some fresh appeal, when they heard the rumbling of a carriage upon the road. An outrider in the queen's livery was galloping ahead.

"What is all this?" said Cauvignac, turning his face toward the road, but without releasing his sister's hand, which he held through the bars.

The carriage, built according to the fashion then in vogue, with massive armorial bearings and open panels, was drawn by six horses and contained eight persons, with a whole household of lackeys and pages.

Behind came guards and mounted courtiers.

"Road! road!" cried the outrider, striking Cauvignac's horse, which, however, was standing with modest reserve well away from the centre of the road.

The terrified beast reared and plunged madly.

"Be careful what you do, my friend!" cried Cauvignac, dropping his sister's hand.

"Way for the queen!" said the courier, riding on.

"The queen! the devil!" said Cauvignac; "let's keep out of trouble in that direction."

And he stood as closely against the wall as possible, holding his horse by the bridle.

At that moment a trace broke, and the coachman, with a vigorous jerk upon the reins, brought the six horses to a stand-still.

"What has happened?" asked a voice with a noticeable Italian accent; "why do you stop?"

"A trace has broken, monsieur," replied the coachman.

"Open the door! open the door!" cried the same voice.

The footmen obeyed, but before the steps were lowered, the man with the Italian accent was already on the ground.

"Aha! Il Signor Mazarini!" said Cauvignac; "he evidently didn't wait to be asked to alight first." After him came the queen.

After the queen, Monsieur de La Rochefoucauld. Cauvignac rubbed his eyes.

After Monsieur de La Rochefoucauld, Monsieur d'Épernon.

"Ah!" said the adventurer, "why wasn't that brother-in-law hanged instead of the other?"

After Monsieur d'Épernon, Monsieur de La Meilleraie.

After Monsieur de La Meilleraie, the Duc de Bouillon.

Then, two maids of honor.

"I knew that they had ceased to fight," said Cauvignac, "but I had no idea they were so thoroughly reconciled."

"Messieurs," said the queen, "instead of waiting here until the trace is mended, suppose we walk on a little way; the weather is so beautiful and the air so fresh."

"At your Majesty's service," said Monsieur de La Rochefoucauld, bowing.

"Walk beside me, duke, and repeat some of your excellent maxims! you must have devised a great number of them since we met."

"Lean on my arm, duke," said Mazarin to Monsieur de Bouillon, "I know that you have the gout."

Monsieur d'Épernon and Monsieur de La Meilleraie closed the procession, talking with the maids of honor.

The whole party were laughing merrily together in the warm rays of the setting sun, like a party of friends out for a holiday.

"Is it far from here to Bourcy?" the queen asked. "You should be able to tell me, Monsieur de La Rochefoucauld, you have studied the country so thoroughly."

"Three leagues, madame; we shall certainly be there before nine o'clock."

"Very good; and to-morrow you will start off early in the morning, and say to our dear cousin, Madame de Condé, that we shall be happy to see her."

"Your Majesty," said the Duc d'Épernon, "did you see the comely cavalier, who turned his face to the wall, and the lovely dame who disappeared when we alighted?"

"Yes," said the queen, "I saw them both; it seems that the nuns know how to enjoy themselves at the convent of Sainte-Radegonde de Peyssac."

At that moment the carriage drove rapidly up behind the illustrious promenaders, who were already some distance beyond the convent.

"Let us not weary ourselves, gentlemen," said the queen; "the king, you know, is to entertain us with music this evening."

The whole party re-entered the carriage and drove away with shouts of laughter, which were soon drowned by the rumbling of the wheels.

Cauvignac followed the carriage with his eyes, reflecting deeply upon the terrible contrast between their noisy gayety and the mute sorrow within the walls of the convent. When the carriage had passed out of sight, he said:—

"I am glad to know one thing, and that is that, bad as I am, there are people who are worse than I; and by Mary's death! I propose to try to make it true that there is nobody better than I; I am rich now, and it will be an easy matter."

He turned to take leave of Nanon, but she had disappeared. Thereupon, with a sigh, he mounted his horse, cast a last glance at the convent, started off at a gallop on the Libourne road, and disappeared in the opposite direction to that taken by the carriage containing the illustrious personages who have played leading parts in this narrative.

Perhaps we shall meet them again some day; for the pretended peace, but ill-cemented by the blood of Richon and Canolles, was a mere truce, and the War of Women was not yet at an end.